Greetings from the shallow end!

I hope you enjoy reading the  Brown, *Swimming Against the Ti*

Life doesn't get any easier for our heroine, but it does get crazier as her father's girlfriend gets nasty, Electra's super-glam Wundacousin Maddy comes on to the scene and Electra fires off an email which starts a calamitous chain of events. Although Electra's world is changing, one thing remains constant. As a way of coping with the sometimes grim realities of life, Elecctra's mind pops up with gloriously shallow thoughts in the midst of deeply serious situations!

I'm often asked whether these books are based on real people and real life. Although the characters are fictitious, they *are* based on people I've met, and all the mad, bad and sad happenings are taken from real-life situations. Whilst at school I used to sit and stare out of the window at school dreaming of *anything* but lessons, then go home and write pages and pages in my diary of who did what to whom, and (usually) why wasn't I part of it? Years later, that dreaming and those diaries are brought to life through Electra and her friends.

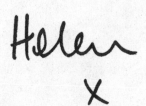

The shallows of Electra Brown's life:

1. Life at the Shallow End
2. Out of my Depth
3. Swimming Against the Tide
4. Taking the Plunge

www.helenbaileybooks.com

SWIMMING AGAINST THE TIDE

Helen Bailey

*Hodder
Children's
Books*

A division of Hachette Children's Books

A Catalogue record for this book is available from the British Library

ISBN-13: 978 0 340 95030 2

Typeset in Berkeley by Avon DataSet Ltd,
Bidford on Avon, Warwickshire

Printed and bound in China by Imago

The paper and board used in this paperback by Hodder Children's Books
are natural recyclable products made from wood grown in
sustainable forests. The manufacturing processes conform to the
environmental regulations of the country of origin.

Hodder Children's Books
a division of Hachette Children's Books
338 Euston Road, London NW1 3BH
An Hachette UK Company
www.hachette.co.uk

In memory of Rufus
7 June 1994 – 9 March 2008
A dog in a million.

Chapter One

I'm outside Burger King, leaning against the window, stressing over whether I can get away with having my belly button pierced without Mum finding out, but if I did, what are my chances of it going wrong and ending up with gross green pus pouring from my gut, which is what happened to Sorrel, though she went to a dodgy place with a parrot in the window which has now closed down, when over the noise of Eastwood Circle Retail Park I hear, 'Hiya Electra!'

It's the unmistakable squawk of The Queen of Sleaze, Claudia Barnes. She's tottering towards me, chest puffed out, shoulders jerked back and her bleached-blonde hair ironed straight and rigid with hairspray. Ambling behind her are Natalie Price and Tamara Lennox-Hill. They're so busy comparing the length of their nails they don't seem to notice they're continually barging into annoyed shoppers struggling to cope with bags and sobbing children.

Bummer! Now that Claudia's seen me it's too late to bolt into Burger King, dive under a table, and crouch amongst the stray chips and dropped chicken nuggets until they've gone, or at least until Lucy and Sorrel arrive. On their own, Nat, Tam and even Claudia are OK, but when they're hunting in packs, you really need your own bezzie back-up as protection from agreeing to throw dodgy parties or pretending you've done things which you haven't, usually with boys, but sometimes with alcohol and *always* with dire consequences. But it's too late to escape, they're nearly level with me and there's *still* no sign of Luce and Sorrel.

'You a Billy No Mates this arvo?' Claudia asks, poking me in the chest with one of her French-manicured nails.

'Ow, Claudia!' She's practically punctured my left boob, though as I've got a mismatched boob situation going on at the mo, a bit of deflation on the left side might help even it up with the right one.

Not only has my boob been assaulted, I'm totally miffed that Claudia could even *think* I might be the sort of saddo who spends the last Friday of the long summer holiday hanging around shopping centres on her own, even if that's exactly what I've been doing for the last couple of hours.

'As if!' I say sharply.

'So, what you up to?' Claudia continues to interrogate me.

I pretend to scan the horizon looking for the girls, but really I'm trying to avoid looking directly at Claudia's chest. This is almost impossible as what with wearing heels and being taller than me, her boobs are practically bobbing in my face. This isn't because she has Mighty Mammaries, but because as well as the boobs-out-shoulders-back thing, I know for a fact she stuffs chicken fillets in her bra, which is why me, Luce and Sorrel secretly call her Tits Out. I rub my sore boob and then realize with horror it probably looks as if I'm feeling myself up, so I go to ram my hand in my jeans pocket but miss, and stick a mitt down my front which must look even worse. 'I'm meeting the girls here for lunch and then . . .' I leave what I hope is a dramatic pause, '. . . and then I'm going to get my passport photie taken. We're going abroad at half-term.'

I casually toss this info into the conversation and wait for Tits Out to ask which bit of the planet I'm off to. I might pretend the Brown family are going on a package tour to Mars via the moon, just to wind her up.

Instead of cross-examining me on my travel plans, Claudia elbows Tam in the ribs.

'Tam's got some fab news, haven't you, Tam?' she says. 'Go on, spill.'

Tammy Two-Names grins.

'You've had your braces taken off?' I ask.

'Yah, but not that,' she drawls, running a pink tongue over her bare straight teeth. 'I'm like, not going back to QB after all. I'll be back at Burke's on Monday.'

The qualifications to get into Queen Beatrice's College for Girls are that you need to be brainy, bitchy and snotty-nosed, but most of all, your parents need to be loaded. Tam qualified on all counts until the end of the first term of Year 9 when her dad's brain went into meltdown and he totally freaked out in the loos at work. He lost his mind, his job and with it his mega-school-fees-salary, so now that the Lennox-Hills are strapped for cash, her older brother Rupe is still at boarding school but Tam is at my school, Flora Burke's Community School, where the only entry qualification you need is a pulse.

'Sorry, Tam, you must be gutted,' I say, knowing however much she pretends to be a Burke, she'd much rather be a Queen Bee.

Tammy tosses her long dark hair and gives the sort of half-snort half-donkey-bray laugh posh girls excel at. 'S'OK. I do miss the uniform though. Burke's is minging.'

A dreamy sigh comes from my left.

'But *we've* got Buff. *He's* worth changing schools for.'

Despite the fact that she's standing next to me, I'd completely forgotten Natalie was there. The gormless expression she always wears coupled with the fact that she rarely says anything interesting makes her blend into the background, something Nat hopes the greasy yellow make-up she trowels on will do for her zits. Sadly for poor Nat, it just makes her face look as if it's smeared with butter. Unlike Tits Out who would probably be thrilled with her nickname, Natalie would be crushed if she knew me and the girls call her Butterface behind her back.

We all melt at the thought of our lush geography teacher, Jon 'Buff' Butler. It's going to be an anxious few days before we start back at school after the long summer break, as until we get our new timetable we won't know whether Buff or Miss Rogers, aka The Hamster, is going to take GCSE geography.

I'll be well gutted if it's The Hamster, who's blonde, small and anxious, and looks as if she's stuffed her cheeks with food. She tried to teach us geography for the first term of Year 9 before Buff came and rescued us, but she was completely unable to control the class. Once, Pinhead, Gibbo and Spud tied Frazer Burns, aka Razor Burns, aka Freak Boy, to his seat by taping his ankles to his chair legs with packing tape. She either *really* didn't notice or pretended not to, but it wasn't until FB tried to stand up and fell over, pulling the chair with him, that she said anything, and that was only, 'Do you need some scissors?'

Anyway, if I don't have Buff as my teacher, it won't just be academic eye candy I'll miss. By staring at Buff's peachy butt as he writes on the board I've obviously absorbed *some* info, as according to my school report geography is *officially* my best subject. If I end up Buff-less I'm going to plead with Mum that I *have* to have private tuition with him after school, which would be fantastico as he might see me in a whole new light. A teenage temptress rather than a fourteen-year-old schoolgirl in a *deeply* unflattering green tartan kilt and thick black sausage-skin tights.

'Going anywhere interesting?' Tits Out interrupts my delicious daydream of one-on-one tuition with Buff, just at the point where he's telling me he can't wait to take me on a field course.

Three sets of eyes are fixed on me, their mascara-drenched eyelashes quivering like spiders having an epileptic fit.

'You like, said you were going away,' Tam prompts.

'Oh, yeah. We're going to America at half-term.'

I try to say this casually, as if our family going abroad is nothing out of the ordinary. In reality, other than a day trip to France as a toddler yonks ago when apparently I was sick in my pram the whole way there *and* back, in fourteen years I've never left the UK, which is why when Mum announced her half-term holiday plan yesterday evening I became hysterically excited and danced around the kitchen chanting, 'We're – Off – To The US of A!' over and over again, pretending to be a cheerleader, but with two long-handled pan scrubbers rather than glittery pompoms.

Claudia raises one of her overplucked eyebrows. 'God, have you never been? I've been *loads* of times.'

Damn her! I wish I *had* said we're jetting to Mars as even Miss Been There Done That couldn't have pretended to be a teenage astronaut.

I'm mega-miffed that Claudia has already been to America, though I don't know why I should be surprised. Claudia Barnes has always done *everything* before me.

Her parents split up before mine.

She was the first girl in my year to wear a bra.

She began to bring in no-shower-period-notes when she was *eleven*.

She's *way* ahead of me in the snogging stakes, though as I have had only one disastrous smothered-in-spit snog with a Frog exchange student called Didier Deville, that's not a hard record to beat.

I've never had a hickey and she's had *loads*; not that I want one, but I haven't even had the chance to get one. She seems to have badges of slaggery on show all the time. And despite the fact that her dark eyebrows don't match her peroxide-yellow hair, she sports fake boobs, ridiculously long white-tipped nails and carries around unopened packets of Marlboro Lights and condoms in her bag, boys *love* her.

Or perhaps that's *why* they love her. They assume she's either been there and done *that*, or wouldn't mind going there and doing *that*, whereas I haven't been there and I certainly haven't done *that*, but then even the most freaky boys don't usually say to their friends, 'Cor! I really fancy that wide-faced, mousy-haired girl with the lopsided baps,' do they? I might share the name of an ancient Greek goddess or a glamour model, but in the looks department I'm *so* not a Greek girl or a video vixen.

'We're going to Miami and then on to New York to visit my Aunty Vicky and cousin Madison,' I say. 'They've got an *enormous* penthouse apartment in Manhattan.'

I wait for Claudia to reel off a list of relatives she has in America, probably even claiming the Statue of Liberty is modelled on one of her family.

'I've been to Miami and New York and loads of other Yank cities too,' she warbles. 'LA, San Fran. Florida . . .'

'Florida is the state in which Miami is a city,' I say, mega-impressed that I've managed to pick up a bit of world knowledge and have corrected Tits Out's geography. It's Buff and his bum again! Geography by osmosis. Just think what I could achieve with private tuition!

'Duh! I know that!' Claudia rolls her eyes. 'I was *going* to say, Florida was great. We went to SeaWorld a couple of years ago and I got soaking wet when Shamu the killer whale swam past. My T-shirt and shorts went *completely* see through. You could see *everything*!'

Any smugness I was feeling over knowing more about geography than Claudia has been completely destroyed and replaced by a rather disturbing image of her wet and semi-naked being circled by a monster whale.

'My passport is like, *totally* chocka with stamps,' Tammy drawls. 'I've been like, *everywhere*.'

'I've been to the Isle of Wight,' Butterface chips in. 'Or was it the Isle of Man?'

Tammy snorts with laughter and I notice that without her oral ironmongery she's actually quite pretty in a horsey type of way, which is gutting as it means even *she's* more likely to get a boyfriend than me.

It's hopeless. I don't even have a *hint* of romance in my life.

I thought Luce might be some use, partly because she's

so gorge I reckoned on getting some *Befriend the Ugly Friend* action, but mainly because she has two older brothers, Michael, who's totally off the radar as he's already in his second year at uni in London, and James, who's in Year 11 at King William's School for Boys, a temple of tasty testosterone and the private school of choice for the hunk of Mediterranean manhood known as Javier Antonio Garcia, aka Jags, or, as I prefer to think of him, The Spanish Lurve God. Jags was actually born in Slough rather than Spain, but The Slough Lurve God doesn't sound exotic enough to match his dark hair, olive skin and *gorgeous* long eyelashes. I am *totally* in love with him and we are destined to be together for ever, but unfortunately he's too busy being cool and gorge and sporty to notice me. I've pulled his jeans down, flashed my bum at him and even fallen at his feet, all by mistake obviously, but despite that, and even with the Lucy–James connection, Jags *completely* blanks me. To him I'm just a friend of James Malone's kid sister, and James is too busy snogging gormy zit-riddled slap-heavy Nat to put in a good word for me with Jags.

At least Sorrel isn't likely to get a boyfriend. She brands anyone with a Y chromosome a lying two-faced cheat like her dad, which is a bit harsh as Desmond Callender didn't lie about a woman like my dad, he lied to Sorrel's *Meat-*

is-Murder mum about scoffing a bacon sarnie. Whatever the lie, the end result's the same. We don't have our dads at home. Mine's living above a dentist's and has a new witchy girlfriend, and Sorrel's is on a beach in Barbados stuffing himself with curried goat.

My moby bleeps.

'Change of plan,' I say, scanning the text from Sorrel. 'I'm meeting the girls at Macky D's instead.'

'I could murder a McDonald's,' Tammy says. 'I'm like, always so starving I might have a worm.'

This throws me into a blind panic. The thought of them coming with me, not Tam's suspected parasitic infection. I haven't seen Luce for two weeks as she only got back from her French hols yesterday and there's masses of goss to catch up on. And although I've seen Sorrel nearly every day during the holidays, apart from the bit at the beginning when we had a row and she stopped speaking to me, if Tammy Two-Names is there Sorrel will just scowl and the atmos will stink and I won't be able to pump Luce for info about whether James has said what Jags has been up to over the summer, and whether Jags has mentioned me, even a tiny bit.

'Can't we go later?' Butterface whines. 'I wanna buy some new shoes.'

'Yeah, let's get the trotters first,' Claudia agrees. 'And then we can munch.'

I could hug Nat with relief, but decide against it to avoid smearing her thick yellow make-up on my clean white top.

Chapter Two

Sorrel is already in McDonald's, sitting at a table near the counter, surrounded by bits of cardboard and crumpled napkins, scoffing the last of what looks suspiciously like a sausage and egg McMuffin.

'Why aren't you in the window?' I ask, plonking myself opposite her. We always try and grab a prime people-watching and bitching seat.

'Just fancied here,' she shrugs.

'And why here rather than Burger King? We always go to BK.'

It's not just the flame grilling we prefer, the loos smell better.

'What's with the Spanish inquisition?' she asks, and just hearing the word *Spanish* sends shivers down my spine.

Sorrel looks unusually smiley, but then she's just scoffed meat, which always makes her happy. The downside of having a rampantly vegan mum is that Yolanda has banned her six kids and current man-about-the-house, Ray Johnson, from eating Face Food, home or away. This means that out of sight from The Meat Police, Sorrel fills her chops with cooked flesh and then swigs minty mouthwash to banish meat-breath, not just from her mum, but from her older sister Jasmine who's a lentil-lover as well as a complete snitch and totally up her own pert backside now she's passed masses of GCSEs this summer and is about to go into our sixth form.

Sorrel dabs daintily at her mouth with a napkin, which is well odd. Usually she smacks her lips, wipes her mouth with the back of her hand and then licks it, extracting every last meat molecule. There's something different about her, but before I can put my not-so-beautifully manicured finger on it, Luce arrives with a cheery, '*Bonjour, mes amies!*'

After two weeks in Provence her hair is honey blonde, her skin is golden brown and she looks even more gorge than usual. If she wasn't my bezzie I'd want to slap her. There's lots of squealing and hugging and whipping off of watch straps to compare tan marks, though frankly I don't know why we bother to go through this ritual. At the merest hint of a UV ray I go blotchy with lobster-limbs, Sorrel is black to start with, so Luce *always* wins.

Luce sits down next to me and folds her long brown legs under the table. My legs are not so much folded as my thighs squished unattractively together like a couple of mottled unsliced salamis.

Sorrel gets up. 'What do you fancy? I'll get it.'

'Are you all right?' Luce asks. Sorrel's standing slightly bent over at the waist. 'You got period cramps?'

'No!' She tosses her braids and almost takes someone's eye out with a flying bead as they squeeze past. 'Now, do you want something or not?'

'Just a vanilla milkshake,' I say. 'I'll give you the dosh later.'

'*Et moi*,' adds Luce, who seems to have forgotten she's no longer in France.

Sorrel heads off to the counter.

'So, how was Frogland?' I ask. 'Did you have a good time?'

We'd agreed that unless it was an absolute emergency, we wouldn't text each other, to avoid astronomical phone bills and the parentals going ape.

'*Fabuleux*!' Luce beams. 'Completely, utterly and totally *fabuleux*!'

This *is* a surprise. She'd been dreading spending two weeks with her family in France, especially her mum, Bella Malone, who's a part-time Home Stylist but full-time

15

Control Freak, Neat Freak, French Freak and the cause of Luce having a bit of a self-harm situation going on.

'But didn't your mum notice?' I whisper, wondering how you'd conceal livid fingernail-induced scars when you're lounging semi-naked by the pool in the baking foreign sun. 'How did you get round that?'

'I just kept my T-shirt on and said with my colouring I was a prime skin cancer candidate and no one said anything,' she whispers back. 'I even swam in one.'

The image of Tits Out in her wet T-shirt pops into my head.

I look over my shoulder towards Sorrel who's in the queue, tossing her hair and jiggling her backside as if she needs the loo and is having to hold on. 'Are you going to fess up about the self-harm thing?' I ask Luce. Neither of us have told Sorrel about it and I still feel a bit bad we're keeping it a secret.

'Eventually,' Lucy nods. 'But I want to be certain that I'm really better first. I still feel I need to see Fiona. I'm going over there, *demain*.'

Fiona Burns is a glamorous doctor who's been helping Luce deal with her self-harm issues. She's also Freak Boy's mother.

I haven't seen FB for weeks, probably because he's been keeping his freaky beaky-nosed head down and avoiding the hoody-bullies like Pinhead, Gibbo and Spud, who hang around near his house, waiting for him.

An image of FB pops into my head. I can see him sitting on the sofa in the conservatory in his swanky house, all alone, his beak buried in a computer mag. Then, bizarrely, a gorgeous tanned hunk pops out from behind one of the potted palms and flashes me an orthodontically perfect white smile. It's Freak Boy's father, Duncan Burns. I'm still not convinced that Hot Dad and Glam Doc didn't adopt FB at birth as if he *is* their biological child, Freak Boy's DNA helix has spectacularly unravelled somewhere along the line, and all that stuff about genetics and fruit flies Mr Hardy taught us in biology is clearly *way* off.

Before I have the chance to quiz Luce any more, Sorrel heads towards us. She's limping, swaying from side to side.

'What's wrong *now*?' I ask as she sits down with our milkshakes and her box of chicken nuggets. 'You got a dodgy hip?'

'How was Frog-world?' Sorrel asks Luce, completely ignoring my question.

'I was just telling Electra, I had a *fabuleux* time,' Lucy gushes.

'So, The Neat Freak backed off and didn't make you

17

line up your flip-flops every night?' Sorrel asks.

'Mum was much more relaxed than usual,' Lucy replies, 'and anyway, most of the time I was hanging out with Pascal.'

'Pascal?' I gasp, elbowing her. 'Who the heck's Pascal?' This explains why she keeps dropping *le* odd French word *dans le conversation*.

She giggles. Her face may be tanned but it can't hide the crimson blush creeping up her neck.

'Just the son of the Fournier family that owned the farmhouse we stayed in.'

She hands me her moby. The screensaver is of a boy with blond spiky hair wearing a red-checked shirt and a cheesy grin. I suppose he'd be good-looking if you were into lads with heads like bog-brushes, but with the exception of Buff Butler I go for more exotic dark-haired types.

'I can't believe you didn't text me!' I shriek. 'We agreed you'd text if it was something really major.'

'Lust alert! Lust alert!' Sorrel chants, looking at Pascal's pic. 'Luce has got a boyfriend! Luce has got a boyfriend.'

'No I haven't!' Lucy says, trying to sound put out but failing miserably. 'And it wasn't really major. He was just a friend who happened to be a boy.'

'But did you kiss him?' I ask, scanning her face for major-snog clues.

Lucy giggles. 'Might have done. *Un petit peu*. At the end of the hols.'

'She's Frog snogged!' Sorrel shrieks. 'Can you believe it? Our Princess of Cool has French kissed!' She picks up Lucy's phone from the table and pretends to lick it going, 'Did you go, *Mwah mwah gorge French bit*?'

'No!' Lucy grabs the phone off Sorrel and snaps it shut. 'I kissed a French boy. That's not the same as French kissing!'

'So, no tongues, Luce?' I giggle. 'Not even the slightest tickling of the tonsils?'

'Stop it!' she orders, going even more beety-red. 'I had my tonsils out, remember?'

She looks fit and well and relaxed and completely different from the girl who only a few months ago rocked on her bed racked with sobs as she told me about gouging lumps out of her skin. I'm really happy for her, but deep down I feel a teeny-weeny bit miffed that Luce is now also way ahead of me in the boyfriend stakes. When it came to boys, Sorrel, me and Luce were like The Three Musketeers. Instead of one for all and all for one, more, none for all and all for none. It's just me and Sorrel now, and The Two Musketeers sounds well odd.

19

'By the way, I've got news,' Sorrel says. 'The Loony Lentil is getting a car!'

'You're joking!' I say, genuinely gobsmacked. Yolanda is *totally* anti-car, not just 4x4 Beast Cars on which she slaps *Gas Guzzler* stickers, but anything which isn't environmentally clean and capable of carrying loads of people like an electric bus.

I have a sudden horrible thought. 'She's not buying an electric bus, is she?'

'If she does I'll leave home.' Sorrel gives a mock glare. 'We're getting it at half-term. She wants your mum's lover boy to take a look at it first.'

'I've got some exciting news too!' I say, the thought of Phil as Mum's lover making me want to heave.

'Someone's asked you out?' Lucy says.

'No, not that.'

'Your boobs are finally the same size?' suggests Sorrel and I give her a sarky smile.

'Mum told me last night we're going to America at half-term! How cool is that? We're going to Miami for a week and then back through New York to see Aunty Vicky and The Goddess Madison in Manhattan. I'm getting my passport photie taken later.'

'Oh no!' Lucy looks crestfallen. 'Pascal might come over then and I really wanted you to meet him.'

I'd been hoping for a bit more enthusiasm to my news. Not only is Luce more interested in Pascal arriving than me going, Sorrel defo isn't listening. She's staring straight past me with a dreamy look on her face. Then she suddenly sits up straight and does more neck jerking and braid tossing.

'Do yous want this? I flipped it meself.'

The sky darkens and I look up to see a lanky black lad in a McDonald's uniform leaning over me as he puts a wrapped burger on the table. He's at least a couple of years older than us, and has a huge diamond stud in his left ear, probably fake, as if he could afford a real rock he wouldn't be working in Macky D's. He pushes the burger towards Sorrel, who instead of grabbing it, unwrapping it and stuffing it in her gob, just leaves it on the table.

'Ta,' she says casually, winding one of her braids around her left index finger.

Big Mac Boy hovers by our table whilst Sorrel ignores him and examines the bead and fingernail combo in forensic detail.

I try to kick her under the table but just manage to slam my toes into a metal post so the table vibrates.

'Let me know if yous want more of my meat,' Big Mac Boy finally says, pushing his baseball cap back from his face. 'S'no probs.'

'OK,' Sorrel shrugs. 'Ta.'

He gives a lopsided grin and lopes off, presumably to flip more burgers.

Luce and I stare at Sorrel.

'What?' she says, giving us a wide-eyed look. 'What's your prob?'

'Oh don't do the innocent look with us, Miss Callender,' I reply. 'No wonder you didn't want to go to Burger King! You've got the raging hots for Big Mac Boy!'

'I do not,' Sorrel snaps.

'Well, he really fancies you!' Lucy whispers. 'All that stuff about giving you his meat!'

I suddenly realize why Sorrel was leaning over the table and walking oddly. She didn't have period cramps, need the loo or have a dodgy hip.

'You little minx!' I giggle. 'You were showing him your booty! You were pointing your butt in his direction!'

'Get lost!' Sorrel says, unwrapping the burger slowly and suggestively. 'I hardly know Warren.'

'Warren! Jeez, Sorrel! You're on first name terms with him already!' I can hardly believe it. What's happened to all the anti-Y chromosome stuff?

'Duh, he's got a name badge on,' she points out sarcastically before adding, 'but he told me his surname's Cumberbatch. I sat next to him on the bus coming here.

He used to go to St Joseph's but he's about to start graphic design at Eastwood Tech.'

'That's where Mum's doing her business course,' I say. 'Oh he *so* has the hots for you!' I show her the burger wrapper I've been fiddling with. Warren Cumberbatch has scrawled his moby number on it.

If there's any doubt in Big Mac Boy's mind that we're discussing him, it must be dispelled by the sight of all three of us staring at him and then dissolving into fits of giggles.

'He's got a ponytail,' I say. 'How can you fancy someone who has a ponytail and smells of chip fat?'

'He probably has to keep his braids tied back for work,' Sorrel says through a mouthful of ground beef. 'Health and safety knows no style.'

'He's your ideal man!' I tease. 'He can give you free meat and when you snuggle up to him he'll pong of fried flesh!'

Sorrel crumples the burger wrapper into a ball and throws it at me, but then reaches across the table, grabs it back and stuffs it into her jeans pocket.

'You're making *way* too much of this,' she says. 'He might fancy me but it does *not* mean I fancy him.'

'OK then, what would he score on the Snogability Scale?' Lucy asks. 'Be one hundred per cent cross-your-heart-and-hope-to-die honest.'

I used to spend hours assigning Snogability scores from 1 to 5 to everybody from the creepiest Zitty Bum Fluff boy (1) to The Spanish Lurve God (5) but now I'm thinking of giving it up. Spending time perfecting the S-Scale is a bit like having hundreds of cookery books when you can't even boil an egg. All theory and no practice, and at the end of it you're still hungry and there's no food on the table.

Sorrel looks across at Warren who's all hot and sweaty shovelling chips.

'Probably a 3, maybe a 3.5 without the uniform,' she says.

'God, this is serious!' I shriek. 'You've never given anyone above a 1.6, not even David Beckham!'

'Pascal scored a *quatre* before we kissed and a *cinq* afterwards,' Lucy sighs.

We're all giggling but at the back of my mind I can't help thinking, *I'm now The Lone Musketeer*.

Chapter Three

'The Little Runt has drunk all the Sunny D,' I moan, staring into the fridge before slamming it shut so hard, an alphabet magnet falls off and skids across the floor. I can't be bothered to pick it up, so I just kick it under the sofa to join all the others nestled amongst the dust. 'Doesn't he realize he's not the only one living in this house?'

'Don't call Jack a runt,' Mum says. She's sitting at the table scribbling on a bit of paper. 'And what's up with you?'

'*Nothing's* up with me,' I snap, rearranging the letters on the fridge to read JACKS A SCROAT. 'I'm just fed up of him. He drinks everything, gobbles all the crisps and biscuits and then makes foul smells that he thinks are funny.' I thought I'd take the opportunity of increasing my list of little-brother-related grievances beyond just drinking all the juice. I'm also narked that he doesn't go back to Hilmartin Junior School until Tuesday while I go back to Burke's on Monday.

'Well, I'm about to go shopping so I'll add juice to my list,' Mum says. 'Anything else you need?'

'Not unless you can get me a boy from Tesco's,' I mutter under my breath.

'A toy from Tesco's?' Mum asks. 'For Jack's birthday? Haven't you got him anything yet?'

'His birthday's *days* away,' I say. He's having a party tomorrow but he's not nine until next Wednesday, so I'll think about what to buy him on my way home from school that day. A handful of football trading cards and a Pot Noodle with a candle rammed into the top should keep him quiet. 'And why do I have to go to his stupid swimming party anyway?' I grumble. 'Why should I spend the last Saturday afternoon of the hols watching scrawny snotty kids trying to drown each other? *He* doesn't want me there.'

'*I* want you there,' Mum says firmly. 'And I've bribed you with a new iPod, remember?'

I really need that bit of technology. I've been MP3-less since some thieving weasel swiped my mine.

'Well, all right, but it's not like you're on your own,' I say, mooching about. 'Phil and Dad will be there.'

As soon as I say the words *Phil* and *Dad* in the same

sentence I realize why Mum needs me. Without me to intervene there's a real risk Mum might push Dad into the pool as revenge for his affair. On the other hand, Dad might push Phil into the pool as, even though he was the one that left, he can't stand the thought of Mum having a boyfriend, especially an ex-army one with a tattoo, a Harley-Davidson and a big yellow AA van with flashing lights.

I stop roaming aimlessly about, flop on the sofa and give a big *I'm fed up and I want you to know it* type of sigh.

'*Now* what's wrong?' Mum asks.

'Nothing,' I say in a tone of voice which is intended to convey the fact that *everything* is wrong.

'Were the girls interested in your trip?' Mum asks.

'S'pose.' I lie back on the sofa and stare at the ceiling.

'Did Lucy have a lovely time in France?'

'S'pose.'

'Oh for goodness' sake, Electra,' Mum snaps. 'Can't you say anything other than *S'pose*?'

'S'pose so?'

Mum gives up and carries on scribbling. Quite frankly I think she could have tried a bit harder to find out what's narking me.

'Lucy's in lurve with some bog-brush-headed Frog she met on holiday,' I say, finally fed up of being blanked by

27

my own mother. 'And Sorrel's got Big Mac Boy sniffing round her.'

'Big Mac Boy?'

'Oh it doesn't matter,' I snap, adding a full eye-roll for maximum effect, which I realize mid-roll is a total waste of a good eye movement as my eyeballs are pointing at the ceiling, not at Mum. 'Like you'd understand.'

'I think I understand you're in a funny mood because your friends now have boyfriends and you don't,' Mum says.

'I am *not* in a funny mood and they *don't* have boyfriends,' I snap back, thinking, *yet*.

Mum gets up from the kitchen table and comes and perches on the arm of the sofa. I'm a bit worried that it'll collapse and she'll topple on to me and I'll suffocate, trapped under mountains of pale flabby breast tissue.

Mum has humungous boobs. The sort of boobs that enter a room seconds before she does. The sort of boobs that make you wonder how she stands up straight. The sort of boobs men and boys stare at in fear and wonder. Mighty Mammaries. Not my sort of boobs at all.

I shuffle up the sofa just out of suffocating bap range, but Mum moves and sits next to me.

She pats my thigh. 'One by one you'll all start to get boyfriends,' she says. 'Perhaps we should have a talk, you

28

know, about things. Stuff. Relationships with boys. *Sex*.'

Oh how butt-clenchingly embarrassing! I thought once you got to fourteen you'd escaped the horrors of a parental sex lesson. *Surely* by fourteen they've realized you know you weren't dropped under a bush by a passing stork.

'Mum! You're like several years too late!' I shriek.

'What?' She looks shocked. 'I'm too late? For goodness' sake, Electra, you're far too young . . .'

I realize with horror that she has *totally* the wrong idea.

'No!' I butt in before she can make any humiliating assumptions about my non-existent love life. 'I mean, I'm doing GCSE biology! I already know everything I'm supposed to know! *I'm* not going to be a pram-face.'

Mum looks relieved. 'Well, that's all right then,' she sighs. 'But is there anything you want to ask me?'

'What's for tea?'

'Electra!'

I can't think of anyone less likely to need to know about the birds and the bees and boys than me at the moment.

'Honestly, Mum, it's fine,' I say.

'Did you get your passport photograph?' she asks, and I can tell we're both grateful for the change of subject.

'I look like a terrorist.'

'Let's see.' Mum holds out her hand and I go and get the pics from my bag.

She peers at them, frowning. 'You look ill, as if you need a holiday.'

'Thanks!' I say. 'That's not a nice thing to say to your daughter.'

I'd gone into the photo booth and told the girls that as this was for a proper government sort of document rather than a bus pass type of thing, I had to take the photograph seriously. I wasn't to smile and my hair had to be off my face, which was *terrible* as my forehead looked so huge in the glass I thought it wasn't going to fit in the screen, and I've also got a line of spots glowing on my chin and across my forehead. But although I banned the girls from actually coming into the booth, it didn't stop them from putting their arms through the curtain and making rude gestures and Lucy shouting out, 'Say *fromage!*' Eventually I managed to get one image without rabbit ears or a V-sign in the picture, but it makes me look totally minging, a terrorist with rampant acne in need of a holiday.

Mum hauls herself off the sofa and puts the photographs on the dresser, and I rush to put a plate over them so Jack doesn't vandalize them with horns and fangs.

'Phil's just waiting to hear if he can get that week off and then we'll book the flights,' Mum says. 'If we fly overnight on the Friday you break up and then get the day flight back from New York on the Sunday, you won't have to miss any school.'

'Like a bit of missed school's a big deal,' I say, flopping back on the sofa and flicking through the TV channels. 'I don't see why I can't skip a day of school either side of the hols. Everyone else does it.'

'So what if everyone else does?' Mum sounds disapproving. 'You know the school frowns on extra days once you've started your GCSEs. I don't want a note home. Oh, and by the way, talking of notes, Madison sent this via your Aunty Vicky's email.'

She drops a sheet of paper on my face. For dramatic effect I leave it perched on my nose, but as Mum doesn't say anything and I'm curious to read what the world's most perfect girl has to say, I blow the paper up in the air and then catch it.

Hi Electra,

Mom tells me u r coming to NYC for a couple of days in October. Mint! Let me know if there's anything special you'd like 2 do when u r here (like shopping, shopping, shopping!). If you want culture we can do shopping AND culture as NY has loads of awesome museums with great shops! I'm really looking forward to seeing you again – I think we were like, 10 – and I can't wait for you to meet Max. You'll get on great! Love,

Maddy xxx (e me direct on madaboutnewyork addy rather than mom's Vhampshire one)

'Is Max their dog?' I ask.

'I think their dog is called Rufus or Rusty or something,' Mum replies. 'Max is probably her boyfriend. I expect she's got half of New York queuing up to take her out. She looks stunning in photographs.'

Oh that's just gr-reat. Maddy and I share DNA, and yet she's a total babe who's practically a model out of *Teen Vogue* whereas I'm plain and sturdy and more suited to a spread in *Farmer's Weekly*. I can just see how *my* holiday is going to pan out. Even American boys who are rumoured to go wild for girls with British accents will ignore me, and when I come back Sorrel will be with Big Mac Boy and Luce will have spent a week snogging Perfect Pascal and I will be *gutted*. But then as Freak Boy shows, having quality DNA on the inside is no guarantee of good looks on the outside.

'Right, I'm off,' Mum says, ignoring the constant heavy sighs I'm giving. She tucks the shopping list into her cleavage. 'Jack's in his room, Phil will be back soon and remember to send Madison a reply.'

'Like I've got anything interesting to say,' I snap back.

I spend about ten minutes lying on the sofa freaking out over the thought of people giving me pitying looks when they compare cousin against cousin, when I suddenly have a brilliant idea. In preparation for my trip to America I'm going to make a plan. A Glam Plan. I have just over six weeks to turn myself from a pale-faced porker into a teenage temptress worthy of the name Electra. Madison may be naturally fantastic, but surely with a bit of primping and pampering I could make the most of what little babe-DNA I possess? With serious dedication, by the time I step off the plane in New York I could be fit and toned and have fantastic highlighted hair and perfect nails and a buffed-to-perfection body complete with a streak-free fake tan. And then I'll come back and tell Tits Out that I snogged a boy called Chuck or Brad, even if I didn't.

With my Glam Plan in place I feel tons better so I go up to my room, the Sty in the Sky (or loft conversion as Lucy's dad who owns Home Malone, the estate agents, would say), push some dirty knickers off the world's heaviest laptop, The Thigh Crusher, and fire up my email.

I start to type:

From: SOnotagreekgirl1
To: Madaboutnewyork
Date: 31st August 15.21

Hi!
Thanks for the e-m. Really looking forward to seeing you too,
going shopping and meeting Max.
Love Electra x

Well, that's not very exciting. Not only am I not a babe,
I've got nothing interesting or witty to say. I sound as
dull and gormy as Butterface but without even a
Snogging Buddy to brag about. I think of Madison
wandering around awesome museums hand in hand
with Max, or snogging him in her swish apartment
whilst hot Yankee hunks queue up outside hoping to be
her next date.

Just to see how it would look I add:

PS. Of course I'm going to miss my boyfriend Jags.

Ooh, it looks fantastico. The adding of Jags on the end
makes it sound really convincing and seeing the words
my boyfriend Jags is thrilling, even if it is a total lie. What
else can I put?

*We've been going out for 6 months and it's **REALLY** serious . . .*

Now you're talking! I am obviously not dull and gormless. I can't be. I've been going out with a Spanish Lurve God for six months and the dot dot dots hint at doing more than just tonsil tickling. So what if it's only in my head?

I sit back and admire the screen.

What if I was to send the email to Madison? It wouldn't make Jags virtually my boyfriend but could it make him my virtual boyfriend, a boyfriend in a parallel universe, the information superhighway? And would it matter even if he was only virtual? It's not like Madison's ever going to meet him. I can make out Mum doesn't know about Jags because she'd freak at the thought of me having a dot dot dot type of boyfriend so it all has to remain top secret. I could go on virtual dates with him, have virtual conversations, even virtual snog-fests by practising on my arm!

The cursor quivers over the *Send* symbol.

My hand is hovering over the keyboard.

What harm would it do? A little white lie that's all. Just a bit of fun.

I pull my hand away.

This is crazy! A lie is a lie whatever colour it is.

Whether it's about a bacon sarnie, a secret woman or a virtual boyfriend, lying *always* end in tears.

But then I think of Madison holding hands with hunks, Lucy French kissing the Frog, Sorrel being all flirty with Big Mac Boy, James snogging Butterface and Tits Out doing *everything* with *everyone*. I'm being left behind. I'm not even a wallflower, more of a wilting weed no one wants.

I jab my right index finger on the *Return* key and press *Send*.

As I watch the little bar move from left to right at the bottom I feel shocked at what I've done. Shocked, but excited.

Finally, I've got myself a boyfriend.

Chapter Four

'I can't believe I've given up my Saturday afternoon for this,' I moan. 'We could have been shopping!'

Me, Luce and Sorrel are sitting in the front row of the spectators' gallery at Aqua Splash, whilst below us in the pool, ten of Jack's friends, all with runny noses, are beating the hell out of each other with brightly coloured plastic floats. Actually, I can't believe the girls have given up their afternoon when they're not even related to The Little Runt and don't have the promise of cutting-edge technology to look forward to. So far, their only perk has been the box of Maltesers Mum bought us, and which are now perched on my denim-clad knee.

'Phil's quite fit-looking, for a wrinkly,' Sorrel says, watching him walk up and down the side of the pool in a pair of baggy swimming trunks covered in lime-green and pink flowers.

'I wonder what score your mum would give him on the Snogability Scale?' Lucy says. 'I'd have to knock off points for the skin-scratching designer stubble.'

'Do *not* use the words *Mum*, *Phil* and *Snogability* in the same sentence, please,' I say. 'It's sick.' I throw a Malteser in the air, catch it in my mouth and crunch it in one smooth movement.

'*You've* just done,' Sorrel points out.

'Pascal looked good in swimming shorts, but then French people are always *très* stylish,' Lucy says dreamily.

'I expect Warren looks pretty hot too,' Sorrel says, and the two of them collapse in fits of giggles whilst I just snap my gnashers on another chocolate-covered honeycomb ball, wishing they'd shut up about Perfect Pascal and Wonderboy Warren. Yesterday, sending that email to Madison seemed exciting. Today, I'm totally freaked I did it. I haven't fessed up to the girls what I've done. I may not have a boyfriend but I don't need to broadcast the fact that I'm also a lying saddo.

'Isn't your old fella supposed to turn up?' Sorrel asks me.

'He'll be at some plumbing emergency.' I throw another Malteser in the air but miss my mouth. The chocolate ball goes flying over the railings, bounces on to the tiles and plops into the water where a snotty-nosed boy sees it and pops it in his mouth.

Mum squeezes herself between the seats as she comes towards us, saying 'Hello' to mothers who have decided to sit out the party with a pile of magazines and a coffee.

'It all seems to be going well,' she says, looking relieved. 'The centre is doing the hot food, but I've put out bowls of crisps and Twiglets and things. If you girls can make your way to the Neptune Room when the boys leave the pool then we'll be ready for when they descend. About half an hour?'

'*Oui*, Mrs B!' Lucy trills.

'She's a bit glam for a pool party.' Mum nods towards the end of the row as a skinny woman in a tight cream dress, high heels and reddish-blonde poker-straight hair sits down clutching a cream handbag to her flat tum. 'I wonder which child is hers?'

Oh. My. God.

My stomach turns over and my heart begins to race.

It's The Kipper! Caroline Cole! Dad's girlfriend! I've been avoiding her since that dreadful night at Dad's flat when I ended up sitting on a wall slapping myself across the chops in the hope that Dad would think she'd hit me so he'd dump her. I can't believe he'd bring that bony witch here!

The Kipper sees us staring and lifts a skinny arm to wave. She's looking particularly orange and Kipper-like today.

'You know her?' Mum asks as The Kipper teeters towards us on spindly sandals, which are gold and fabulous but completely inappropriate for a kid's pool party at the local leisure centre.

'It's Dad's latest totty,' I say through gritted teeth. 'The one after Candy.'

I'm thrown into a blind panic as to how I should introduce her to Mum, but before I can decide between, 'Mum, this is the evil fish who hates me,' or, 'Mum, this is the evil fish who I hate,' The Kipper sticks out a bony claw and says, 'I'm Caroline and you must be Ellie. You and your daughter are practically identical!'

Mum laughs and obviously takes it as a compliment that she's been compared to her teenage daughter, whereas I am furious that I'm the spitting image of a middle-aged woman with a weight problem, minging clothes and shapeless hair. I love my mum but I *so* don't want to look like her. The Glam Plan is scheduled to start tomorrow and it obviously can't come quickly enough.

'And you are?' The Kipper asks, beaming at the girls.

'Lucy,' Lucy beams back.

'Sorrel,' grunts Sorrel, not looking up from her moby.

'Sorry we're late,' The Kipper says. 'Rob and I were just ordering a new car and doing some last-minute shopping for our holiday. We're off to Spain tomorrow for two weeks' sun and sand.'

That explains her alarming orange colour. She must have just had a spray tan. I hope for the sake of the others on the beach it calms down by the time she gets there or it will be like lying next to a radioactive bottle of Lucozade.

There's an awkward silence and The Kipper starts to sway on her tarts' trotters so alarmingly, I'm both worried and thrilled at the thought she might topple over the rail and fall on to the tiles below. Unlike a Malteser, she probably wouldn't bounce but shatter into loads of tiny bones.

'Well, I'd better go and make sure everything's ready,' Mum says. 'Nice to meet you, Caroline.'

Mum heads off, and as I watch her squeezing her big butt and wide thighs between the red plakky seats it occurs to me that The Kipper and Mum couldn't be more different.

'Mind if I sit here?' The Kipper asks. 'My feet are killing me.'

Without waiting for an answer she parks her bony bum next to Sorrel, who's fiddling with her phone and constantly sighing.

'Haven't you texted Warren yet?' I ask. 'He wouldn't have left his number if he didn't want you to get in touch.'

'Is Warren your boyfriend?' The Kipper asks.

I'm bummed that she's sitting here, double-bummed that she hasn't realized she's not welcome and triple-bummed that she's butting into *my* conversations with *my* friends.

'Nah,' replies Sorrel. 'Just some lad I met.'

'Oh I expect he'll be a boyfriend soon,' The Kipper purrs. 'A good-looking girl like you won't be single for long. Or you, Lucy.'

The girls giggle and I'm mega-mad because this is obviously a jibe at me not having a real boyfriend because I look like a middle-aged frump. If it wasn't a waste of delicious confectionery I'd pelt her with Maltesers.

'Your bag is fantastic, Caroline,' Lucy gushes. 'I've seen lots of celebrities with them. Just in magazines, of course.'

'Here, have a look.' The Kipper passes her bling bag to Sorrel who hands it to me. It's a cream Chloé with dangly bits and a huge gold padlock. Before I hand it to Luce, I sniff and stroke the butter-soft leather. It oozes luxury and money and must have cost a bomb.

'Ooh it's lovely,' Lucy sighs when she gets her tanned mitts on it.

'I'd kill for a bag like that,' I add, thinking that

if by some miracle The Kipper comes to a sticky end perhaps I'd inherit it, as what would Dad do with designer leather?

'Well, if ever you need to impress anyone, just let me know. I'd be happy to let you borrow it.'

I look around to make sure that The Kipper has said this to me, not to Luce or Sorrel or to some random woman behind us, but before I can stare into her cold glassy eyes to get the truth, she hangs over the railings and points at the pool.

'Look, there's Rob,' she says.

The girls are sniggering behind their hands, and when I look down, I see why.

Dad's at the side of the pool in the smallest, tightest pair of bright-red Speedos I have *ever* had the misfortune to see. As he walks along, his moobs bounce and his gut wobbles and it's all absolutely *gross*.

Phil, who's been patrolling the poolside in his floral shorts, sees Dad and walks over to him. He stretches out his hand, but Dad doesn't shake it, he just pulls his tummy in and jerks his shoulders back the way Tits Out does. Dad's taller than Phil, but *much* porkier, though both of them are slap-heads, Dad because his hair's fallen out and Phil because he has an army-style buzz cut.

Phil goes back to one side of the pool and Dad goes

back to the other, and they just strut up and down like a couple of peacocks, pretending to keep an eye on The Little Runt and his friends, whilst giving each other the odd furtive glance. I'm *so* relieved. Obviously there's going to be a lot of posing and preening but no punching.

'I think I'll just pop to the ladies,' The Kipper says, getting to her feet. 'I need a pee and a powder. See you later!'

'Thank God for that!' I gasp as she wobbles away. 'I thought she'd never go. *Now* do you see how evil she is?'

'I thought she was very sweet,' Lucy says. 'She wasn't a bit how I imagined.'

'Yeah, you made out she was like some kind of paranoid psycho,' says Sorrel. 'She seemed cool.'

'But didn't you get her jibes about me looking like Mum and you two getting boyfriends and not me?' I'm furious The Kipper has impressed the girls. 'She's always trying to twist the knife!'

Sorrel and Luce give me exasperated looks.

'Are you sure it's not you who's para?' Sorrel asks.

'She said you could borrow her Chloé!' Lucy says. 'How great was that?'

'She's evil!' I shriek. 'Am I the only one who can see it?'

Lucy puts her hand on my arm. 'Electra, do you think it might be you rather than Caroline that has the problem?'

I give her what I hope is a prime *Are you mad?* look.

'It's just, well, you called Phil The Impostor and now you like him, and then Candy Baxter was The Bitch Troll until she and your dad split up and then you missed her, and now you hate Caroline The Kipper . . .'

'What are you trying to say?' I ask, yanking my arm free. 'That I'm lying?'

'No!' Lucy sounds shocked. 'Just that maybe you hate *anyone* your parents get involved with.'

'She's saying that the prob's with you,' Sorrel adds unhelpfully.

I'm about to have a mega strop when a buzzer goes and the lifeguard signals for the pool to clear. Dad and Phil start waving at the boys, telling them to get out.

'Come on,' I say. 'Twiglet duty.'

I'm just stuffing the empty Malteser box in my bag when I hear raised voices and look down to see Phil and Dad squaring up to each other. Dad has his tummy sucked in and is giving Phil evils. Phil is flexing his shoulders, looking like a soldier ready to go into battle, although wearing flowery swimming trunks would be rotten camouflage from the enemy, unless the battle was in a flower bed. I'm trying not to look at Dad's indecent Speedos, which are a biology lesson all by themselves. It looks as if he's stuck an apple down the front of them. A tiny one.

'Do you think there's going to be a fight?' Lucy gasps, as Dad pokes Phil on the shoulder and Phil staggers backwards.

'It's the battle of Mrs B's luvver boys!' Sorrel says, sounding more excited than she has all day. 'Old against new!'

Dad's making a fool of himself. It's pathetic to watch a coot-head with moobs, a pot belly and obscene swimming trunks trying to take on Phil the tattooed muscle man. It's not just embarrassing. It's deeply sad.

'I'm getting Mum,' I say, but before I can get out, there's a huge splash. Dad and Phil are in the pool, powering through the water, creating huge waves.

I stand watching, horrified, as neck-and-neck they somersault at the end and start another length.

Everyone around me is laughing. I'm not. I don't want to see Dad humiliated by Phil. I don't want to see Phil beaten by Dad. I just want them to stop, shake hands, get dry and help pass around the savoury snacks.

I'd rather hoped Dad's moobs might act as inbuilt floats and help him at least keep up, but by lap three he begins to lag behind Phil. There's a flash of floral backside as Phil does his turn whilst Dad is still approaching the end, and by the fourth and final length, Phil is already bobbing about at the finish as Dad swims up. As some of the mothers in the gallery clap, Phil goes to slap Dad on the shoulder but Dad pushes him away and clambers out of the pool, showing a humiliating amount of hairy butt-crack as he does so.

'I need a pee,' I say. I can't get out quickly enough. 'I'll see you in the Neptune Room.'

My bladder isn't bursting. I just need to escape for a bit. It's not just seeing Dad lose the race and almost losing his swimming trunks that's upset me. Seeing The Parentals and their partners all together in one place has made the whole divorce thing seem so much more real. When you see everyone together you realize that's it, they're over, for *ever*.

I head down the stairs and towards the exit to escape the smell of chlorine and wet towels. I'll take a few gulps of car-park air to clear my head and then go back to help out.

The automatic doors slide open and I dart round the corner and lean against the brick wall taking deep breaths of . . . smoke?

It's The Kipper, puffing on a cigarette.

When she sees me she blows a smoke ring towards me and takes another deep drag on her cancer stick.

I don't know what to say but feel I need to say *something*, so I blurt out the first thing that comes into my head.

'Did you mean it about me borrowing your bag?'

Even though I hate her, I wouldn't say no to having the bling bag for a few hours. Claudia and co. would be green with envy.

The Kipper says nothing but gives me a cool, glazed look before tossing her hair off her shoulders and flicking ash on to the ground.

'Inside, you said I could borrow your bag.' I nod towards the bag of the beauty slung across her bony arm. 'Did you mean it?'

'As if,' The Kipper snorts.

'Then why did you say it?' I ask. 'Why do you always say one thing when you mean another?'

'So everyone thinks I'm nice to you,' she drawls.

'But you're not,' I say. 'You're evil to me.'

The Kipper takes another drag, bellows smoke and gives a hollow, brittle laugh. 'Yeah, I know that and you know that but nobody believes you because they think you're just a kid who still has issues over Mummy and Daddy not being together.'

She makes quote marks with her fingers when she says *issues*.

I think about what Lucy and Sorrel said earlier. If my own bezzies don't believe me when I tell them The Kipper's mean to me, I've zero chance convincing Dad.

'When Dad finds out what you're really like he'll dump you,' I snap.

'Oh I don't think that will happen, do you, Electron?'

'Why do you hate me so much?' I say, feeling more gutted that I can't get my hands on her Chloé than the fact that she's deliberately called me a negative particle. I can be *very* shallow.

The Kipper tosses her fag end away and grinds it into the ground with her gold sandal. She's probably fantasizing about my head being under her foot too, stamping my wide pimply forehead into the tarmac.

'Hate you? I don't hate you,' she laughs. 'You're just like an annoying wasp on a picnic, buzzing round and causing trouble until someone finally manages to swat you.' She reaches into the bling bag, pulls out a small spray of breath freshener and squirts it into her mouth. 'So buzz off, Wasp Girl, before you get swatted!'

I watch her sway away on her gold tarts' trotters.

I don't mind her calling me Wasp Girl.

She's obviously forgotten wasps can sting.

Chapter Five

'I've told you, Ellie, *he* started it. He was very hostile!'

'You should have walked away!'

'I tried to swim away but he jumped in after me.'

'Then you should have jumped out, not started some childish race!'

'I am not going to jump in and out of a swimming pool just because your ex-husband decides he has a point to prove!'

I cough loudly. There's nothing wrong with my throat but I've been in the kitchen for at least thirty seconds without anyone noticing me.

It's Day One of The Glam Plan. There are fifty-five days between grotty me and glam me and I'm dressed and ready for action, but Mum and Phil don't notice as they're *still* arguing about yesterday's incident at the pool. I stand around posing, which gets zero response, try another attention-attracting coughing fit and finally sit at the table and dramatically swipe away the box of Shreddies and the sugar packet, but *still* they keep bickering. It's doing my head in.

'I've told you, he's not yet my ex-husband!' Mum almost shouts, slumping next to me at the table. She stirs her tea so fast I'm freaked the spoon might get caught up in a beverage vortex and spin out and up and poke her in the face. 'You should have let him win. Rob's a proud man and he'll be hurt he hasn't won. And if he's hurt it'll come out as anger. He'll use this against me in the divorce, I know he will. He'll start being deliberately awkward.'

'Especially with the evil lawyer he's got,' I mutter.

'What about his lawyer?' Mum says, *finally* realizing I exist.

'You met her yesterday,' I say. 'That bony orange woman. Dad's girlfriend. Caroline Cole.'

'As in Cole from Hammond & Able?' Mum shrieks. 'Your father brought his lawyer to his son's birthday party? Why didn't you tell me?'

'You never asked,' I shrug.

I talk about The Kipper as little as possible and Mum talks about Dad as little as possible so the fact that Dad is seeing the solicitor handling his divorce from Mum never came up.

'Oh this is just great!' Mum snaps. '*You* humiliated him at the pool, *she's* getting all friendly with his lawyer and I'm the one who has to cope with the fall-out!' Her head jerks between Phil, me and her cup of tea. 'As if I haven't enough to worry about, what with starting college on Thursday!'

'*I'm* not friendly with her,' I say. 'She's a bony bitch.'

'Who's a phoney snitch?' asks Jack, coming into the kitchen holding Theo his rabbit.

Mum glares at me and mouths *language*.

'Dad's girlfriend,' I say. 'The woman in the cream dress at your party.'

Jack looks blank for a moment and then says, 'I thought she was pretty.'

I don't believe it! Even The Little Runt has been taken in by The Kipper. Men!

'Can Dad come to America with us?' Jack asks, putting Theo on the floor.

'I don't think that's a good idea,' Mum says sharply, looking across at Phil. 'And take Theo outside. I'm fed up of stepping in bunny poop in my bare feet.'

Jack chases the little black rabbit around the kitchen which just means poo pellets are deposited one by one across a wider area.

'I should hear tomorrow whether I can take that week

off,' Phil says. 'Half-term can be a bit difficult if you don't book it months ahead.'

'Er, like, hello? Has anyone noticed what I'm wearing?' I say, fed up of being ignored.

I've got totally gorge pale-pink tracky bottoms on with *Sporty* written across the bum, a white long-sleeved T-shirt (good for hiding the salami arms) and some wicked trainers which have silver mesh on the top and a pink stripe round the heel. I look The Business. At the party, Mum gave me the iPod she'd promised me, a pink nano, but when Dad saw her do it he obviously didn't want to be outdone so he shoved some money into my hand and whispered, 'Buy yourself something nice,' which was fantastico for two reasons, one because I needed the cash, and two because he did it in front of The Kipper whose mouth went so pinched and twisted, even she couldn't have forced a ciggy into it.

Me and the girls chucked a few more snacks into a bowl and the moment the first parents arrived to take away their brats I pleaded for my freedom, and we shot to Eastwood to spend my dosh in the tiny Topshop. I'm now totally kitted out and ready to go, and thanks to Mum's iPod and a downloading sesh last night, I'm wired for sound.

'Very nice,' Phil smiles. 'Are you going running?'

53

'Running is so last year!' I snort. 'I'm going for a power walk.'

'Well, power walk your way over to Aqua Splash,' Mum says, getting up to clear the table. 'Jack left his swimming shorts there.'

'Like, no way!' I shriek. 'It's miles away. I have to build up my walks slowly, and anyway I am *not* touching his stinky trunks.'

Mum glares at me. 'What is it those sporty adverts say? JUST DO IT!'

When it comes to sport, the world is divided into two sorts of people. The people that duck when a ball hurtles towards them and the people that dive to try and catch it. I am a ducker not a diver. In other words, I am not sporty.

I'm never picked for the netball team because I never jump to get the ball, mainly because I'm too lazy, but also because when I jump my skirt flies up and shows everyone my sturdy thighs. I'm not bothered about girls seeing upper-leg flesh (other than Miss North, the games teacher, who we are sure is lesbionic) but the netball courts are right next to the footie pitches and I don't want to be humiliated by scummy lads shouting, 'It's the Sturdy Salami!' Hockey is OK as long as I don't have to run and can just put my stick out and trip someone up. Tennis would be good if I could have my own ball slaves, otherwise I just get too exhausted running after stray balls to play any actual tennis. Badminton has the advantage of being inside and with a lighter racket than tennis but, as with balls, I duck when the shuttlecock speeds towards me, which isn't helpful.

So I might not be the sportiest girl in the school but this morning, in my new tracky and trainers, I look it.

I slam the front door of 14 Mortimer Road, overcome an almost irresistible urge to flash my bra at Mrs Skinner next door who's snooping behind her net curtains, skip down the steps of the house into the street and march along, swinging my arms with a spring in my step and my earphones pumping music into my head.

The Glam Plan is going brilliantly. Not only am I exercising, I've cut down the calories by shunning the Shreddies, turning my back on the toast and passing on the Pop-Tarts.

And now I'm absolutely starving.

I don't want to faint on Day One. I might bang my head on the pavement. I'm not so much worried about a major brain injury – I presume Mum would cancel the trip to America if I was lying comatose in a hospital bed – but what if I got a big gash down my face or broke my nose?

I couldn't face The Goddess Madison looking as if I'd been in a fight.

I nip into the newsagent's for a Snickers bar. The peanuts will give me a bit of protein and I'll make up for the calorie-fest by eating less later.

As I chomp on the nuts and toffee I think how mega disappointing it's been that although I'm a vision of pink and white sportiness and have gone the long way round, I haven't seen anyone I know. I might as well take a short cut through the park. I still won't see anyone but it means I can get the stinky shorts and go home. If I'm to arrive in New York in a blaze of gorgeousness I've got a busy schedule of exercising and exfoliation, toning and tanning and filing and flossing ahead of me.

I don't remember the last time I was in Victoria Park on my own. It's always full of winos or druggies or people that are best avoided, but I'm reckoning that there isn't much stranger danger at eleven o'clock on a sunny Sunday morning. There are kids playing football, families on bicycles, a couple of dog walkers, some Goths sleeping on a park bench. It's actually quite nice, and as long as I watch where I'm walking to avoid mud and dog poo, I'm *totally* safe.

'ARGH!'

I've been assaulted! Someone has tried to grab my butt in broad daylight with kids around! It's only by skilful staggering that I manage to stay on my feet.

I spin round to see a stinky wet rug with a black nose, four legs and a panting pink tongue. The mutt has seen my pink-clad butt and made a beeline for the word *Sporty*. I'm covered in muddy paw prints which totally penk and now the ruddy dog is wagging its tail so fast, bits of greenish mud are splattering me.

'Go away!' I scream, twisting this way and that. 'Bog off, dog!'

This makes the dog think I'm playing and sends him even more mental. He's now barking at me, so as well as being mud-splattered I'm getting a heavy whiff of toxic dog-breath.

'Get lost! Go home! Drop dead!'

The wretched dog keeps bouncing up and down with its muddy wet paws. I now have paw prints over my boobs as well as my butt. I love dogs and I'd love a pupster of my own, though as I couldn't even look after our guinea pig without it being murdered by a passing fox, I'm never going to be allowed one, but if I was, I'd have a well-behaved well-groomed dog, maybe one with a diamanté collar which I could carry in a designer handbag.

I'm still yelling and thinking to myself that Mum was right, the park isn't a good place to go on your own, and that this wasn't the sort of exercise I had in mind for Day One of The Glam Plan when someone comes running towards me brandishing a lead. I rip out my earplugs and hear yelling.

'Archie! Off! Off!'

It's Freak Boy. His voice sounds deeper than I remember, but perhaps that's because of the running-and-shouting combo.

'Can't you keep that dog under control?' I yell as FB clips the lead on Archie and drags the yapping mutt away. 'Look at the state of me!'

To prove how muddy I am, I grab my sweatshirt and hold it out to FB which looks as if I'm presenting my baps to him which was *not* what I intended, especially as my chest smells rank. 'I'm filthy!'

'I'm sorry.' FB hangs his head and tries to hide behind his hair, which has grown out of its pudding-bowl look and is quite long. 'It's goose poo. He was rolling in it by the pond and then he suddenly ran off. He must have recognized your smell. Dogs have twenty-five times more smell receptors than humans.'

My smell! What's Freak Boy trying to say? That even without being plastered in goose turds I stink, or that his unruly dog hunts down girls wearing Anaïs Anaïs? I then think how tragic it is that my perfume doesn't have the same effect on boys as it does on Archie, and that Jags doesn't leap out of a pool and come tearing across a field to jump on me.

'My clothes are ruined!' I moan. 'What if I see someone I know?'

'Well, I know you and I still think you look . . .'

I wait for Freak Boy to say something nice, even though I don't really want him to as it would be creepy. But still, a girl has to get her compliments where she can. I'd accept lovely, gorgeous, or even at a pinch, nice.

'. . . presentable.'

Presentable! Presentable! What sort of a word is that? Who under the age of twenty says *presentable*?

'Do you . . . er . . . want to walk Archie . . . with . . .?'

'I'm going to Aqua Splash,' I say before Freak Boy can finish his sentence, which I'm sure is going to end in the word *me*. It's bad enough I look as if I've rolled in crap without it seeming as if Freak Boy had something to do with it. 'I've got some stuff to collect.'

'Oh well.' FB looks disappointed and for a nanosecond I feel sorry for him.

'Will you be back at school tomorrow?' I ask him, 'or did you get terrorized?' Last term he was bullied so badly by Pinhead, Gibbo and Spud he mentioned his parents might move him.

'I stayed in most of the time so I expect they found someone else to taunt. I'll be in on Monday.'

I feel a flood of relief that FB's coming back to school and then a wave of disgust as it really shouldn't bother me one way or the other if he's there or not.

I try to give him an *Am I bovvered?*-type look, just in case my face has given away the fact that for a nanosecond I *was* bovvered, but FB is staring down at Archie, who's pawing the ground and sniffing.

There's an awkward silence before FB says, 'Well, bye then.'

As he walks off, head down, shoulders hunched, I wonder whether I've been a bit of a cow. I could have suggested he walked to Aqua Splash with me, but after all that stuff at the end of last term when people got the wrong end of the stick and thought I fancied him, I need to be careful no one sees us and believes the ugly rumours.

I'm just marching through the car park when I see a group of boys standing around the entrance to the pool. If I hadn't been mauled by the stinky mutt I'd have done a Tits Out, yanked my shoulders back, stuck my chest out and sauntered past them wiggling my bum, hoping that at least one of them might glance in my direction, if only to read the writing across my backside. But as I look and smell like a goose-loving tramp, I'm just going to keep my head down and walk straight through them in the hope that no one notices me.

'God, you smell ripe!'

It's Lucy's brother James, all tall and blond and tanned from the French sunshine.

And then I see Him.

Bronzed and gorgeous, standing in khaki cut-off shorts and a white T-shirt, his dark hair wet but drying slightly at the ends so it's beginning to curl gently, his lips pressed around a can of Red Bull.

Jags.

The Spanish Lurve God.

My virtual boyfriend.

As he's a bit on the short side I hadn't noticed him until the others moved to get away from my smell, but as soon as I realize who it is I keep my head down and study his gorgeous legs, admittedly stumpy, but shapely and very sporty with just the right amount of hair-to-skin ratio. Neither baby smooth nor gorilla legs. Perfect from head to toe.

'Other than penking like a rugrat's nappy, what you up to?' James asks.

No need to lie now. No need to come out with a Shakespeare quote or pretend that I'm interested in some obscure rock band just to impress Jags. I've got a legitimate reason to be here. I'm not hanging around hoping to accidentally-on-purpose snap Jags with my mobile phone or pretend I'm about to play badminton. I'm not stalking him. I'm here to collect lost property.

'Oh, I've just been for a run.'

What?! Where did that come from? I can't believe I've just said that. It might explain the splattered tracky though.

'We've just been playing water polo and now we're going for a jog,' James says. 'Fancy another few k's?'

'Sure.'

No! I can't remember the last time I even ran for a bus! And *please* let k's mean KitKats not kilometres. It's all too much for Day One of The Glam Plan. I need to work up slowly to my gorgeousness.

Jags throws his can into the bin and just as I'm wondering if I can go back and dig it out as a souvenir, we're off.

It's no good.

I can't go on.

I'm going to die.

My throat is rasping, my heart is pounding, my forehead is sweating so much it's running into my eyes, I've got double vision, I need water and my pits are *gushing*.

And we've only just left the car park.

It's not the running that's knackered me, but the combination of trying to run whilst sucking my gut in, clenching my butt cheeks and trying to keep my iPod from popping out of my top. I'd tucked it into my bra, but for small boobs they're surprisingly jiggly, probably on account of the push-up bra I'm wearing rather than a sports jobby, and the pink case keeps creeping over the edge of my top like some weird metallic third nipple.

And what's even worse is that Jags and James have run off without me! I've now officially got boys running *away* from me.

I stagger into the park and collapse on the nearest Goth-free bench. I'm coughing so much I have to spit out the phlegm, which is gross, but I reckon that exercise-induced gobbing is just about acceptable. I need time to get myself together for when they come round again. Perhaps if I can stop dying and keep the iPod under control I might be able to join them, though I don't know why I'm bothering. I stink, I can't run far and I'm out of breath.

I cough and spit out another ball of mucusy saliva, which lands on my trainers.

'Are you all right?'

It's Freak Boy and Archie.

'I was just having a rest,' I say, watching the frothy bubble of spit soak through the silver mesh into my socks. 'I've been running, with friends.'

'I thought you were going to the swimming pool?' FB says.

'*I* thought you were walking your dog,' I snap, and then realize he still is.

I can see James, Jags and the others hurtling towards me. I'm desperate for Freak Boy to go before they get here, but he doesn't seem to get the hint. He sits on the bench next to me. As he does so, Archie suddenly grabs on to my left leg and starts . . . there is no other word for it . . . humping my shin.

'Get him off!' I shriek, wriggling my leg which just makes the dog clutch it even harder. 'Get him off me. He's mating with my leg!'

FB jumps up and leans over me trying to pull the rutting dog off.

'In broad daylight too!' James Malone laughs as he, Jags and the others run past roaring with laughter.

Chapter Six

As I swing out of the end of Mortimer Road, Tits Out is already at the bus stop round the corner in Talbot Road. She's probably been up for hours, straightening her hair, touching up her white-tipped nails, plucking her eyebrows, stuffing her bra. We're not due in until ten on the first morning of the new school year, but whereas Claudia has taken the extra hour to glam herself up, I stayed in bed until Mum blew a whistle in my ear, nearly bursting my eardrum.

We all have to wear the same uniform, a minging green tartan kilt, white shirt, green tie and a green blazer, but somehow Claudia makes hers look different. She's hitched up her skirt into a mini-kilt, showing acres of faked-bronzed thigh between its hem and her black over-the-knee socks. Her white shirt is tied in a knot around her waist and she's turned the collar of her blazer up and kept the huge knot of her tie low down. She looks tarty but classy tarty. As I walk towards her I pull out my shirt and try knotting it, but my belly pokes out over my waistband which is *so* not a good look and another reason why perhaps a piercing in that area is best avoided.

'What are you doing with your hand down there?' Claudia jeers as she sees me trying to ram my shirt back into my skirt. 'Having a good fiddle?'

'I'm still getting dressed,' I say, ignoring the stony looks of a couple of wrinkly coffin-dodgers at the bus stop. 'I slept in.'

'Talking of sleeping, Jags says you were involved in some rampant rutting with Razor Burns in the park yesterday.' She pokes me in my side with her elbow. 'Electra Brown! Shagging on a Sunday. In public!'

I daren't even look at the wrinklies. They're probably fanning themselves with their bus passes to get over the shock.

'His dog was humping me.' I say this sarkily but am secretly thrilled that although The Spanish Lurve God shows no evidence of even knowing I walk on this planet, he still recognized me enough to tell Tits Out that a smelly doormat was trying to get his bits away with my leg. 'Did Jags say he'd seen me?'

'Not really,' Claudia says. 'He said he'd seen the beaky boy with James's kid sister's friend so I guessed it was you and him.'

Not quite the recognition I'd hoped for then.

'Why were you with Jags anyway?' I ask, though I can hardly bear to hear the answer. I'm still not convinced she and Jags weren't in my bedroom during my disastrous birthday party, but I'm not one hundred per cent sure as I was practically unconscious from OD-ing on coloured buzz juice.

'Nat texted James 'cause she hadn't heard from him after his hols, and then he texted back and said she was dumped, just like that! Nat wanted me to ask Jags to ask James to find out why.'

I didn't actually think Natalie was going out with James Malone. I thought they just had an arrangement whereby they ate each other's faces at parties if there were no other willing lips.

'And?' I ask. 'Why did he dump her?'

'Apparently he met some girl in France,' Claudia sniffs. 'Poor Nat, she can't compete with foreign birds.'

'But he'll hardly ever see this French bit,' I say. 'Why can't he still be Nat's snogging buddy?'

'Dunno.' Claudia puts her hand out to stop the bus. 'But Jags says James says he can't see Nat when he's made a commitment to this French tart. Nat spent most of yesterday arvo in bits.'

The bus rumbles up and the moment the doors open Claudia pushes past the coffin-dodgers who are staring at us like we're devil-kids. I wait to let them totter on which takes so long one of them could have died in the process, so by the time I get to the top deck Claudia is already next to Butterface, who's blotchy-faced and puffy-eyed. Even an extra-thick coating of yellow make-up can't disguise the fact she's obviously been blubbing for hours.

Sorrel lives five stops further back so she's already behind them, staring at her moby. She barely looks up as I squeeze in next to her. Apparently she finally sent Big Mac Boy a text. It took her from Friday lunchtime to Sunday afternoon to decide what to say. In the end she went for *Hi*. He apparently texted back *Hi 2 u 2*, and now we're all waiting for the next thrilling instalment of this riveting exchange of romantic messages.

'Claudia told me James dumped you,' I say to Nat, who bursts into tears and swivels round to face us. It's a horrific sight. Her tears are making tracks through her make-up and she hasn't got waterproof mascara on. It looks as if a couple of tarantulas are marching down her cheeks.

'Do you think Lucy knows what's been going on?'

Butterface sobs, leaning over the back of her seat. 'I want to know all about this French tart.'

'Why's she got a face on?' Sorrel mutters.

If she could be bothered to look up she'd realize that, actually, Natalie's face is sliding *off*.

'James Malone dumped her for some bit he met in France,' I say.

Nat starts wailing even louder, making strangled snorting sounds. People start staring.

'You wouldn't get me busting my tear ducts for some lad,' Sorrel says sourly.

'Just leave it, Nat,' I say, hoping that her nose isn't going to run and drop on to my skirt, though at least with the tartan print it wouldn't show, not unless snot dries yellow or white. 'He's not worth it.'

'I've told you, Nat, he'll get bored of having no one to snog at parties,' Tits Out says over her shoulder. 'It's not like this cow lives local. When he's got the raging horn and she's not here he'll be sniffing around you, Nat, mark my words.'

'I don't want him now,' Natalie sobs. She fishes a tissue out of her bra and blows her nose, covering it in yellowy-brown grease.

'Then what are you worrying about?' Sorrel says. 'Get over yourself.'

'I wanted to be the dumper not the dumpee!' Nat wails.

'If I'd known he'd found some friggin' foreign froglet I'd have dumped him first!'

I text Luce to warn her not to stand by the school gates if she doesn't want to be ambushed by Butterface asking awkward questions about her brother's love life, but to wait in the loos until we find her.

'Listen, Nat, there are masses of fit lads out there other than James,' Claudia says, rooting around in her bag. 'You'll have a better one in a couple of days.'

She makes it sound as easy as buying a new top. The old one doesn't fit you any more so you just go out and find a new one. How come I can't find anything to fit me? If there are masses of fit lads out there, why do I have to resort to a virtual boyfriend?

Claudia hands Butterface her handbag mirror. When Nat sees how minging she looks she wails even more, but gets out her make-up bag.

'I'm never going to get over this,' she says, holding a bottle of foundation in one hand and slapping it on with the other. '*Never.*'

'It's not as if you were officially going out with him, Nat; you only snogged him,' I say. 'Did he ever call you his girlfriend?'

Butterface starts wailing again, which wrecks the slap she's just put on.

'But we snogged loads of times so I just assumed,' she says. 'I mean, how many times do you have to snog before you become someone's official girlfriend?'

Lucy's leaning against a basin in the toilets waiting for us. It's already littered with hair from pre-lesson hair primping and preening.

'What's the problem?' she says. '*Pourquoi le* loos?'

'Butterface is out to interrogate you over your bro's love life,' I say. 'James dumped her, by text.'

'I didn't know he was officially going out with her,' Lucy says. 'I thought they just snogged.'

'Well, she thought she was his girlfriend and she's gutted,' I say. 'She wants to grill you about it. You have been warned.'

'*Merci.*' Luce strokes her already glass-smooth hair with her hand.

'You never said James had a girlfriend,' I say, unhooking the chandelier earrings I wear to and from school, replacing them with tiny fake-diamond studs. 'Since when?'

'Since the start of the summer. I was trying to forget.' Lucy pulls a face. 'All the time we were away it was *Fritha this* and *Fritha that.*'

'Fritha doesn't sound very French,' I say, looking in the

mirror and thinking it's going to take more than just a Glam Plan to make me look OK unless The Glam Plan includes extensive reconstructive facial surgery. 'I thought she'd be called Claudette or Antoinette or something.'

'What makes you think she's French?' Lucy asks.

'Because your bro told Nat he'd met a bird in France,' Sorrel butts in.

'That's the reason James gave for dumping her,' I add.

'Well, he didn't meet her in France and she's not foreign,' Lucy says. 'That's why he was like a love-sick puppy when we were away. He was in France and she was in England. Fritha Kennedy is in our year but at QB's.'

Chapter Seven

'Today is the day when school gets *really* serious.'

Our headmaster, Mr Thomson, stands on the stage in the school hall doing his impression of a teapot, one hand on his right hip, his left arm waving over the crowd of Year 10s sitting below.

'Today you will embark on work for your GCSE exams, the results of which will be with you for the rest of your life.'

It's exactly the same speech as previous years, except then it was about SATs and GCSE choices. As I've heard it all before, I tune out as The Teapot drones on about coursework and modules and consistency and commitment and doing things that will look good on forms, until I snap to with the sound of a moby ringing. It's trilling away next to me but luckily it's not mine. It's Sorrel's. She's obviously forgotten to switch it to vibrate and tuck it in her bra.

It's pretty dire for a moby to ring during school time,

but in an assembly with The Teapot is probably about as bad as it can get.

The best thing in such extreme circumstances would be to ignore it and make sure your face is giving a *What jerk has left their moby on?* look, hope that by the time a teacher has waded into the crowd to try and find out where it is it will have stopped, and bank on everyone around you looking innocent and claiming sudden and severe hearing loss.

But Sorrel doesn't ignore it. She starts scrabbling manically in her bag. By the time she's got it out, it's stopped ringing but some teacher I've never seen before with a bushy ginger beard has come stomping through the row and is holding out a stubby-fingered hand. He's very short and if he had a fishing rod he'd look exactly like a garden gnome.

'I'll turn it off,' Sorrel says, clutching the silver rectangle. 'It won't happen again.'

'Och no, you'll give it to me, lassie,' snaps The Ginger Gnome. He's clearly Scottish. Perhaps he took the job because he was attracted to the tartan uniform. 'You can have it back after school.'

I shoot Sorrel a sideways glance and see she's giving him one of her best *I dare you* stares, which doesn't seem to bother The GG in the slightest, possibly because he's used to being stared at, what with being the spitting image of a garden gnome.

The Teapot stops talking and starts glaring. Sorrel clutches her phone and The GG keeps his hand outstretched. Everyone holds their breath at this pupil–teacher standoff.

Then, in one quick darting movement, The Ginger Gnome grabs Sorrel's phone and puts it in his pocket.

Now, I meant to *think* the next thing that came into my head; at the most mutter it under my breath. I didn't mean to *say* anything out loud, but the shock of going back to school must have scrambled my brain as I find myself gasping, 'He's mugged you!'

The Ginger Gnome glares at me and I notice his left eye is *seriously* bloodshot.

'You are?' he demands.

'Electra Brown,' I squeak, looking down because the gross eye is making me feel sick, and also because The GG's breath is as rank as Freak Boy's dog's.

'Well, that's not a name I'm likely to forget,' he snaps, and I wish, yet again, that I'd been called something simple like Jane Brown rather than the name of the self-catering apartments in Faliraki, Greece, where I was conceived on my parents' honeymoon.

'And you?'

I guess he must be asking Sorrel because the toxic wind from his mouth isn't blowing in my direction.

'Sorrel Callender,' she grunts.

'Well, you can both come to see me in Room 3A on the upper level after school.'

As he stomps off down the row, the sea of pupils quickly parts to let him past, presumably glad to step out of the stinky-breath slipstream.

I can feel anger vibes from Sorrel as Mr Thomson continues with his assembly which is now about doing the Duke of Edinburgh's Award scheme and how it can help you get into uni.

'Listen carefully for your form rooms, which will stay the same for the rest of the year,' The Teapot says. 'Your tutor will give you timetables.'

'Who do you think we've got?' Lucy whispers, looking at the row of teachers who look as fed up to be back at school as we are.

'Dunno, but thank goodness we haven't got The Penguin,' I whisper. Mrs Frost is standing glaring at the side of the hall, dressed head to toe in black except for a white shirt. Actually, her water retention problem has got worse over the summer so she's more Killer Whale than Penguin. She told us last term she'd be taking another form group next year, but my joy at not having her was short-lived as she teaches English language *and* literature for all Year 10s, so I'm stuck with her and her blobby body for another two years.

'Form 10.1 you are in Room 3A Upper with Mr McKay,' booms The Teapot.

Sorrel and I look at each other in horror.

The Ginger Gnome is our new form tutor.

'So, is everyone clear about what they're doing and where they're supposed to be doing it?' The Ginger Gnome bellows. 'And it's *sir*, not Mr Mckay or Mr One Eye or even Mr Go Die. I've heard them all before.'

There's sniggering and mutterings of, 'Yes, sir,' and the sound of shuffling of papers but I just feel a sense of rising panic as I look at the pile of paperwork in front of me.

I am now *seriously* freaked about schoolwork. How am I going to cope with proper exams if I can't even understand the timetables The GG has just given out? There seems to be one for homework, one for coursework and one to give to Mum, which has parents' evenings and things on. The timetable isn't just a bit of paper, it's now in something called *A Planner* and is on a two-week rotation, which means you have to remember not to turn up for history with Mr Moxon on Wednesday morning just because you had it last Wednesday morning, as you're now probably due in French with Mademoiselle Armstrong. There are blank grids that we're supposed to fill in but I'm not sure why, a list of school trips, and a timetable of things going on in the rest of the school, like, *Hello?* Why should I be interested that the tots in Year 7 have an art exhibition in December? And lesson-free study periods, the one thing I was looking forward to in Year 10 have been scrapped, as last year's Year 10 were spotted at the chippy rather than the library.

The Ginger Gnome said that we should aim to spend between two and two and a half hours on homework *every* day. Does that include Saturday and Sunday or just Monday to Friday? Ordinary people have weekends off so why shouldn't we? It's slave labour. I can't see how I'm going to fit it in *and* have a life.

If I leave school at ten to four and spend half an hour outside the newsagent's with everyone else then that takes me to twenty past four, when we usually go to Eastwood Circle to mooch around for a bit. In the winter we stand underneath the hot-air vents in Marks & Spencer until the security guards chuck us out, but in the summer we just hang around the benches by Debenhams or sit in Burger King, though I expect Sorrel now wants to go to Macky D's because of Warren the Wonderboy. By the time

I've got home it's six-ish when Mum does tea. Then I watch the TV and get on the computer and message the girls, or phone the girls or text the girls and then it's at least eight-thirty, which means if I start then I could be doing homework until eleven at night, which can't be healthy. I'm sure Mr McKay has got it wrong and is just saying this stuff to freak us.

Sorrel's mad about the moby mugging. As we were going up the stairs to the form room she was giving it all, 'I'm going to go straight up to that ginger minger and demand my moby back,' but it was all hot air and she kept her head down.

I flick through the planner: English lang and lit with The Killer Whale, maths with a new teacher called Mrs Chopley, history with Poxy Moxy, art & design, Miss Ainsworth, French with Mademoiselle Armstrong aka The Big Geordie, business studies with Mr Lyndsey, biology, Mr Hardy . . . I start to write the days of The Glam Plan in it even though I'm sure the school didn't intend us to use it as a personal grooming record.

And then, as I turn a page, life suddenly feels one hundred per cent better. There's another reason other than going to America to keep up with The Glam Plan.

Buff Butler *is* my geography teacher.

* * *

By the time we'd had our assembly and our extended form session with all the timetable stuff, we really only had half a day's school to endure. Real school starts tomorrow. For my French set, the bottom one, there was supposed to be a conversation lesson but The Big G was off ill, so we just sat in the language lab and larked about. And now, after final reg, me, Sorrel and Luce are standing in front of The Ginger Gnome's desk, waiting for Sorrel to get her moby back.

'Well? Haven't you got homes to go to or coursework to start?' The GG asks, stroking his bushy beard.

As well as being our form tutor, Mr McKay is also the new Design and Technology Head of Department, but looking at him, I wonder whether it's safe to let him around D&T equipment with that quantity of facial hair. Surely he's worried it will accidentally get clamped in a vice or ignite with a blowtorch?

'You've got my mobile,' Sorrel says flatly. 'You confiscated it.'

'And?'

I shuffle to one side as, like Mrs Frost's water retention problem, The GG's breath has got worse during the day.

'*And*, I'd like it back, please,' Sorrel says in a tone of voice which implies *Are you stupid or what?*

'And I'd like it back, please, *what*?' Mr McKay barks.

Sorrel just stands there. Her evil glares don't seem to be making The Ginger Gnome quiver in his dodgy brown slip-ons.

'What's the magic word?' Mr McKay prompts.

I'm desperate to say *Abracadabra*, and have to bite my lip really hard to stop myself.

'I'd like my phone back, please, *sir*,' Sorrel almost snarls.

The GG slaps it in Sorrel's outstretched hand and turns towards me.

'And what do you have to say for yourself . . . who are you again?' My name might be recognizable but what with Jags and now The GG, my pasty face obviously isn't.

'Electra Brown, sir. I'm sorry I said you mugged Sorrel. It was more of a snatch, no I mean a grab, a teacher's snatch, which is OK . . .'

I've got to get out of here.

'And you,' he says to Lucy. 'What have you done wrong?'

'N . . . n . . . nothing,' Lucy stammers slightly. 'I just came to watch.'

The GG does more beard stroking and I'm convinced that small bugs will fall out of it, land on the desk and start scuttling across the woodgrain-effect plastic top.

'Och, go home and get out of my sight,' he snaps. 'This is going to be a long year. For all of us.'

Chapter Eight

We didn't go home of course. We went shopping.

'Why don't you just go in and ask if it was him phoning?' Lucy says to Sorrel as we get off the bus at Eastwood Circle and Sorrel makes a beeline for McDonald's.

'I can't do that!' she shrieks. 'I don't want him to know I'm wondering whether he was Withheld Number.'

'You said you didn't give a flea's fart whether it was him or not,' I say. 'I don't know why you don't fess up to fancying the pants off him.'

'I do *not* fancy him,' Sorrel says, slicking on some lip gloss as we get near the big yellow M. She pushes me towards the door. 'But let's go in, just in case he's there.'

We hang about inside pretending we might order. We hang about outside in case he's hanging about outside. We even go round the back to see if he's having a break by the bins. But there's no sign of the ponytailed burger flipper.

'That's it!' I shriek as a fat rat climbs out of a pile of rubbish and scoots past me. 'I'm on Warren-spotting strike.'

'Me too,' Luce shudders.

Even Sorrel has to agree that hanging out with vermin is beyond the call of bezzie-duty, so we abandon our search and begin to wander.

Ahead of us Tits Out, Tammy Two-Names and Butterface are loitering by the bench outside Debenhams.

When Luce spots Nat she ducks into Superdrug and we dart in after her.

'Look, I'm just going to go home,' she whispers, peering round a display of special-offer panty liners. 'I can't face the third degree over my bro's love life.'

'Oh, Luce!' I moan. 'Don't be such a wimp. Nat's going to find out she was dumped for a Queen Bee rather than a French Tart sooner or later.'

'*Oui*, but not from *moi*,' Lucy says. 'Anyway, I want to send Pascal an email to tell him how the first day back went. See you *demain*!'

She giggles and scurries out of the shop with her head down.

Sorrel and I continue to wander towards The Tarty Trio.

83

Groups of Burke's sixth-form boys are hanging around, Claudia and Tam are laughing and doing lots of inappropriate hair tossing, but Nat still looks grumpy and gormy. She's perched on the back of the bench with her feet on the seat, sucking on a lollipop stick.

'Cheer up, Nat,' I say, wondering whether she *has* cheered up and her face has just settled back into its usual blank look. 'Great tarts' trotters!'

She's dumped her socks and black school flats for bare legs and spindly red metallic sandals.

'I bought these on Friday and James had dumped me by Sunday,' she says, close to tears. 'He never even got to see them and they make my legs look gorge!'

She sticks a pin out and the sixth formers examine the price ticket stuck to the sole of one of the sandals.

'Talking of seeing people, did you get a bollocking from the Red Devil about your moby?' Claudia asks Sorrel. 'Did you get it back?'

Tits Out has taken off her school tie and has undone her shirt so, what with her chicken fillets and her push-up padded bra, it looks as if she's got a couple of bald-headed men nestling down there.

Sorrel waves her moby in the air. 'Like he'd *dare* to keep it.'

I take off my tie and go to unbutton my shirt but have

84

just decided there's no point when Tammy Two-Names suddenly starts waving madly.

'Over here! Over here!'

Three girls are sauntering toward us. Even without their grey and red uniform they are unmistakably Queen Bee Bitches. They're all in leggings and little skirts with big belts slung around their tiny waists and armfuls of jangling bangles. I recognize a couple of them from when they came to my party and trashed the house, including the bitchy tall one who put Mum's bra on her head and sniggered over how big and grey it was.

'Hi, Tams,' says The Bra Bitch. She sneers at us and wrinkles her nose like there's a really bad smell in the air, and for a moment I have a stab of paranoia that despite a long hot shower yesterday I've still got a whiff of goose poo about me. 'I see you're back at Burke's. You must be, like, well gutted.'

Tammy shrugs. 'I don't know what's going to happen,' she says, obviously hedging her bets between annoying her old friends and *really* annoying her new ones.

'I think you're stuck there now, Tams,' says another snooty girl. 'Not unless your dad stops being a mentalist by, like, Thursday.'

'*We* don't go back until then,' Snooty Girl 3 crows.

I glance at Claudia, who's looking a bit miffed that the

85

Burke's sixth formers are staring at the posh girls rather than her. She sticks her chest out even further and gets a packet of fags and condoms out of her bag. If this brandishing of slag accessories was meant to keep the sixth formers sniffing around it hasn't worked, as they sling their rucksacks over their shoulders and saunter off, laughing. Claudia looks annoyed and stuffs the unopened packets back in her bag.

'Thank God they've gone,' The Bra Bitch gasps, tossing her glossy long brown hair. 'My boyfriend gets like, *mega* jealous if he even *sees* me near other boys.'

'He does,' agrees Snooty Girl 2.

'I didn't know you had a boyfriend,' Tammy says admiringly. 'Since when?'

'Since like, the start of the summer,' says The Bra Bitch. 'He's like, *totally* into me.'

'He is,' nods Snooty Girl 3, looking so snooty I want to ram a couple of eyeliner pencils up her nose.

The Bra Bitch does more hair tossing. I rather hope Sorrel might start tossing *her* braids. A swipe across the chops with a burgundy glass bead would, of course, be a tragic accident, but would wipe the smug look off The Bra Bitch's zit-free face.

'Do I know him?' Tammy's practically panting for info. 'What's he like?'

The Bra Bitch waits for a moment, the dramatic pause presumably because she's about to reveal the name of a stunning hunk which will have us all reeling with jealousy. I have a flash of panic that it might be Jags, but then feel sure that The Bra Bitch wouldn't go out with someone so much shorter than her.

'James Malone? He's in Year 11 at KW, but he's like, sixteen at the end of September.'

Oh. My. God. The Bra Bitch is Fritha Kennedy!

Butterface, who's been sitting sulking on the back of the seat, jerks her head up. There's nothing gormy and blank about her face now. It's twisted into a snarl.

'James Malone?' she shrieks, still with the lolly stick in her mouth. '*You're* seeing James Malone?'

'Yah.' Fritha Kennedy manages to look up at Nat whilst looking down her nose. 'I've been going out with him all summer. Like, what's it to you?'

'Well, newsflash!' Tits Out snaps. 'He's been two-timing you with Nat *and* with some French bird he met on holiday.'

'Which one of you is Nat?' Fritha sneers.

'Me!' Natalie yells. 'So he's been three-timing you!'

'Oh you sad, daft, cow!' Fritha mocks. 'He just told you that to like, get rid of you. I was like, there when you sent that pathetic text, and it was like, me that texted you back

87

from his moby. Didn't you realize, it's *me* he's seeing!'

'And you're not French?' Nat squeaks.

'As if!' Fritha snorts. 'God, Tams, are these the sort of brain-dead chavs you have as friends?'

At which point, *everything* goes mental.

'You've stolen him, you stuck-up cow!' Butterface shrieks. She tries to get off the seat to lunge at Fritha, but as she does so the heel of one of her sandals gets caught between the slats of the bench and she tumbles to the ground with a terrible scream.

'Oh get up, chav-brain,' The Bra Bitch snaps.

I don't know whether she actually kicks Natalie or just points a silver ballet-slipper-clad foot towards her, but Tits Out sees her do it.

'You snotty bitch!' Claudia screams and pushes Fritha, who pushes her back.

Claudia then grabs Fritha's hair whilst Snooty Girl 2 tries to bop Claudia over the head with her bag, and Snooty Girl 3 whips out her moby and starts filming everything.

Tammy tries to pull Fritha away and Sorrel, who fancies being in the police when she leaves school, starts shouting, 'Break it up! Break it up!' I stand there wondering what to do as I've never been involved in a proper fight before and I'm freaked. I'm just wondering if I should go and get help or whether it will look as if I'm a wimp and am running away when I realize Nat's still lying at my feet, on her side, crying and moaning and clutching her face.

'Nat, get up!' I scream, as the bundle of scrapping girls stagger towards us. 'Get up! You're going to get trampled.'

Nat doesn't move.

'Nat! Get up! Get up!' I'm really hysterical now. I reach down to grab her hand to try and drag her to safety.

There's a gurgle as she rolls over on her back.

I'm freaked that there's loads of blood gushing out of her mouth on to the pavement, but doubly freaked when through the blood I see a white lolly stick poking right through her left cheek.

Chapter Nine

'It's nice to see so many familiar faces as well as new ones,' Jon Butler smiles as he stands at the front of the class. He's obviously been somewhere hot as he's very brown and his floppy blond hair is beautifully bleached. 'When I read your name out, can you put your hand up so I can see who you are? It might take me a few lessons to instantly put a face to a name, so if I call you Peter when you're really Paul, don't get upset.'

I don't normally like drawing attention to myself in class, but the thought of Buff's eyes being solely on me for a few seconds is thrilling. I duck under the desk, fiddle around in my bag, and come up again wearing chandelier earrings to try and disguise the width of my dish-face and a slick of clear lip gloss for a perfect pout. There's not time to sort out the hair, so I just spit on my hands and smooth it down. I'm just in time as after Claudia's name is called out Buff says, 'Electra Brown?'

'Here, Mr Butler!' I put my hand up, but keep my nails hidden as they're looking a bit rank as there's not yet been a nail day in The Glam Plan.

To my horror, Buff doesn't look up but just mutters, 'Electra', marks the register and then calls out, 'Frazer Burns?'

Freak Boy barely puts his hand up but Buff looks up and smiles. 'Hello, Frazer. Nice to have you back in my class.'

Even Freak Boy gets more of a look-in than I do! How tragic is that?

Everyone Mr Butler calls out seems to at least get a glance from under those long eyelashes. Everyone except me. How come *I'm* not noticed by Buff?

'Natalie Price?' Buff calls out.

Silence.

'No Natalie today?'

A murmur runs around the class. Everyone's heard about the run-in with the QB girls, though the story has now grown to become that the QB lot pushed Nat off the seat, stamped on her head, nicked her phone and ran off before the ambulance arrived, that last bit being true. Claudia went to see her after school yesterday and said she had a big white blood-soaked bandage on her face, like a sani-pad stuck to her cheek. I might call her Pad Face on a temporary basis.

'Natalie had a terrible accident on Monday night, Mr Butler,' Tits Out says, batting her eyelashes so hard it looks as if she's allergic to bright light. 'She twisted her ankle, wrecked a great pair of shoes and has a facial injury caused by a lollipop stick. She won't be back for about a week.'

'Ooh, that sounds nasty,' Buff says. 'If you see her, give her my best.'

'I will, Mr Butler,' Tits Out says breathily.

Buff finishes off the register and then announces with a wide smile, 'For those of you who didn't have me last year, I'm Jon Butler.'

The girls giggle at the thought of *having* Buff Butler, but he either ignores us or doesn't notice. He turns to the whiteboard, points his muscly butt towards the class and as he writes his name on the board in thick black marker, I notice the hair on his forearm looks like spun gold.

'My real name's Jonathan but it's a bit of a mouthful and I'm not keen on the word *Johnnie*.'

Everyone giggles. Perhaps now we're in Year 10 and no longer kids he's flirting with us. Perhaps he realizes his secret weapon in getting his pupils great grades is his lush looks. It's certainly much better to be taught by academic eye candy than someone like The Ginger Gnome. I mean, if The GG was teaching you geography you couldn't look at him because he looks so weird and his bloodshot eye's so gross. And you wouldn't want to go near him to ask him questions after class because you'd suffocate from his breath. Whereas even when Buff is going on about coursework and interaction of people with their environment and using words like *rural* and *urban* and *migration* and talking about the field trip next year it sounds interesting, *especially* the field trip. Not that the thought of traipsing around in a cold river with a tape measure exactly thrills me, but four days and three nights in a chalet in the middle of nowhere with Buff does. I'm going to have to really think about my wardrobe for that one, as I don't know *anyone* who looks glam in an anorak and wellies.

I spend the rest of the lesson staring intently at Mr Butler, pretending to listen to him whilst imagining myself being stranded on a riverbank, unable to get across the rushing water, until Buff gives me a piggy-back, clutching my meaty thighs around his six-pack.

'Electra, could I have a word please?' Buff nods towards me as everyone files out.

My first thought is *I'm in teacher trouble*, but unless he was mind-reading and logging in to my racy daydreams about him, I haven't had a chance to do anything wrong. Yet. Perhaps Buff was ignoring me earlier because he knew he was going to pull me aside after the lesson and tell me how thrilled he is that I'm in his class. Perhaps he does fancy me and was deliberately playing it cool just to throw the others off the scent, not wanting to make his lust obvious. Of course *nothing* can happen between us. That would be too weird and, possibly, illegal, but it's pretty thrilling to think that if something could happen, it would.

I give my best smile, pull my shoulders back, stick my meagre chest out and walk to the front of the class.

'Yes, Mr Butler.' I toss my hair in what I hope is a casual yet clearly attractive way rather than looking like I'm jerking my head around.

'Electra, those earrings you're wearing are very nice . . .'

I knew it! He's paying me a compliment. He's seen me in the chandeliers and realized there's so much more to me than being just a schoolgirl in his class.

'. . . but they are totally inappropriate for school and against the uniform code. Don't wear them in school again, OK?'

Buff smiles, but whichever way you look at it, I've been

told off by him and it feels *totally* humiliating.

'Sorry,' I mumble, and scurry out with my shoulders hunched and my satellite-dish face burning hot.

'What did Mr Butler want?' Lucy asks. She and Sorrel are waiting for me outside.

'I got told off. Come on, let's get out of here,' I say, scooting along the corridor whilst unhooking the earrings and dropping them into my bag. I hate having naked ears but I'll look for the studs later.

'You got a bollocking *already*?' Sorrel says, catching up. 'What for?'

We go into the dining hall and join the queue, which is very short because it's a healthy lunch day, so most of the kids are buying burgers and chips off Flyin' Brian through the school fence. Now that the vending machine is full of apples and milk rather than chocolate and cans, Brian's doing a roaring trade three times a day.

'My earrings are, apparently, inappropriate for school,' I say tartly. 'Buff told me to take them off.'

'Well, they do practically touch your shoulders,' Sorrel says. 'You were asking for trouble.'

'Like you were, leaving your moby on in assembly?' I point out.

'Gosh, I wouldn't have thought Mr Butler would have cared about such things,' Lucy says. 'He seems much more laid back than that.'

'He might be good-looking but he's still a teacher,' I say. 'Behind the smiles and the rippling muscles he's just like the rest of them. A petty earring Nazi.'

I don't really think Buff's petty, but I feel pretty silly about the earrings and hurt that he's told me off. I also feel totally humiliated that I did an impression of Tits Out in front of him. Maybe I should try and change subjects? We haven't even had a proper geography lesson yet, so perhaps if I tried to get into another class, *anything*, I wouldn't have to face Buff again. And maybe I would learn *more* by having an ugly teacher as my limited brain power wouldn't be wasted on trying to impress teacher totty. I briefly wonder whether I could swap geography for D&T as there's no *way* I'd ever look on The GG as anything other than a gargoyle, but the thought of having to make things like a CD rack out of perspex puts me off.

'Get the chicken,' Sorrel urges, nudging me in the ribs. 'And make sure they're not hiding chips under the counter.'

Sorrel's mum won't give her any money for lunch, as she makes her packed lunches from café leftovers such as curried lentils stuffed in wholemeal pitta bread. Sorrel says these not only taste disgusting, but make her produce lethal-smelling farts all afternoon, and given that for all but French and maths I sit near her, I'm happy for her to dump the lentils and provide fart-free food.

We head towards Claudia and Tammy. It seems odd not to see Butterface with them.

'What did Jon want?' Tits Out asks as I dump my tray down next to Tam.

'Told me to take my earrings out,' I say. 'I've gone right off him.'

'This is my teacher bait,' she says, wiggling her chest as if I couldn't fail to notice that without her blazer her black lacy bra is clearly visible under her white shirt. 'He wouldn't dare tell me to take my bra off, well, not in public!'

For a moment I feel sorry for Mr Butler, trying to teach the class about mountain ranges whilst most of the girls in front of him are working out whether he can see their mountains, or in my case, uneven humps. But then I remember the telling-off and don't feel sorry for him at all.

Tits Out starts stabbing away on her moby. 'I'm just sending Nat a text to say Buff sent his love.'

'But he didn't,' Sorrel sneers. 'He sent his best, not his love.'

'Same as,' Claudia shrugs. 'It'll cheer her up. I'm going to go and see her again after school. Any messages? Anyone want to come?'

'Tell her I said to get over it,' Sorrel says pinching a piece of my anaemic-looking chicken. 'I'm going to see if Warren's working.'

'I'd come with you except it's my little bro's birthday and I have to put in an appearance,' I say. 'And I've got to buy him a pressie.'

'Count me out,' Lucy says. 'I've got extra Français after school and Pascal thinks I should go so we can really communicate.'

'I'll come,' Tammy says.

Claudia looks shocked. 'God, Tam, I don't think you should, I mean, what with your whole snotty QB connection and everything. It might cause Nat to have a relapse, burst her stitches open or something.'

'She might attack you,' Sorrel adds, waving a knife towards Tammy's freaked face. 'Retribution by proxy.'

'She'll get over it,' I say. 'James *and* the accident, but maybe not the shoes.'

'I've told her that as soon as she can put some slap on the scar she should be back out there and hunting for hunks, even if she limps,' Claudia says. 'She's not going to find a lad stuck at home or even in here.' Tits Out rolls her eyes. 'I mean, other than teachers, is there anyone here that you'd even snog let alone shag?'

We look around the sad wasteland of zero talent that is

our canteen. It's a pretty sorry bunch of Zitty Bum Fluff Boys and nerds.

'They're all just kids, they'd never get a job in McDonald's,' Sorrel says, as if working on a chip counter is the ultimate in hunk-employment.

'Pascal's our age but then he is French,' Lucy says. 'Foreign scores extra points.'

I think of The Spanish Lurve God and can't help but agree.

'Let's like, give marks out of ten to the next lad that comes past,' Tam says. 'One for *Not with a barge pole*, and ten for *Let's see your barge pole!*'

We all giggle and then I see who's heading towards us, head down, tray in front of him, unaware that he's about to walk straight into a coven of cackling witches ready to trash his looks and his personality with a crappy score.

'Doesn't *that* just prove my point about minging lads at Burke's?' Claudia says, nodding towards FB who's almost level with our table. 'Top Male Minger.'

Tammy giggles. 'I'm going to give Razor Burns his score. Nul points!'

'Stop it, Tam!' I growl. 'Stop being such a bitch.'

'Lighten up!' Tits Out trills. 'It's just a laugh, unless you'd secretly shag Razor!'

'Hey! Razor!' Tammy calls out. 'WHAT THE?!!'

'God, Tam, I'm so sorry!' I start fussing around, helping a juice-soaked Tamara pick bits of cucumber and tomato out of her lap. 'I don't know what happened!'

As I stood up somehow my entire tray of chicken salad and apple juice tipped on to her lap, *just* as FB passed by.

Chapter Ten

I'm lying on my bed listening to the rain drumming on the roof, hugging a hottie because of period pains, wondering if I should repaint the bedroom walls from Babe pink to Goth black, and thinking of things I've done with Jags – in a virtual sense – to tell The Wunder Cuz, when there's a Mum-shriek from downstairs.

'Electra! If you want any washing done, bring it down.' There's a pause. 'And check for tissues!'

I haul myself off my bed, get on my hands and knees and start sniffing bits of clothing on the floor to see whether they're dirty and worn, or clean and just abandoned. Some of the stuff on the floor isn't dirty from wearing, but I've tried it on, decided it wasn't right, couldn't be bothered to hang it up, left it on the bed, needed to move it to get *into* bed, put it on a chair, needed to sit on the chair, bunged it on the floor as a temporary measure, where it stayed and then got dirty rolling around with the dust balls on the laminate strips.

I grab an armful of assorted clothing and go downstairs. Clutched to my chest it does whiff a bit.

Lying on the mat, in the hall, is the post. As I pick up the soaking bunch of envelopes I drop a pair of knickers. In picking up the knicks I drop a bra. For a few seconds there's a continual movement of penky underwear between floor and arms until I wonder whether the laundry is actually so stinky it's running away on its own.

Eventually I get both underwear and post under control. There's a couple of bills, an official-looking white one addressed to Mum, some pizza leaflets and a postcard with a bull pawing the ground looking murderous. I'd be murderous if a man dressed in embroidered cut-off trousers and pale-pink socks started flicking a red sheet in front of me. The card must be from Dad. He's back from Spain tomorrow, Sunday. But when I turn it over, I don't recognize the handwriting. It's in blue ink and all thin and spidery.

Hi E & J

Having a lovely time soaking up the sun and relaxing.

Food good. Wine even better. Hotel wonderful.

Wish you were here!

Love Caroline and Rob xx

The Kipper has written *our* postcard! She's added a kiss too! Phoney! And what's with the fake *Wish you were here* bit? Wish I was there so she could force me to wear a red T-shirt and chuck me in front of a rampaging bull, I bet. I fold the card in four, tuck it into the back pocket of my jeans and go down to the kitchen.

'Post for you.' I drop the letters on the kitchen table and go to dump the washing on the floor by the machine until Mum shoots me a look which leaves me in no doubt that I should actually put the clothes *into* the washer.

I'm just ramming fabric into the drum, when Mum gasps, 'Oh!' and I hear a chair scrape back across the floor tiles.

When I turn round, she's slumped at the kitchen table holding a piece of paper, her hands shaking.

'Mum, you all right?' I ask, alarmed. 'What's happened?'

'I'm fine,' she sighs, dropping the letter on the table and running her hands through her hair. 'But I could do with a cuppa. Pop the kettle on, love, will you? And maybe get out some choccy biccies?'

'What is it?' I say, rinsing out two used mugs just enough to look clean. I wonder whether the postcard from Dad has dropped out of my pocket and upset her, but when I feel my backside, the pocket on my right butt-cheek is still bulging. 'Is it to do with Dad?'

'Sort of,' Mum says as I practically scald myself by

fishing the teabags out of the mugs with my fingers rather than using a spoon. After I've slopped some milk in, I take them to the table with a packet of chocolate Boasters wedged under my left armpit.

'Thanks, love.' Mum cups the mug between her hands. 'I've just got the decree absolute through the post. Your father and I are officially no longer married.'

'Well, that's good, isn't it?' I say, crunching a biscuit. 'That's what you wanted.'

'I suppose so.' She gives a mammary-heaving sigh. 'It was just a shock to see it there in black and white, even though I knew it was on its way.' She puts down the mug and grinds her eyes with her palms. 'This time last year I was married and happy and . . .'

'. . . and you had no idea Dad was having an affair,' I say. And then wished I hadn't.

'Even so. It seems so final.'

'If you could change things, would you?' I ask her. 'If you could turn back time . . .'

'You mean, do I wish I was still married to your dad?' Mum says, nibbling round the edge of a Boaster. 'Of course I wish things had turned out differently, but it's too late.' She taps the divorce papers. 'All those years and it comes down to this.'

I take another biscuit. It's Day Fifteen of The Glam

Plan, but there's no point in even *thinking* about having a low-calorie day when it's raining, you've got your period and your parents have just got divorced. 'You've got Jack and me,' I say. 'And Phil.'

Mum pats my hand. 'I know, love, I'm very lucky. We're still a family, just a different sort of family, and I'm enjoying this part-time college course and . . .'

High above the kitchen I can hear my moby trilling in my room.

'It'll be the girls,' I say. 'Bella's dropping them off later. Luce said she'd ring when they were on their way. I can ring her back and tell them not to come.'

'No, I'll be fine,' Mum smiles. 'I've got to go out and pick Jack up from football, take him to a party and then do some shopping. I'll drop the bags back here before I collect Jack. I can give the girls a lift home on the way if you like.'

I get up and give Mum a hug and, as I do so, I glance at the washing machine, whirring away in the corner.

'I'm sorry, Mum . . .' I start.

'Electra, love, it'll be fine.' Mum kisses my arm. 'People get divorced all the time. There's nothing to worry about.'

'No, there is,' I say, looking at the water swirling behind the glass doors of the washing machine. 'I've left a *stack* of tissues in my clothes.'

105

'After everything they've said about wanting me to learn French, how could they do this to us?' Lucy cries as she hurtles through our front door flicking rain from her shoulders. 'I don't need to learn Irish!'

'What's happened?' I ask as Sorrel follows her in. Behind her, in the street, I see Bella Malone roar off in her big silver Range Rover.

'It wasn't exactly *entente cordiale* in the Beast Car,' Sorrel says, dumping her sopping jacket over the banister. 'Pascal isn't coming over at half-term as The Family Malone are heading to Ireland to see rellies.'

'Even Michael's been ordered to come,' Lucy wails. 'None of us want to go but they're forcing us!'

'Oh, Luce, I'm so sorry!' She's standing in our hall looking so wretched I'm worried she'll start scratching herself again. 'What's Pascal said? Is he upset?'

'Very,' Luce sniffs, taking off her coat and hanging it up on the coat hooks. She tries to be different from her mum but she's clearly still the daughter of a Neat Freak. 'He emailed to say he's *très . . . très . . .*' she searches for the right word, 'gutted!'

As we troop down to the kitchen where I'm still trying to pick bits of tissue off wet washing, Lucy's moaning about life being unfair and Sorrel's muttering that she wants to go into town and see if Warren is working.

'We could just nip in and see,' she says, flinging herself on the sofa. 'You don't actually have to buy a burger.'

It's been more than two weeks since they met, and although Warren gives her the odd burger when he's on flipping duty, there's still no sign of him asking her out, and even Sorrel can't claim that a free box of chicken nuggets leaning against the bins round the back is a hot date, especially since they're always on the look-out for rats.

'It's all right for you,' I say. 'You get free meat. We either boost Macky D's profits or we have to sit and watch you scoff. Anyway, I thought we were going for a walk. That was the plan.'

Lucy is next to her, hugging a cushion to her chest, staring at the pic of Pascal on her moby. 'I don't feel like it. I feel like crying.'

Sorrel is also staring at her phone. I can see over her shoulder she's flicking through the three texts from Warren. Never have the words, *Hi 2 u 2, Cool* and *Mint* been examined in such forensic detail.

Looking at my friends making eyes at their mobies annoys me, though obviously having period pains doesn't help my general mood.

'*Every day* something goes wrong!' I moan. 'How am I

supposed to keep up with The Glam Plan?' My school planner is on the table as I'd scooped it up from the bedroom floor where it had been hiding under the dirty laundry. I flick it open. 'Day Fifteen is supposed to be an E day but I can't E if it's raining, I've got gut-ache and you're not up for it!' I've been putting E for exercise, FM for French manicure, FT for fake tan and so on in the diary, but so far, it's been a bit half-hearted with plenty of FMs and FTs but absolutely no E. 'I've got three weeks to get stunning, four if you count the fact that I'm not seeing The Wundacousin until the Friday.'

'None of your plans ever go according to plan,' Lucy says. 'I thought you were going to stop planning plans.'

'This one's important,' I say. 'Madison is a stuck-up Teen Queen and I will *not* be thought of as a genetic throwback.'

'I can't believe you're stressing over seeing a cuz,' Sorrel says. 'I can see you stressing over a lad, but not a rellie.'

'I keep telling you,' I say, irritated that neither of them seem to understand the seriousness of the situation. 'She's a goddess! She probably looks good in an anorak. She cheerleads with pompoms and I cheerlead with pan scrubbers. She has a fab boyfriend and . . .' I nearly add that I only have a pretend boyfriend, but manage to keep my potty mouth under control.

The girls give me odd looks.

'Stay here and I'll prove it.'

I leave them mooching over their mobies and go upstairs, to the box room that Dad always used to call his office. It was pretty crammed when he was living here, but now it's one enormous filing tray, except nothing is ever filed, just piled. There's stacks of paper, empty envelopes, cards for decorators and articles ripped out of magazines and newspapers.

I'm looking for old Christmas cards. The Hampshire's Christmas card always has a picture of the Wunder Cuz on the front. Modelly Madison making snowballs. Skipping Madison tripping through crisp autumn leaves. Smiley Madison the cheerleader. The Glam Plan *has* to work. I don't want to be thought of as the unfortunate cousin who doesn't know how to shake a pompom properly.

But standing in the cramped room surrounded by paper-dross I don't know where to start, and I'm not going to spend my afternoon sifting through piles of rubbish just to prove to the girls that my cousin is a total Teen Queen while they're downstairs gossiping about their boyfriends. They'll just have to take my word for it that my cousin is so gorgeous and perfect and completely wonderful she can practically walk on water and heal the sick.

I'm about to go back down when on top of a pile of

takeaway leaflets I see the words *County Court*. I vaguely recognize it as the paperwork Mum got in the post this morning. Looking at it I can see why she was upset. It looks so formal, so final, so bleak. Eleanor Charlotte Brown seems to have been *the Petitioner* and Robert Brown, *the Respondent*, so I guess Mum divorced Dad. There's no mention of why they split up, no mention of Dad's affair with Candy Baxter. I think next to Dad's name instead of *the Respondent* there should be the phrase, *the Cheating Liar*.

And then I see the words:

The marriage solemnized on the 18th day of December . . .

18th of December! They've got that wrong. Mum and Dad were married in late September, not December. I know this for a fact because I was conceived whilst they were on honeymoon and my birthday is the 5th of July which is approximately nine months after the wedding. Someone has made a mistake. If they've got the dates wrong, maybe Mum and Dad aren't officially divorced.

My heart starts racing.

It's a sign! A sign that it's not too late for the parentals to get back together! With this mistake Mum and Dad have been given a last chance to turn back time.

Chapter Eleven

Sorrel waves as she darts through the rain to the front door of 5 Forge Road. We've already dropped Luce off, and now we're on our way to collect The Little Runt from his party.

'Mum,' I say as we pull away. 'I think Dad and you are still married.' It's the first time we've been on our own since I went snooping in the study, and I've been itching to spill my discovery.

'What?!' The car swerves into the middle of the road and back again before bouncing off the kerb. You'd think I'd remember by now not to drop bombshells when my mother is in charge of a four-wheeled killing machine, especially in bad weather. 'What makes you say that?'

'I was looking for a photie of Madison to show the girls, when I found your divorce paperwork. It says you got hitched in December, not September. They must have got the dates wrong.'

'Ah,' Mum says.

'So if the forms are wrong, you could be like, still married on some legal technicality! It's fate! A second chance! Candy was a mistake, The Kipper's never going to last and I mean I like Phil but—'

'Electra, stop.' Mum pulls over to the side of the road and turns off the engine. 'There's no mistake.' There's a tense silence. 'We did get married in December.'

'Not September?'

She shakes her head. 'You know I said I didn't go to university after A levels?' Her voice sounds strained and wobbly.

'Yeah, 'cause you'd miss Dad too much.'

'Well, I did go, to Newcastle in fact, to study English, but I left at the end of the first term because—' She stops in mid-sentence. 'Not because of your father. Well, sort of because of your father, but more because . . . oh, ignore me. It's nothing.'

I can tell it's not nothing. Your mother doesn't pull over to the side of the road, turn the engine off and look as if she's having her nails ripped out with hot tweezers for nothing.

'Mum! I thought we had a pact!' I shriek. 'Aren't you

supposed to be treating me as a grown-up? Aren't we supposed to be talking to each other more?'

'I know.' She bangs the steering wheel and gives a deep sigh. 'OK. The reason I dropped out of university after the first term was because by Christmas I was three months pregnant with you.'

Well, I wasn't expecting that! I'd thought some dozy court official had typed the wrong date in, or Mum had given them dodgy details by mistake. Never in a million years did I suspect the truth which is, 'YOU WERE PREGGERS WHEN YOU MARRIED DAD?'

'Electra, calm down!'

'CALM DOWN! AFTER YOU LECTURED ME ABOUT BEING CAREFUL WITH BOYS AND NOT BEING A PRAM-FACE YOU GOT PREGNANT *BEFORE* YOU MARRIED DAD?' I'm in full-on window-shattering mode.

'No, Electra,' Mum says sharply. 'I didn't get pregnant *after* I lectured you, I got pregnant before I married your father, which is *why* I was lecturing you.'

I am *totally* gobsmacked. I can't believe that my goody-goody mum walked up the aisle aged eighteen, a preg-head. That's only four years older than me!

'But why change the date?' I ask. 'What's with the porky pies?'

'It was your grandma's idea,' Mum says. 'She was

113

ashamed I'd got pregnant, ashamed I'd dropped out of uni, ashamed I wasn't married. She told everyone except immediate family that we'd had a quiet wedding in September rather than a very quiet wedding in December with me holding a big bouquet to hide the bump. The story just stuck and after a few years we forgot about it. It didn't seem important.'

'Didn't seem important! You change the date of your wedding and it doesn't seem important!' My voice is at bat-squeak level.

Mum says nothing but just sits and stares ahead of her.

'So I wasn't conceived on your honeymoon in the Electra self-catering apartments then?'

Mum shakes her head. 'No, but we did go there for our honeymoon, which coincided with Christmas. We were the only people staying; it was cold and windy, there was no hot water and I had *terrible* morning sickness!' She laughs at the memory, but I'm not laughing. This has turned *everything* I believed on its head. Mum and Dad didn't get married because they couldn't live without each other. They got married because they hadn't got their contraception sorted out. And if I didn't start life in Greece, where then? I could have been called Mini or Sofa or Park Bench! It's probably best I *don't* know.

'Would you have married Dad if you weren't preggers?' I ask.

'Probably not.'

'*What?*'

Mum pulls her seat belt away from the Mighty Mammaries and turns to me.

'Look, I'm not saying I wouldn't. I'm just saying if things had been different I *probably* wouldn't have. I would have carried on with university, seen your dad when I could, and then I'd have probably met someone else and he'd have probably met someone else and, I don't know, we'd have probably drifted apart.'

As well as a lot of probablys floating about, there's a definitely that I wasn't planned.

I look out of the passenger window. There's nothing to see because of the lashing rain and the steamy glass. I wipe the window with my hand but it fogs up immediately and leaves my palm wet and mucky. I need to ask Mum a question but I'm freaked I won't like the answer.

'Did you ever think about not having me?' I say. 'You know, getting rid of me?'

'Oh, love, that was never an option!' Mum cries. She tries to give me a hug, but the combination of her huge boobs and her fastened seat belt means she can't get to

115

me, so there's just a weird straining noise. She gives up and holds my hand. 'Electra, you were loved from the start, by both of us.'

We jump out of our skins.

Someone's banging on Mum's window. Everything is steamed up and we can't see who it is.

'Lock the door!' I scream. 'Lock the door!'

Phil's always telling Mum to lock the doors when she's driving, especially at night, and now I can see why. We're about to be carjacked by some gun-toting drug-crazed maniac. The door is opening . . . we're going to be attacked . . . Mum's going to be dragged away and thrown in the back of a van . . .

'What's wrong?' Phil peers into the car. Through the open door I can see the yellow lights of his AA van flashing in the gloom. 'I saw you as I was passing.'

'Nothing's wrong,' Mum smiles. 'We'd just stopped for a chat.'

'Oh, Ellie!' Phil sounds exasperated. Even I can see that stopping on the side of the road in the pouring rain without leaving your lights on is probably not the safest place for a life-changing chat with your daughter.

Phil offered to run me straight home, which seemed a better option than sitting in the car with The Little

Runt, no doubt hyperactive from gorging himself on cake at the party.

'Won't you get into trouble?' I ask, as in front of us Mum moves out in the road. I can tell she's done the whole mirror, signal, manoeuvre routine knowing that Phil's behind her, otherwise she'd just head out into the traffic, ignore the blaring horns and hope for the best.

'I think you count as a damsel in distress,' Phil says. 'You certainly seemed a bit distressed. Everything OK?'

I stay silent. It's all very well begging your mum to treat you as an adult, but sometimes the consequences are hard to take.

The windscreen wipers are on full blast, left and right, left and right. I feel hypnotized watching them.

'Did you know Mum was already preggers when she married Dad?' I finally ask.

'Yes, yes, she told me. Does it matter?'

I shrug. I know one thing. 'It means that I was an accident. Jack was planned but I was just one big fat inconvenient mistake they were stuck with.'

A hot tear plops out and runs down my cheek followed by several more. Then my nose starts running and I wonder why you can't have a good sob without snot being involved.

'Oh, Electra, come on.' Phil hands me what I thought

would be a wad of soft tissues but is oily scratchy paper. 'Remember when I met your mum?'

I nod, sending snot flying from both nostrils. We broke down on a dual carriageway because Mum filled the car with petrol instead of diesel and Phil was the AA man who rescued us.

'Well, that was a mistake, but if it hadn't happened, we'd have never met. Doesn't that just prove that sometimes, like you, mistakes can be wonderful?' He reaches across and gives my arm a sympathy squeeze.

We drive on in silence. The rain lashes down and the wipers go at top speed. My eyes and nose feel sore, not just from blubbing but because the paper Phil gave me is one notch down from sandpaper, so that when I blew my nose I took some skin off at the same time. This inadvertent exfoliation will put The Glam Plan back days. I start to sob again, even louder, not because I'm a mistake but because I'm thinking about how rank I'm going to look in New York.

Chapter Twelve

Sitting behind the reception desk, bent over a computer, a blonde girl with shockingly dark roots is pecking away at her keyboard.

'Sign in, please,' Root Girl says, pushing a pen on a bit of string in my general direction without looking up.

'I'm here to see my dad,' I say. 'I'll just go through.'

It's months since I've been to Dad's warehouse and I wonder what's happened to Geriatric Joan who used to feed me gnasher-wrenching toffees when I came round after school.

'There's no one here called Mahdad,' Root Girl says, still pecking away. 'You could try the unit next door.'

'Rob, Rob Brown,' I say irritably, wondering if she might notice me if I actually climbed on to the desk and stamped on her stubby fingers.

'And you is?' she asks, finally glancing up, chewing gum.

She doesn't look unfriendly, just mind-numbingly bored. Like I am in maths. I've spent almost three weeks working out how many more days there are to the end of school (too many), estimated the number of black and white squares on different parts of Mrs Chopley's jacket (front, back, collar, lapel, sleeves, total jacket approximately 129) and thought about how many chair legs there are in the entire school (no idea and like, who cares?). Once I've finished counting the number of dead flies trapped between the double-glazing unit in the form room and multiplied it by the estimated number of windows in the entire school, I'll have nothing left to do.

'I'm his daughter,' I say sharply. I can't imagine that many fourteen-year-olds in green blazers pop in after school to buy a couple of spare toilets and a shower unit.

The girl manages a thin smile whilst still chewing. 'I didn't know Rob had a daughter, but now you mention it, I can see it. Yous look alike.'

Oh that's just great! First The Kipper thinks I look like my middle-aged porky mum, and now Root Girl thinks I look like my middle-aged, porky coot-head dad!

She taps on a phone with a pencil. Good tip that. Saves the nails. I'll add it to The Glam Plan so that my nails are totally fantastico by the time I see Madison. I'm on Day Eighteen but as I've not exercised, am still packing in the calories and can't be bothered to body-buff, if the worst comes to the worst I'll distract attention from my figure and face by waving amazing nails in front of me all the time.

'Your daughter's here,' Root Girl says. There's a bit of a pause. 'Yeah, in front of me . . . all right, I'll tell her.'

The girl smiles. 'He'll be a coupla minutes.'

I'm fiddling with my moby when I realize Root Girl is staring at me. Perhaps she's lesbionic and goes for the whole girl-in-a-uniform thing.

'Soz,' she says when she realizes I've clocked her looking. 'I used to go to Burke's.'

'Bet you're glad you've left,' I say, relieved she wasn't eyeing me up.

Root Girl sighs and starts cleaning under her nails with a letter opener. 'Nah, not really. At the time I just pratted around, couldn't wait to leave and now, no offence to your old dad like, it's the same here but wiv zero mates.'

I'm about to suggest to Reception Girl that she could try counting the number of leaves on the plastic plant in reception to pass the time, when Dad appears. Two weeks in Spain with The Kipper have left him looking like a flaky boiled lobster. Not a good look on anyone but *especially* Dad.

'What are you doing here?' he says, hugging me. 'I

thought we were meeting up later for a pizza.'

'I need to get back to do some homework,' I say, which is true, but the real reason I've taken two buses and walked for ages through a scrubby industrial estate to get to Dad's office is because it's a Kipper-free zone. I was going to meet him in town for a post-holiday catch-up, but I suddenly had the terrible thought that The Kipper might try and gatecrash the evening and sit cooing over Dad whilst kicking me in the shins.

'What's happened to Joan?' I ask as I follow him through the warehouse.

'Retired,' he says over his shoulder. 'Took Binky her cat to live in Eastbourne.'

Mum and Dad started Plunge It Plumbing Services from an old ice-cream van when they first married. Then they got a Portakabin, and then lots of Portakabins and now the company fills an enormous warehouse on the outskirts of town. It's like being in IKEA, but instead of having sofas and scatter cushions piled on the shelves, there's toilets and pipes and huge boxes labelled *Stop Cock 15mm* and *Black Ball Float*.

Dotted around the edges are offices filled with people packing and unpacking things. They glance up through the glass windows as we walk past.

Dad shows me into his office. It's covered in paperwork

and catalogues and bits of metal things and looks like a bomb's dropped on it.

'How's school?' he asks, sitting down and putting his feet on his desk.

'Grim,' I say, flopping on a chair opposite. 'I'm counting fly corpses already.'

'Well, this should cheer you up.' He pulls an orange cellophane-wrapped box from under a pile of papers and pushes it towards me. 'Caroline chose it. It was produced locally.'

'Thanks.' I unwrap the cellophane and open the box. It's a glass bottle shaped like a donkey and is filled with liquid the colour of pee. 'And thanks for the postcard. You had a good time then?'

'Fantastic.' Dad beams at the memory. 'Caroline found us a really lovely hotel, five star, a bit pricey but worth it, and of course going outside the school holidays was a dream. I'll get her to email you some photos if you like.'

Like I'm really interested, I think to myself.

There's a plastic stopper up the donkey's bum. I pull it out and dab some perfume on my wrist and take a sniff. Rank! It *is* pee. The locals have probably forced donkeys to pee over buckets before they siphon it into bottles to flog to evil orange witches.

'Caroline fancies a trip away in January, you know,

to get some winter sun on the old bod.' He slaps his gut which wobbles under his polo shirt. 'She fancies the Caribbean.'

'We never went on holiday with you,' I grumble. 'You never wanted to take any time off to be with us. The most we got was the odd week in Center Parcs and you weren't there half the time.'

'I was building the business up,' Dad says. 'It's taken time to employ people I can trust and get the industrial contract side up and running.'

'You know we're going on holiday at half-term?' I say. 'To Miami and then New York to see Aunty Vicky's lot.'

'Ah, about that.' Dad folds his arms across his chest so that his moobs push together. It's tragic he's got more of a cleavage than I have. 'I know that's what your mother is *planning*.'

'No, it's more than planned,' I say. 'It's booked and paid for. The flights and everything.'

'Well, I haven't given my permission yet.' He tosses a paper clip in the air with one hand and catches it with the other, not looking at me. 'I haven't decided whether you can go or not.' He tosses the paper clip again, but this time it lands on the floor.

'Like, we need your permission to go away!' I snap. 'As if!'

I'm nuclear furious. It's obviously OK for your father never to go away on holiday with his family because of work, but then the moment he's got some tarty totty he decides he can leave the office for two weeks of sun, sex and sangria at the drop of a paper clip.

'Well, actually, Electra, you do,' Dad says in a triumphant tone of voice. 'For you and Jack to leave the country I have to give your mother permission and I haven't decided yet whether I'm going to.'

I am *totally* gobsmacked.

'That is *so* unfair!' I shriek. 'It's not just me that wants to go away. Mum needs a break too.'

Dad takes his feet off the desk, gets up and walks over to his office window. I'm sure he's not really checking that there's still plenty of U-bends or toilet handles on the shelves. He's avoiding my eyes, which are firing death rays towards his flabby butt.

'Listen. I've got no problem about my family going away on holiday,' he says. 'I do however have a problem with my family going away with a tattooed pool-oik who spends his life lying on the hard shoulder looking up at broken half-shafts!'

Phil.

He's mad at Phil.

Mum was right. The fact that Phil won the swimming

race has rebounded on us. Mum was married to Dad for almost fourteen years before he left. She might not have known he was having an affair with Candy, but she certainly knows him well enough to know he's a *really* bad loser.

'You're just jealous!' I say jumping up. 'Jealous that Phil beat you at breaststroke. Jealous that Mum's with Phil and is happy. Jealous that we're going away together. It's *pathetic*.'

'It was butterfly, not breaststroke,' Dad snaps back. 'And he cheated by jumping in first. He got a head start.'

'Oh for God's sake, Dad!' I snap. 'Get over yourself!'

'That's enough!' he shouts, turning back from the window and facing me. He really should wear a higher SPF in the sun. The combination of anger-induced high colour and sunburn makes him look like an overripe tomato about to explode. '*You're* old enough to look after yourself, but what sort of an influence is this bloke on Jack? I don't want my son riding around on a motorbike, wanting a tattoo and going into the army.'

Dad's getting a bit ahead of himself. Jack's nine. It'll be a few years before he's likely to be on the back of a Harley-Davidson in army fatigues with a skull and crossbones surgically inked on his arm.

'You should have thought of that before you left,' I

snap. This isn't the happy post-holiday, showered-with-posh-duty-free-perfume reunion I thought it would be. It's turned into a full-blown parental war with Eau de Urine. Just when Mum and I are getting on better, hostilities break out with Dad. I'm tempted to lob *You never wanted me in the first place!* into the argument, but decide to keep this devastating bit of ammo as my trump card for another time.

Dad and I ignore each other. The atmosphere bristles with tension.

'So, are we going out for something to eat or not?' Dad finally asks.

'As if!' I practically spit back. I'm hoping my face is saying *Don't you dare try and get round me with the offer of a pizza or Tex-Mex* even though I'm starving and might crumble at the chance of a Chinese.

'Well, at least let me give you a lift home in my new car,' Dad says, his voice softer. 'I only got it yesterday. And if you come in the car, I promise I'll think about letting you go away.'

I'd like to have flounced out and shouted, 'I'd rather walk over broken glass than see your car!' but Dad's always driven a plumber's van so I'm curious to see his new motor, and it's such a long trek home, and I'm starving, so I grunt, 'OK.'

'I'll just go and see Barry to tell him that I'm leaving early and I'll be right back,' Dad says. He taps a few keys on his computer, picks up his jacket from the back of his chair and heads out into the warehouse.

Whilst Dad's seeing Barry, I hang about his office. There's nothing to look at unless you're interested in a calendar with pictures of blonde girls with impossibly round boobs holding waste pipes, so I go and sit at his desk. He's got the same swively chair he had all those years ago in the first Portakabin. It's old and worn, but when I was about seven or eight I used to love to sit on it with my legs dangling off the floor. Using the edge of the desk to push off from, I'd spin round so fast I'd feel dizzy and sick. Then when I'd stopped feeling dizzy and sick, I'd do it all over again.

I'm about to push off and swivel for old times' sake when Dad's screensaver pops up on his computer. It used to be a picture of me and Jack in the bath both covered in bubbles. I'd be about seven and Jack was three-ish. There weren't any digital cameras in those days so Dad had the picture scanned and made into a file. We both looked cute, if I say so myself. But there's no sign of that picture. Instead, there's a snap of The Kipper, sunglasses perched on her head, diamond studs glinting in her ears, laughing as she holds up a glass of sparkling pink champagne.

When Dad changed the screensaver a message probably popped up saying, *Are you sure you want to delete this file?* He could have so easily chosen *No* and kept us. But he didn't. With a click of a mouse we were deleted and replaced by *her*.

'Ready?' Dad asks, standing in the doorway.

I stuff the bottled donkey pee into my bag and follow him out. Root Girl has already gone, hopefully to the hairdresser's. She's probably been counting the seconds until five-thirty in the same way I wait for ten to four at school.

In the car park, Dad sticks out his hand. There's a couple of beeps and the orange lights of a low-slung dark and sporty soft-top flash ahead of us.

Dad's bought himself a sports car.

A total bling car.

A Porsche.

A mid-life crisis accessory.

'I thought you liked driving the van?' I gasp, following him towards The Black Bullet. 'I thought you said it made you feel like a proper plumber?'

'Well, it was time for a new toy,' Dad says as I climb in and put my seat belt on. 'And Caroline was uncomfortable in the van surrounded by pipes, putty and paperwork.'

The car smells of new leather rather than the pine-tree air freshener Dad's van smelt of, and the doors close with a low clunk instead of the sound of a tin can being crushed.

'What do you think?' he says proudly as the roof lowers. 'Swish, eh?'

He reverses out of the parking space.

'It's only for two. What would happen if The Kip . . . Caroline was here. Where would Jack and me sit?'

Dad lets the leather steering wheel run through his hands. 'There's a couple of seats in the back. You wouldn't want to sit there for long, but you could just about squeeze in.'

We head out through the industrial estate with its boxy warehouses and sprawling factories. Dad flips the indicator, turns left on to the main road and, as he puts his foot down, the car roars into life.

I'm sitting in a bling-tastic car with the roof down and the wind in my hair hurtling along and am I happy?

No.

I want to cry.

I don't want to be squeezed into Dad's car *or* his life. I want to be the child that used to be on the screensaver covered in bubbles. I want to be the child who came round after school and ate toffees and made herself sick

130

spinning on the office chair. Then I didn't know what it was like to stress about GCSEs or coursework. I wasn't worried about mismatched boobs or freaked about lying about my non-existent love life. *No one* had boobs or boyfriends. And back then I didn't know I was the mistake that forced my parents into getting married.

I burst into tears.

'What's wrong?' Dad asks, alarmed. 'Don't you like the car? Has a bug flown into your eye?'

'I want to be seven again!' I sob.

Chapter Thirteen

It's Wednesday evening and I'm in deep trouble.

I've been pushing full-speed ahead with The Glam Plan as it turns out Dad can't stop us from going on holiday so we *are* going to America and I *will* see The Goddess Madison. I'd written FM down in my planner, which I thought meant that today, Day Twenty-Five of the fifty-five-day Glam Plan, I needed to give myself a French manicure. I was just blowing on my nails (the left hand is fab, but the paint job on the right is well dodgy) when I realized that it actually meant French, as in *Bonjour*, and the M wasn't for manicure, it was for maths. In other words, today was about two sets of homework not one set of nails.

I rang Luce and, after a few emails between her and Pascal, managed to bung down enough French answers to keep The Big Geordie happy, but now it's nine o'clock and I've only just started the maths homework Mrs Chopley set us. I rang Sorrel but she was out hanging around The Oaks, the block of flats where Warren lives, in the hope of bumping into him. He didn't give her his address, she looked him up in the phone book and as there was only one Cumberbatch listed, it has to be him. She's practically stalking him, which is maybe why he's *still* not asked her out. He probably thinks she's a meat-crazed bunny boiler.

I stare at the typed sheet in front of me.

A slug crawls at a speed of 21cm per hour towards a row of lettuces. It eats several rows and then returns over exactly the same distance, but at only 7cm per hour.

What is the slug's average speed over the entire journey?

I've been looking at the question for so long the slug could have crawled there, stuffed itself on the lettuce buffet, crawled back, and started out for seconds.

There's another five of these Brain Extenders to finish before tomorrow. I really don't care how long it's going to take Anne to overtake her friend Bob on the motorway, or what 100kg of raspberries weighs three days after they've been picked and are going to mush. I've had enough of every night being taken up with schoolwork I either can't do, should have done days ago or just can't be bothered to start. Homework is taking up valuable Jags-dreaming time, although oddly, since I sent that email to Maddy, I haven't heard from her, so I haven't had to make up any more virtual juicy Jags-action.

I wander down to the kitchen where Mum's sitting at the table doing her own homework. She seems to be taking her part-time business studies course much more seriously than I'm taking full-time school.

'What do you know about the speed of crawling slugs?' I ask, flicking the paper in front of her face.

'I know nothing,' Mum says in a fake foreign accent, pushing the questions aside.

'So if I said to you, a slug is crawling at 21cm an hour . . .'

'What's that in inches?' Mum asks. 'You know I don't do metric.'

'I don't know but it doesn't matter!' I say. 'The speed isn't important. It could be 1000cm per hour . . .'

'That would be a very quick slug,' Mum says, still flicking through a textbook. 'A turbo-charged slug. But then they do seem to make for lettuces with astonishing speed.'

I'm getting irritated now.

'OK, forget the slugs. Let's move on to the soft fruit. You have a bowl which contains 100kg of fresh raspberries . . .'

'That's one massive bowl,' Mum says. 'You couldn't get that on our kitchen scales.'

'So there's this 100-kilo mega-unable-to-get-on-to-the-scales bowl of rotting raspberries . . .'

'What's that in pounds and ounces?'

'Mum! I'm serious! Are you going to help me or not?' She's being deliberately awkward and it's not funny.

She puts down her pen and closes her book. 'Electra, I've told you. I'm happy to help you with your homework but I can't tell you the answers. You've got to work them out for yourself.'

'But *everyone* gets their parents to do their homework and coursework!' I wail. '*Everyone* knows that!'

'And what happens when they sit in the exam room and their parents aren't there?' Mum asks. 'What then?'

'They sit and think, well, at least my parents helped me get twenty per cent so far,' I say acidly. 'At least *their* parents gave them a flying start.'

I flop on the sofa, stick my feet on the coffee table, make a paper aeroplane with the maths questions and throw it into the air. It immediately dive-bombs on to the floor and gets a crushed nose. I can't do *anything* right.

'Listen, love, if you're really struggling, perhaps we should think about getting you some private tuition,' she says. 'What do you think?'

'I could do with some help in geography,' I say enthusiastically. 'I could ask Mr Butler if he'd do some stuff in the evenings with me.' I have completely forgiven Buff for being an earring Nazi and humiliating me. You can't be angry with top teacher totty for long.

'But I thought geography was one of your better subjects,' Mum says. 'That nice teacher of yours said you were doing well.'

'That's *why* I need extra lessons with him,' I say. 'To make sure I *still* do well.'

The phone rings and I jump up to answer it, stamping on the hated maths questions on the way.

'Hello, Electra love.'

'Granddad!'

Granddad Stafford *never* calls. Grandma does all the talking.

'Do you know anything about the speed of slugs?' I ask. He used to be a bank manager so he's bound to be good at maths. 'I'm stuck on my homework.'

Mum is at my elbow signalling at me to give her the phone.

'I just need to have a word with your mum,' Granddad says. His voice sounds tired and old but then he is old so he's probably permanently knackered. 'Is she there?'

'She's next to me, but if you think you can help me with

136

my slugs, will you get Mum to put you back on?'

I don't hear what Granddad says as Mum snatches the phone out of my hand which is *so* rude.

'Dad?'

I leave Mum to Granddad and go back to the sofa and start refolding the paper aeroplane, trying to make it more aerodynamic. After careful tweaking, I launch Paper Dart Mark 2, the same but with little spoilers on the wings. The modification has no effect as it dive-bombs, spectacularly, on to the telly.

'No!' Mum shrieks, which I think is a gross overreaction to the crash-landing.

I turn round to see her clutching the edge of the dresser, swaying like she's standing on a boat in stilettos during a storm. I jump up and drag a kitchen chair from beside the table and carry it to her, just in time as her legs give way and she sinks on to it.

'But why didn't she tell us?' Mum cries. 'How long have you known?'

She motions at me to get a pen and I grab the one I'd been using for homework and hand it to her, along with the damaged paper aeroplane. She unfolds it and starts jotting down notes.

'So, what happens next? . . . OK . . . When will you know more? . . . Right . . . And then after that? . . .'

OK . . . Does Vicky know? . . . Yes, I'll telephone her later . . . Yes, probably . . . I'll drive up tomorrow . . . No, Dad, I will . . . Listen, I can miss a day of college . . . I'll ring you in the morning . . . OK . . . Give her our love and tell her I'll see her tomorrow . . . Bye, Dad . . . Love you.'

Mum puts the phone down.

She's so slumped her boobs are practically touching her knees, but the unsupportive bra and pull of gravity probably isn't helping.

'Mum?' I say, butterflies flitting around in my stomach. 'What's happened?'

She pushes her hair back across her head with both hands and bursts into tears.

'Oh, Electra! Your grandma has bowel cancer.'

Chapter Fourteen

After the bowel bombshell, I led Mum to the sofa, poured her a glass of red wine and, as we'd run out of tissues and kitchen roll, raced upstairs to the bathroom and grabbed a stack of loo paper. By the time I came back down, Mum was sobbing her heart out so much her boobs were rising and falling at such an alarming rate they were practically slapping her under her chin.

'He never rings so I knew, I just knew in the pit of my stomach that it was bad news,' she'd gasped between mammary-heaves. 'The moment you said the word *Granddad*, I just knew.'

'What a bummer!' I'd said, which isn't really the right thing to say when you've just been told your gran has bowel cancer, but was the first thing that came into my head.

Mum wasn't just upset about the cancer, but that

Grandma had known for ages and kept it to herself, which explains why she kept putting off our summer visit. In the end Granddad insisted we were told as, although she's had chemicals to poison the out-of-control cells and radiation to fry those that stubbornly refused to die, she's still got to have an op, and maybe even more treatment.

Mum's driven up there today and is going to stay tonight and go to the hospital with them tomorrow, Friday, so she can find out what's going on. Phil's looking after us until she's back, so me and The Little Runt have been warned to be on our best behaviour.

'Glad to see that you're finding my Year 10 lessons as interesting as you did my Year 9, Electra Brown,' Frosty booms from the front of the class.

It's the last lesson of the day and she's caught me in mid-molar-revealing yawn. She starts bearing down on me, waddling along the row on her fatty splatty feet, her black cardigan flapping.

'Sorry, Mrs Frost,' I say, just as another yawn starts to gather momentum at the back of my throat. She's almost next to me. I mustn't yawn again.

Uurrp!

Oh that's just great! My yawn has morphed into a burp right next to Frosty's giant gut!

'Do you even know what text we're studying?' she snaps.

'Of course,' I say confidently, praying that I won't yawn, burp or emit any other bodily noise in her vicinity.

'Then perhaps you'd like to remind the class!' Frosty demands.

What a daft question. I've been reading the book for weeks and am actually quite enjoying it, though I think I'd enjoy it more if we could just read it rather than forensically dissect it sentence by sentence.

'It's *How to Kill a Mockingbird*.'

The moment I say it I know I've made a major gaffe.

The class sniggers and I want to hide. I know it's not *How to*. I know it's just *To Kill*, but my brain's shut down.

I'm tired and it's not just a day of school that's wiped me out. After I left Mum to phone Aunty V I'd tried to get back down to Mrs Chopley's Brain Extenders, but every time I looked at a question my mind would substitute a different one such as, *If Dorothy Stafford's 1cm tumour doubles in size every month, how long before she pegs it?* The other question which kept floating in and out of my stressy head was, *How do you know you've got cancer in your butt?* I mean, with boob cancer you hear about people finding lumps in their baps so they whizz off to the docs, who then do tests and things. But how do you

141

know if you've got a lump in your bottom? Your inner bottom. Maybe your *upper* inner bottom. I mean, I know that butt and bowel isn't the same thing, but they are close together. And then it got later and later and I was still thinking about tumours and bums, and *still* hadn't worked out how long the stupid slug was taking to get to the lettuces, and before I knew it I'd fallen asleep over my desk and woke up at 2 a.m. with a stiff neck wondering how I was going to explain to Mrs Chopley that I hadn't answered a single question. My usual trick of getting the answers from someone on the bus on the way to school isn't so easy with Mrs C. She gives marks for the working out. But when I said, 'I'm sorry, Mrs Chopley, I had some bad news last night about my grandma. She's very ill,' and showed her the question paper on which Mum had scribbled words like *tumour*, *oncologist*, *colostomy bag* and *op*, she looked all concerned and said, 'Hand it in on Monday, Electra,' and didn't question why the paper had odd wing-shaped creases in it.

'I'm sorry, Mrs Frost, I had some bad news last night about my grandma. She's very ill.'

'How very convenient for you,' The Penguin snaps back, which is a horrible hurtful thing to say. I don't need an ill relative to get me out of homework. Usually I can do it all by myself.

She waddles off and I pretend to read but I can't concentrate on Scout and Jem, as I keep thinking about Grandma. She's the complete opposite of Dad's mum, Nana Pat, who'd be straight round to the doc's saying, 'Doc, I've got a pain in me arse,' or whatever it is you get when you've got a problem in there. Grandma S is very prim and proper, especially about bodily bits and functions, using words like *front bottom* to describe girly bits. I was angry with her when I found out she'd made Mum and Dad lie about their wedding, but now I think of her having to explain that she has something wrong with her insides to doctors who will poke her and prod her and stick instruments up her bottom, not realizing that she must be finding the whole thing excruciatingly embarrassing.

'Electra?' Lucy is standing next to me looking all concerned. 'Are you OK?'

At last the lesson has finished and the classroom is emptying.

'I'm just worried about my gran,' I say, gathering up my stuff and heading towards final reg.

'What's wrong with her?' Tammy asks.

'She's got cancer,' I reply. 'Bowel cancer.'

'My aunt had bowel cancer,' Tammy says. 'She had like, bits chopped out of her and everything.'

'But she's OK now?' I say. 'She's better?'

Tammy looks embarrassed. 'Oh, er, no, she pegged it, but not from the cancer. She got knocked over coming out of the hospital.'

I don't think I've ever been to the school library in my own time. I've had to go for school projects and things, of course, and when we were younger and first went to Burke's we'd go to the library and flick through copies of *National Geographic* and snigger at pictures of men with rings in their bits and women with boobs so dangly you could tie knots in them, but then we grew up, and anyway, you can get much more snigger-worthy pictures on the Internet.

But after everything that's gone on, I didn't feel like hanging around the shops, gossiping with the girls, or going straight home to see Jack and Phil, especially as I'd promised Mum I wouldn't be mean to The Little Runt. I wanted somewhere quiet where I could think, maybe even snooze.

The only people in the library are the geeks and nerds who are clustered round tables, bad-haircut heads down, scribbling away or flicking through textbooks. I am *so* not going to join one of their tables. It could be the slippery slope to total Geekdom. Today the library, tomorrow sensible shoes and short nails.

I roam around for a bit until I find an empty chair wedged in a corner between some towering bookshelves. I settle myself in, and to give my reason for being in the library some added authenticity, I grab a book from the shelf next to me, balance it on my knee and settle down for a snooze.

It's good here. Quiet. Peaceful. It's a shame they won't let us bring food and drink in or I'd spend more time here, just relaxing not studying.

'I didn't know you were interested in nuclear and particle physics.'

Freak Boy is standing in front of me looking all excited, which is a bit weird to be honest.

'Er?'

I haven't the foggiest idea what he's talking about. He points to the book on my knee. *Principles of Charge Particle Acceleration.*

'Oh, I just like to read around the subject,' I say breezily. 'Get a rounded view of the topic.'

I am deeply disturbed that I said that. It's the sort of showy-off-trying-to-impress-with-my-stunning-intellect statement I'd make if Jags was here. But it's a Freak, not a Lurve God next to me and, without realizing it, I've tried to impress FB. I am totally disgusted with myself.

'Wow, Electra,' FB gasps. 'I had no idea that was your thing. Especially sixth-form stuff too.'

I pat the cover and nod. It's probably better if I keep my mouth shut so that I don't come out with some other ridiculous statement like I'm building a nuclear reactor in my bedroom.

'I'm sorry your gran is sick,' he says. 'I overheard you telling Tamara it's cancer.'

I nod again. I feel like one of those nodding dogs on the back ledge of a car, but it's too risky to speak.

'If you ever need any help or want to talk about anything, you know where I am,' Freak Boy says. 'Anything at all.'

Chapter Fifteen

'Hello!' Phil greets me from the stove wearing a pink flowery apron. It looks well weird, not just because of the apron but because I'm still not used to seeing a man cooking in our kitchen. Dad didn't cook and he'd *never* wrap flower-covered PVC around his bod. 'Did you go to the library again?'

'As if!' I snort.

No one goes to the library on a Friday afternoon, not even dorky saddos. One sesh in nerd-land was enough to send me scurrying back to my usual routine of wandering around the shops with the girls.

'Have you heard from Mum?' I ask, peering into the saucepan. It's something with mince and tomato sauce and it smells delicious.

'She rang about half an hour ago. She should be back any moment. Now at this stage it can either turn into chilli or spag bol. Which do you fancy?'

'Chilli,' I say.

'Spag bol,' shouts Jack, who's sitting at the kitchen table laying out his football cards in neat rows.

'You're only saying that because I said chilli.' I grab a card with David Beckham's photo on it and wave it in the air. 'If I'd have said spag bol, you'd have said chilli.'

'Give it me back, Poo Head!' Jack screams. 'I want Becks back!'

'You can have Becks if you vote for chilli!' I shout.

Jack gets up and tries to grab the card from me but I dance round the kitchen and pretend to snog it before handing it back to The Little Runt.

'It's got gob all over it!' Jack yells, horrified. 'You've gobbed on Becks!'

Above us the front door slams. Jack and I race up the stairs to the hall and rush towards Mum to give her a hug. I get there first, not just because I have longer legs, but because I pushed The Little Runt out of the way on the stairs. I'd promised to be nice to him whilst Mum was away, but now she's back, all bets are off.

'What a lovely surprise!' Mum says, kissing me on the head and hugging Jack. 'I feel I've been missed.'

'You have!' we chant.

'How's Grandma? How's Granddad coping? What

did the docs say?' I bombard her with questions as she's taking her coat off, adding it to the pile at the end of the stairs.

'Just let me get in, have a pee and then I'll tell you,' she says, heading upstairs to the bathroom. 'I'll be down in a moment.'

When she comes into the kitchen, Phil gives her a kiss and hands her a big glass of red wine. She goes to the sofa, slumps down and kicks off her shoes. I perch on one arm, Phil leans against the other, and Jack goes to the sink and puts Becks under the tap, presumably to rinse my spit off.

'So, how was she?' Phil asks.

'She's aged twenty years overnight.' Mum shakes her head. 'She's lost a lot of weight and gets very tired easily. Even talking tires her out.'

I have to ask, and it's better to get the gory medical details over with before tea rather than during it. 'How did she know she'd got it?'

Mum sips her wine. 'She said she'd had digestive discomfort for ages. I thought she just meant a stomach upset, but when we went to the oncologist it turns out she'd had chronic diarrhoea with blood in it for months before she plucked up courage to see her GP.'

I think of the mince in tomato sauce on the stove and

wished I hadn't asked. I don't think I can eat it now.

'So what happens next?' Phil says, topping up Mum's glass. 'Did they say when they might operate?'

'Well, the good news is that the chemo and radiotherapy have shrunk the tumour so they're on course to do the op for the 23rd of October.'

My brain starts whirring. The date sounds familiar. Is it someone's birthday? Is that when I'm supposed to be going on a virtual date with Jags?

'That's half-term,' I squeak. 'When we're in America.'

Mum sighs. 'Yes, I'm sorry, love, I know how much you were looking forward to going away, but we're going to have to postpone the trip. I can't leave the country whilst Mum's so ill.' She looks up at Phil. 'I'm sorry. The timing couldn't be worse. Do you think you can change your holiday rota, maybe for Christmas?'

'Let's think about going away another time.' Phil squeezes Mum's shoulder. 'This is much more important. We'll sort something out.'

'Oh, Electra, for goodness' sake!' Mum rounds on me. 'Don't you think I was looking forward to this trip too? Don't you think I'd rather be sitting in SeaWorld watching a whale than sitting in a hospital ward watching over my ill mother?'

'*What?*' I shriek. 'I haven't said anything!'

It's true. I've just been sitting quietly on the sofa feeling gutted that my holiday is slipping away from me, guilty that I feel so gutted, wondering if I'm ever going to find out whether cousin Madison has inherited the Stafford Mighty Mammary gene, but also thinking that at least it gives me extra time for The Glam Plan. On the other hand, can I keep up the Jags lie until Christmas? By then we'll have been dating for nine months and they'll definitely have to be lots of dot dot dotting by then.

'You haven't said anything but you're sitting there looking as if you've chewed a wasp,' Mum snaps.

'Has Poo Head chewed a wasp?' Jack pipes up. 'Has it stung her tongue?'

'I'm sorry,' I say, meaning it. 'It wasn't just SeaWorld I was looking forward to. I wanted to spend time with Madison, get to know her.'

'No, I'm sorry.' Mum gulps more wine. 'I'm just a bit wound up and the drive back's taken it out of me. But if it's not seeing Madison you're worried about you needn't be. I talked to Vicky last night. She doesn't want to be three thousand miles away when Mum's going under the knife. She's coming here, with Madison, for half-term.'

Chapter Sixteen

'What's the panic?' Sorrel says, sliding into a seat opposite me. 'You sounded well freaked on the phone. I stuck the kids in front of a DVD and left.'

I've convened an emergency meeting with the girls in Starbucks at Eastwood Circle. It's not our usual Saturday lunchtime hangout, but I can't stand the thought of Sorrel mooning over Warren if we go to McDonald's and I can't risk bumping into Tits Out and co. in Burger King.

'I am in *serious* trouble,' I say as Luce arrives.

'*Quelle* sort of serious?' Luce asks. 'Parent serious or pregnant serious?'

'Well, obviously I'm not preggers!' I hiss, 'but I have done a *terrible* thing.'

I hunch over the table, look around me and peer over the top of my hot chocolate.

'I pretended to cuz Madison that I've got a boyfriend,

which was fine when we were going to America, but now instead of me going there, she's coming here!'

'Why?' Luce asks.

'Because Grandma's butt op is during half-term! Mum and Aunty V are going to look after Granddad and Grandma and Phil's going to look after me, The Little Runt and The Goddess Madison,' I say in a gabbled whisper.

'No, she means why did you lie about having a boyfriend?' Sorrel asks.

I want to tell them it was because Sorrel might have Warren, and Lucy defo has Pascal, and when I found out Madison has Max it made me feel a total saddo having nobody, though, on reflection, pretending to have a boyfriend makes me Queen of the Saddos.

'I dunno,' I say. 'It was sort of a typing accident.'

'What, your fingers went crazy on the keys?' Sorrel laughs, sitting back in her chair. 'A case of deranged digits?'

I glare at her. This isn't something to be laughed at. If there's one thing worse than having no boyfriend, it's pretending that you have a boyfriend and then being exposed as a liar.

'How long have you had this fantasy boyfriend?' Lucy giggles.

'More than six months,' I add, and then slowly bang my head on the table, which is really what I should have done before I sent that wretched email as it might have knocked some sense into me.

Lucy pats my arm. 'So, just pretend you've split up with him and then your cousin will never know,' she suggests.

For a moment this seems like an excellent plan until I think of a major flaw.

'But what if she meets him?' I say. 'What if she bumps into him and finds out who he is?'

Sorrel rolls her eyes. 'Duh. You can't meet someone who doesn't exist!'

My face must give the game away.

'He does exist, doesn't he?' Lucy gasps. 'Who is he?'

'Oh my God it's Jags, isn't it?' Sorrel screeches, drumming on the table with her hands. 'You've been pretending to go out with that greasy El Dwarfo for six months!'

'Keep your voice down!' I say, flicking some chocolate-speckled milk froth across the table at her. 'It's hair gel, not grease and by now it's seven. What am I going to do?'

I've been in complete turmoil since last night's announcement, made worse by an email from Madison overnight which said she was gutted that Grandma was ill but that every cloud has a silver lining and it meant she could come over and see where I lived. *And I'll be able to meet Jags! I bet he's amazing*, she'd written. *I bet he'd be amazed to learn he's been going out with me for so long.*

'Hi, babes. I came as soon as I could.'

It's Warren in his McDonald's uniform. With stressing I hadn't notice him come in.

Sorrel looks all coy. 'Hiya.'

'What's the bother? Your text sounded well serious.'

'It's Electra that's in trouble,' Sorrel says, and I really want to kick her. This isn't anything to do with him, but she's obviously used my emergency as her Warren-bait.

'Yous pregnant?' Warren asks me.

Sorrel punches him on the arm, which saves me punching him in the face, and giggles. 'As if! No, she's pretended she's got a boyfriend when she hasn't and now her Yankee cuz is going to find out 'cause she's coming over here.'

Oh that's just great. Tell the whole of Starbucks that I'm a lying saddo, why don't you, Sorrel?

'So, get someone to pretend to be your fella,' Warren says, as if this is the easiest thing in the world for a dish-faced salami-limbed girl like me. For goodness' sake, if I could get someone to *pretend* to be my boyfriend I'd *have* a boyfriend.

155

'I don't know anyone,' I say.

'I could pretend,' Warren offers. 'If yous like.'

I think of Jags, all sporty and Spanish and, admittedly, rather short, and look at Warren, lanky, street-cool with his braids and chunky jewellery.

'It wouldn't work,' I say. 'Jags is Spanish.'

'There are black people in Spain too,' Warren says, and I feel stung that he thinks that I think because he's black he can't be a Spanish Lurve God.

'It's not that,' I mutter. 'You're much older.'

Big Mac Boy's phone rings. It seems to be someone from Macky D's finding out why he's gone AWOL from the deep-fat fryer.

'Listen,' I hiss whilst Warren negotiates an early break. 'When Madison's here, whatever happens, as far as you're concerned, Jags was my boyfriend and then we split up, OK?'

I see Jas come in, all tight jeans, tight top and swaying hips. She must be on a break from New Look. As she heads towards the counter she stops at our table.

'Who's looking after the twins?' she snaps at her sister.

'Senna,' Sorrel replies, not looking up but slowly tracing a figure of eight in a pile of sugar on the table with a silver-tipped fingernail.

'She's too young to look after a couple of three-year-

156

olds on her own!' Jas barks. 'Mum is *so* not going to be pleased with you.'

Sorrel shrugs. 'I had to go out. It was an emergency.'

'Some emergency,' Jas sneers, looking round the table at us. 'You'd better get home pronto or I'll ring her.' She strides off to the counter.

If looks could kill, Jas would be slumped on the floor gasping her last breath through over-glossed lips the way Sorrel glares at her.

'Cow,' she says, fiddling under her seat to get her bag. 'I'd better go.' She gives a coy smile to Warren. 'You coming?'

'Nah, babes,' Warren says, shuffling to let her out and then sitting back down. 'I'm on my break.'

Sorrel looks mega-miffed and stomps out.

The three of us sit in silence until Warren asks, 'Is that Sorrel's sister?'

Jasmine is heading towards us holding a steaming cardboard cup.

'Yeah, and she's a right stroppy cow,' I say. 'She never lets us use her staff discount in New Look.'

Jas pauses briefly by our table, presumably to check that Sorrel has gone home and isn't hiding underneath.

'You get better service in McDonald's, babes,' Warren says to her. 'Well, you would from me.'

'Shame I'll never know,' Jasmine says teasingly, raising a beautifully arched eyebrow. 'I don't go into places that sell murdered animals.' She flicks her straightened raven hair and saunters towards the exit, and I'm tempted to point out the BLTs she must have stood next to when she got her drink.

Warren can't take his eyes off her. He's practically drooling.

Finally he lets out a long low whistle. 'Man, that is one hot bootilicious babe.'

Chapter Seventeen

'You said if I needed anything to just ask,' I say, standing on the doorstep of Freak Boy's posh house in Compton Avenue late on Sunday afternoon. 'Well, I need some help.'

I'd felt terrible crunching up the gravel drive and ringing the doorbell, but I was desperate and didn't know where to turn or who to talk to. Luce wouldn't be any help, Sorrel wasn't answering her phone, Phil was out and I can't talk to Mum at the moment, not when she's already made her feelings on the subject clear.

FB shows me in and Archie comes bounding up but thankfully doesn't grab my butt or hump my leg.

We go through to the designer kitchen with its gleaming stainless-steel cooker and sleek black granite worktops. It only needs a bowl of perfect fruit and a recipe book propped open and it would look straight out of *Homes and Gardens*.

159

'Are your parents in?' I ask. There doesn't seem to be any sign of Dunc The Hot Dad Hunk or Glam Doc.

'They've gone to friends for Sunday lunch,' FB says. 'They'll be back in an hour or so.'

'And you weren't invited?'

'I knew it was going to be boring, lots of talk about house prices and pensions so I said I'd rather stay here.' Freak Boy flushes so red, his beak glows. 'I'm glad I did now.'

I *so* don't want him to get the wrong idea about why I'm here.

'I came because there was no one else to talk to,' I say. 'You're the only person who can help.'

'That's OK,' FB says gravely. 'Your gran being so ill must be hard. Apparently one in three of us will be affected by cancer in our lifetime.'

Oh. My. God. He thinks I'm here to talk about Grandma's butt cancer. He thinks I need a great emotional talk, possibly accompanied by some sympathetic hugs or, at the very least, hand patting. He's got it all wrong!

'I'm stuck on my maths homework and it needs to be in tomorrow. I was hoping you could help.'

I'd spent ages staring at the questions, getting nowhere. There's only so many times you can use the illness of a close relative as an excuse, and I can't go back to school and say I *still* can't work out the wretched slug's speed. FB's in the fast maths stream so he'll find Mrs Chopley's Brain Extenders really easy.

FB looks a bit taken aback. 'Oh. OK. Well, what's the problem?'

I pull the bit of paper out of my bag. It's almost disintegrating, what with being used as homework questions, a paper aeroplane, medical records and then stuffed in my bag along with half a Snickers bar that I was keeping until second break, but has left rather nasty brown smears across the page.

'It's chocolate,' I say, feeling I need to give an explanation as to why it looks like loo paper.

FB studies the questions.

'Well, the first one, the slug speed question is very simple,' he says. 'It's just distance over time. In other words, how far has the slug travelled and how long has it taken it to do it?'

He hands me back the paper and I stare at it feeling thick and panicky, wondering whether a male slug crawls faster than a female.

'It doesn't say how far away the lettuce patch is,' I mutter. 'How am I supposed to know if I don't know the distance between slug and salad?'

FB smiles. He's got a lovely smile. I mean, he's still very

161

odd-looking, but when he smiles all his dodgy-looking features come together quite nicely, especially now his hair's grown out of its pudding-bowl look, though even if you were pulling my teeth out with pliers and no anaesthetic I'd never admit it in public.

'Don't laugh at me,' I snap. 'It makes me feel stoopid.'

'Sorry,' FB says, going red, cutting the smile and going back to looking freaky and beaky. 'The question says it would take the slug an hour to go 21cm but once the slug has eaten it can only do the same distance at 7cm per hour.'

'In other words, three times as long,' I say. 'Once it's stuffed itself with greenery it takes three hours the second time.'

'Brilliant!' FB says.

I feel both pleased I'm getting somewhere and deeply embarrassed that something which sounds so easy I find so hard.

'So, how far has it travelled?' FB asks.

'Two lots of 21cm,' I say. '42cm.'

'You really are good,' FB says. This is rather over the top, congratulating me on being able to add 21 and 21 together, but still. 'And how long has it taken?'

'An hour there and three hours back, four hours.'

'Great! So distance over time . . .?'

'42 divided by 4.'

'Is?'

'I need a calculator.'

After much fiddling around on my moby, I divide 42 by 4 and come up with, 'The wretched critter's average speed is 10.5cm per hour!'

'Hooray!' FB laughs, looking quite cute in an About-to-Turn-Freaky-at-Any-Moment sort of way. 'Now, shall we try the raspberries?'

FB made a very good teacher. He didn't tell me the answers, which quite frankly was what I'd hoped for when I went round, but showed me how to work out each question step by step. It took us just over an hour to finish all the Brain Extenders, with a break for a can of Diet Coke halfway through.

'Well, thanks,' I say, jumping off the stool at the breakfast bar. 'I'd better be off and write this up neatly.'

'There's just one thing that puzzles me,' FB says, also getting up. 'For someone who's interested in the speed of a particle in a nuclear reactor, it seems odd that you couldn't work out the average speed of a slug in a garden.'

'Er . . .'

'The book you were reading in the library?'

'Oh that.' I lean against the counter. Freak Boy might

look odd but he's defo not dim, and the sort of boy who can rattle through questions about soft fruit and slugs can obviously see straight through my particle physics lie.

'Why did you pretend to be doing AS physics stuff?' FB says. 'There are easier subjects.'

'I just did,' I mutter. 'Sometimes I say things I don't mean just to impress people and it gets me into trouble,'

'*You* tried to impress *me*?' FB sounds shocked. 'I've told you before, you're well out of my league.'

I hate that he thinks I was trying to impress him.

'I didn't *mean* to impress you, not like I did my cousin,' I say. 'Which is why I'm now in deep goose poo.'

'Go on.' FB climbs back on his stool.

I sigh and sit down next to him.

'I was supposed to be going to America at half-term and I pretended to my cousin over there that I had a boyfriend, except I don't, and because Grandma is ill, Madison, that's my cuz, is now coming over here in three weeks and she might find out I've lied to her.'

'That's worse than lying about particle physics,' FB says. 'What are you going to do?'

I drum the black granite worktop with my fingers and think how good my nails are looking at the moment. At least that part of The Glam Plan seems to be working.

'Sorrel knows a burger flipper at McDonald's,' I say. 'He

suggested that he pretends to be Jags, but it won't work because he looks too old.'

'Jags?' FB says. 'Isn't that the lad who helped me when I bust my ankle?'

I nod and allow myself a smile at the delicious memory of Jags standing in a white T-shirt framed in the summer sun looking fit, tanned and gorgeous whilst FB rolled on the floor in agony after Pinhead, Gibbo and Spud had pinched his trainers and strung them over the telephone wires.

'I could pretend to be your boyfriend,' FB says. 'I mean, if you want me to.'

I thought there was nothing worse than having to make up the fact that you don't have a boyfriend. Then I discovered there *is* something worse and that's being exposed as having a fake boyfriend. That now pales into insignificance when you are seriously considering pretending that the school's most unfortunate boy is your virtual Spanish Lurve God. How low can I go?

'Do you know any Spanish?' I say. 'I'm desperate.'

FB shrugs. '*Adios*? *Paella*? *Olé*?'

'*Olé*? What good is *olé*?' I giggle.

'Well, it might come in handy if you find yourself facing a bull in Spain whilst wearing a red coat!' FB says.

We both dissolve into fits of giggles. There's a red and

165

white tea towel looped over the oven door. I jump up and grab it, holding it out like a matador's cape. FB gets off his stool, pretends to paw the ground and snort like a mad bull and then charges headlong towards the tea towel. I whip it away at the last minute, shouting 'Olé!' as FB charges straight into Glam Doc and Hot Dad who have come into the kitchen.

'What's going on here?' Dunc The Hot Dad Hunk laughs. 'You two seem to be having a good time.'

'He's just pretending to be my Spanish boyfriend,' I mutter, wishing for like, the millionth time in my life that my mouth didn't work independently of my brain, and completely freaked that I've found I rather like the idea of going out with Señor Burns, Jr.

Chapter Eighteen

'Could you at least squeeze out a smile?' Mum asks, scanning the crowds streaming towards us in the arrivals hall. 'A scowl isn't a nice welcome.'

'Like this?' I give what I hope is a premium sarky sneer.

Seven weeks ago I was looking forward to half-term. I thought I'd be on my way to America all buffed and polished from weeks of working on The Glam Plan, ready to meet Teen Queen Madison. I imagined meeting Max, all sporty and straight out of an Abercrombie & Fitch advert, and casually throwing into the conversation snippets of information about Jags so that everyone was totally aware that I had a Spanish hunk waiting for me back home and had done dot dot dot. I dreamt of going back to school with (probably false) tales of meeting American hunks who fell in love with my accent and cute British ways, and who fought each other for my email address. If it was warm in Miami I might even have had a bit of a red-flush-type tan on the salami limbs, which would be fantastic to flaunt around school in October. It was going to be *amazing*.

As it is, instead of swanning around the States, I'm spending Saturday evening crushed next to a railing at London's Heathrow Airport, nose-to-armpit against people who've obviously never been near a can of deodorant, whilst getting whacked in the face by a man waving a cardboard sign saying, *Mr Gonzalez*.

I fiddle around in my bag, get out my lip gloss and slick some on, accidentally-on-purpose elbowing Sign Waver in the ribs in the hope that he might move along a bit and take his rank pits out of my personal space. I don't know why I'm bothering really. A slick of Cherry Glaze gloss isn't going to turn me into the sort of teenage temptress I envisaged when I started on The Glam Plan forty-nine days ago. It's failed spectacularly, firstly because I'm naturally lazy, and secondly because once I found out Madison was coming over here and I wouldn't be paraded in front of her friends as some sad specimen, it was a great excuse to give up any thoughts of exfoliating and exercising. In fact, I've gone backwards in my glamorousness, as a couple of nights ago in a desperate attempt to banish the zits I committed the number-one skin sin. I squeezed the life, but not much pus, out of every face-swelling I could find, including underground brewers, so now I've got scabby lumps, pussy lumps and gross blotches. My face is covered in so much slap I look like Butterface's twin sis.

I might start The Glam Plan again after The Goddess has gone back to Yankeedom. If it became a way of life I might find myself a proper boyfriend so I wouldn't have to lie. Anyway, about that. I've decided no more dishonesty. I'm going to be totally upfront with Madison and tell her that in a moment of GCSE-stress-induced madness I made the whole boyfriend thing up. If she hates me, so what? As a stuck-up-her-butt Teen Beauty Queen we're clearly going to have zero in common and I can put up with her looking down her nose at me for a week. Boys have been giving me that look for years.

'There they are!' Mum leans over the barrier and waves frantically. 'Vicky! Madison!'

I'm freaked that the weight of Mum's Mighty Mammaries is going to topple her over the barrier so that she lands in a heap in front of the passengers streaming off American Airlines flight AA142 from JFK New York, all of whom look as if they've spent eight hours squashed together in a speeding tin can, 37,000 feet above the

169

earth. They look crumpled and confused as they drag their suitcases towards the exit, scanning the crowds for a friendly face.

Except two of the passengers don't looked crumpled and confused. Victoria and Madison Hampshire look calm and cool and fresh and clean, and even neater than I can manage at the start of the day. Madison looks exactly like she does in photies, maybe even more glam and glossy. She's wearing a knitted beige hat, huge gold hoop earrings, a black jacket and has a black and white skull and crossbones scarf casually tossed around her shoulders. As she's tall the scarf-tossing and the hat-wearing look stylish and effortless. I'd look as if I was about to hike up Mount Everest.

As Mum and Aunty V shriek and hug, The Wundercousin raises a slim silver camcorder and films the big reunion.

'Electra!'

Aunty V stops hugging Mum and starts crushing me. As I gulp lungfuls of her expensive-smelling perfume, all I can think of is that Madison is getting a close-up shot of my wide face being squashed into Aunty Vicky's chest. It does answer one question though. Aunty V *definitely* doesn't have the Stafford Mighty Mammaries, but does that mean The Wundercuz does? I shoot Madison a sideways glance, but she's still filming and I'd be *totally* humiliated if she filmed me ogling her baps.

Aunty V stands back with her hands on my shoulders, looking me up and down. She's not a bit like her younger sister. I can't imagine her ever wearing elasticated trousers or having raggedy nails or letting her sleek brown bob grow out of shape.

'You haven't changed a bit, Electra!' she smiles.

Oh gr-eat! Don't most rellies say, 'Gosh, you've grown up!' or, 'Don't you look amazing?' According to Aunty Vicky I'm stuck looking like a podgy ten-year-old.

Mum shoots me a look that seems to indicate I'm not being welcoming enough.

'Hi, Madison,' I mutter.

'Call me Maddy.' From behind the camera she flashes me a bright, white, even smile. Even under the harsh airport lights her skin looks perfect and the hair tumbling from underneath her hat is chestnut glossy.

Cow.

'Cool camera,' I say, as we head towards the car park whilst Mum pushes the luggage trolley, accidentally ramming it into any ankles that are in her way as she and Aunty V rabbit away.

'Actually, about that. I should have warned you,' Maddy says. 'My school wouldn't let me take time out

171

unless I turned this trip into a project, so I hope you don't mind, but I'm planning on making a video diary about you.'

'Me?' This comes out as the sort of squeal so high-pitched only dogs and men with scientific instruments can detect it.

'I want to spend the week hanging out with you, doing exactly the sorta things you'd do if I wasn't here. Kinda like a week in the life of a typical Brit teen.'

'Uh,' is all I can manage to croak. I can't see how sleeping in, texting, messaging, mooching about the shops, sitting in BK or Macky D's, trying on shed loads of clothes we can't afford, going to the cinema to try and get into films we're too young to see, lying around in my bedroom perfecting the S-Scale and reading magazines trying to decide if one day Victoria 'Bobble Head' Beckham's neck will snap and her head will fall off is going to make a riveting project for The Teen Queen and her friends. Put like that, it doesn't make a riveting half-term for me either.

'And then I'm going to edit it and present it to my school.'

This just gets worse and worse!

I can't believe this is happening to me! I can't believe that my life and my bod is going to be filmed and then presented to Miss Perfect's classmates like some reality TV series but without decent lighting and a make-up woman on hand. If I'd have known my every moment and flaw was going to be scrutinized on the big screen I would definitely have stuck to The Glam Plan. I'd have been buffing and brushing and toning and tanning not just for me, but for England and St George!

The arguments between Mum and Aunty Vicky start almost the moment we've pulled out of the car park. Maddy and I sit in the back in silence as Mum tries to negotiate the traffic whilst Aunty Vicky interrogates her younger sister over Grandma's illness.

'I cannot believe that you haven't seen Mum and Dad since New Year!' Aunty Vicky says. Her accent is very odd, half English, half American, and totally mental. 'Perhaps this wouldn't have gotten so far if you'd seen them more often. You might have noticed Mum was ill.'

'So you're saying this is all my fault?' Mum asks. 'When did you last come over here? It's taken Mum nearly dying to get yourself on a plane.'

'They came to New York last Christmas, remember? And we do live three thousand miles away.'

'We intended to go in the summer but Mum kept putting us off!'

'And now we know why!'

The bickering goes on and on. Sometimes I think how nice it would be to have a sister instead of The Little Runt, but then I remember Sorrel, Senna and Jasmine always at each other's throats, and Mum and Aunty Vicky in competition with each other, and stop wishing for something I'm never going to have.

I tune out just as Aunty Vicky is grilling Mum about Phil and whether he's really suitable to look after two teenage girls and a nine-year-old for a week, and has she had a police check done on him to make sure he's not a secret pervy paed, and try again to sneak a peek at Maddy's chest. In the warm car she's unbuttoned her jacket and loosened the scarf. I would say that in the dark, from this angle, her boobs look more like rolling hills than an enormous mountain range, probably perky, rounded, natural and *exactly* the same size.

'Have I like, dropped something on me?' Maddy asks brushing her chest. 'I noticed you looking at the airport. If there's like, food or something on me or spinach in my teeth, just say. I'd rather know.'

I can hardly say I'm comparing your boobs to mine. I don't want her to think I'm a perve as well as plain.

'I'm just looking at the view,' I reply, which is such a stupid thing to say as we're in a tunnel.

'So,' Maddy says. 'When am I going to meet Jags?'

I am *so* not going to fess up to being Queen of the Saddos in the back of a car with my mother's ears flapping.

'Ssh!' I hiss. 'We've broken up. He dumped me.'

Chapter Nineteen

I'm lying in the dark freaking out about the spiders that could be nesting in the piles of knickers and stuff under the bed. I was supposed to tidy my room to make space for the airbed, but I just kicked the clothes on the floor under the bed and now I'm convinced that the multi-legged beasties will wait until I'm asleep, leave their knicker nest and scuttle across my face. Freak Boy once said that the average person swallows seven bugs in a lifetime. Sleeping next to a spider infestation probably doubles that figure. Still, it's just for one night. Aunty V is having the sofa bed in the front room tonight, but then we're going in two cars to Grandma and Granddad's tomorrow for Sunday lunch, leaving Mum and Aunty V there for the week. So if I can get through one night without any arachnid-swallowing I'll be back in my own bed and Maddy will have the sofa bed.

'Phil's lovely,' Maddy says into the dark. 'Your mom's lucky after all the heartache over your dad.'

'S'pose so.' I turn over and the airbed makes a farting noise. From above me, Maddy giggles.

'It was the airbed!' I say.

'Are you sure you don't want me to sleep down there?' she asks. 'I'm happy to.'

Mum would go mental finding out that I've shoved Maddy on to the floor to take her chance with the bedroom wildlife.

'S'OK.' As an anti-spider measure I'm trying to keep my mouth covered by the sleeping bag so this just comes out as a muffled robotic sound.

I hear Maddy shift up in bed. The time in New York is five hours behind the UK, so although it's nearly one o'clock here and I'm knackered, Maddy's body clock is still set to eight in the evening. Despite the long flight, she's awake and perky.

The evening turned out OK, even though it was a short one by the time we got home and had something to eat. Phil and Aunty Vicky got on really well nattering away, Jack did keepy-uppy with his football in the kitchen until it got out of control and he hit the ceiling, bringing plaster down on Aunty V's head, and Maddy filmed everything from us eating soup and sarnies to Jack having

177

a stompy-foot temper tantrum when Mum told him it was bedtime.

So far I've managed to keep away from Maddy's camera by either being behind her, having my behind pointing *at* her or being completely out of filming range. She's so perfect, even looking at her annoys me. No wonder she's going out with an Abercrombie & Fitch model. AND unless she's doing a Tits Out and double-filleting her bra, she defo has the Stafford Mighty Mammary Gene. No one with a waist that small has boobs that naturally big.

'Do you still see your dad,' Maddy asks, 'or is he out of the picture?'

'I'd see him more if The Kipper wasn't always hanging around,' I reply.

'The Kipper?'

'His latest girlfriend. She's orange, skinny, smokes and she's got glassy dead eyes so she reminds me of a bony smoked fish. She hates me.'

'Why?'

'Dunno. She just does. She's either Mary Poppins or Cruella de Vil, depending on whether we're on our own or not. That's why no one believes me when I say she's a witch.'

I clamber out of the airbed and, balancing on my

knees, lean over to the bedside light and switch it on, blinking for a moment.

'Look, this is how much she loathes me.' I go over to my chest of drawers and get the glass donkey perfume bottle and give it to Maddy. 'She could have given me Gucci or Calvin but no, she gave me Eau de Donkey pee. Go on, unplug its butt.'

Maddy takes a sniff and gags. 'This isn't donkey pee, it's mule musk!' she squeals. 'They've probably stuck a mule over a bucket and squeezed its glands!'

'That's pretty much what I thought!' I giggle.

I turn off the light, get back into the farting airbed and pull the sleeping bag around me.

'I'm glad you're still laughing,' Maddy says. 'You seemed kinda quiet and detached earlier. It's OK. I didn't think you rude or anything, but the Jags thing explained it. You must be gutted, especially as you'd . . . well . . . it was *really* serious. How did it end?'

This is my chance to fess up. It's dark, she can't see me, we hardly know each other and she's only here for a week.

'Electra?' Maddy prompts.

'By text, a few days ago.'

Stop it, I think to myself. *Stop it right now, Electra Brown! Stuff a fist in your mouth, not as an anti-spider measure but to stop your potty mouth from running away with itself.*

'What a total jello-spine!' Maddy sounds shocked. 'What did it say?'

'*Adios*,' I reply. 'He said he'd met a Spanish girl in Spain, but it turns out she's from another school round here.' I seem to have set my mouth to automatic-lie mode.

'The total numbnuts!!' Maddy shrieks. 'If I bump into him this trip I'm going to tell him *exactly* what I think of him!'

Chapter Twenty

'For goodness' sake, the stuffing goes into its *lower* regions, Electra, not its neck!' Grandma S barks at me.

I know where it's *supposed* to go, but standing in her kitchen with a fistful of sage and onion stuffing I'm wondering whether I really can put my hand up a plucked chicken's butt and then eat it. The chicken, not the hand obviously. Normally Grandma S telling me what to do would irritate the hell out of me, but it's good that, however she might look, her personality hasn't changed.

It was a shock when I first walked into the living room and saw her. Her usually pink skin was slightly yellow and she'd lost such a lot of weight the sofa seemed to gobble her up in gold nylon-velvet. I wondered if our visit was too much for her so soon after the first lot of treatment, and a couple of days before the op, but when it was my turn for a hug, although her skin felt dry and paper thin, I could feel her boobs were still huge and felt relieved that not everything had shrunk.

Although Grandma isn't cooking lunch, it hasn't stopped her from sitting on a stool by the door, barking instructions.

'Victoria! If you don't get a move on peeling those potatoes they'll start sprouting.

'Eleanor! Don't bin the carrot ends! You know they go on the compost heap!

'Madison! Are you sure it's safe to make a trifle and use that camera at the same time?'

I can imagine Grandma barking at Mum and Dad, 'We'll say your wedding was in September!' and no one daring to challenge her. Perhaps I don't blame Mum and Dad for lying after all.

'Electra! That chicken won't stuff itself! Get on with it.'

I take a deep breath and shove my fist up the chick's bum. As I do so, I catch Maddy's eye, and we both pull faces and try not to giggle. She might look glam and gorge, but so far she hasn't been anything like the stuck-up-her-butt Teen Queen I thought she would be. I'm defo going to fess up about the whole Jags lie, but it hasn't been the right time yet. To get to Grandma's we had to get up at eight, but with the whole time difference thing it didn't seem fair to start explaining the complicated ins and outs of my virtual love life at her equivalent of three in the morning.

'Electra!' Grandma snaps. 'Have you finished the stuffing?'

'Yes!' I swing round, but although my hand went into the chicken's bum smoothly, it doesn't come out easily, and I end up standing in the kitchen with a raw chicken perched on the end of my arm. When I see its pale, plucked skin and skinny legs dangling from my wrist I shriek and throw my arms in the air, which releases the bird sending it flying straight into Grandma Stafford's chest after which it slithers down her body, bounces off her bony knees and lands with a splat on the floor at her feet.

We all stand round staring at the lump of flesh splayed across the yellow lino. With green-and-white-speckled egg-bound breadcrumbs leaking from its butt it looks like some sort of crazy roadkill. And Maddy has captured it *all* on camera.

She's the first to move. She laughs, picks the chicken off the floor with one hand and drops it to the sink, still filming.

'Hey, Gram-ma. It's supposed to be good luck to be hit by bird droppings. I guess it's even more lucky to be hit by an actual bird! You're gonna be just fine!'

Everyone laughs and I want to hug my cousin for knowing when to say just the right thing at just the right time, but I've got chicken bodily fluid on my hands and I don't want to spread salmonella.

'Thanks!' I mouth as I squeeze next to her at the sink, elbowing her big boobs by mistake, which feel squishily real. I push my hands under the running water. She winks at me and nudges me in my boobs with her elbow, which means she's not felt anything squishy, just bony. I don't care. A wink and a boob nudge is as good as a hug between cousins.

The moment Phil pulls his titchy blue Toyota out of Magnolia Close, I dissolve into floods of tears. I'd been holding them back until we were out of sight of Grandma and Granddad, but that final image of them standing on the drive with Mum and Aunty Vicky on the doorstep behind them, everyone waving, was too much and the flood gates opened.

Next to me in the back seat Maddy is crying too, tears splashing the silver camera resting on her lap.

Jack starts wailing, but I think it's just because there are so many tears flowing in the car he feels he has to join in. He doesn't know what he's crying about. He's certainly not crying about whether this might be the last time the family is all together like I know Maddy and I are.

'Come on, everyone,' Phil says brightly. 'Your grandma's a tough old bird. She'll be fine.'

Grandma *was* strong before the cancer, though I don't think she'd like the phrase *tough old bird*. She'd probably prefer something like *elegantly* robust, but now she's like a frail sparrow but with the squawk of a crow.

It's been an emotional day but a good one.

It was the first time Grandma had met Phil and they seemed to get on OK, although that's probably because she thinks anyone has to be better than Dad.

Mum, Aunty Vicky and Grandma talked about old friends and school friends and drank lots of tea that Maddy and I kept making for them.

Granddad, Jack and Phil took themselves off to Granddad's shed until Aunty Vicky called them in for lunch and then they came back with Jack holding a wooden rocket with a rubber band around its base, though Mum said it was best not to launch it in the house but to wait until after lunch and go out into the garden.

The chicken was delish and there was much joking about writing a Stafford family recipe for roast chicken starting with *First toss the bird around the kitchen*, which confused Jack, Granddad and Phil, who'd been in the shed, but caused all the females to giggle between ourselves and say, 'Nothing!' when they asked us what we were sniggering about, and Maddy managed to prop the camera up on a towering pile of books on the sideboard so she could film and eat at the same time, and everyone forgot that Grandma had cancer and was going into hospital tomorrow until we were just about to start on pud when Jack piped up, 'Granny, if your botty cancer makes you die, will you say hello to Granddad Kevin in heaven for me?'

The table went quiet, everyone stared at their bowls, and I thought the cream on the top of the trifle might curdle, the atmosphere was so tense.

Jack isn't old enough to know that there's a time and a place to mention that your paternal grandfather died by falling into a pit of wet concrete on a building site, and a couple of days before your maternal grandmother goes under the knife isn't one of them.

'Maybe Granddad Kevin was too heavy to float to heaven because he was covered in concrete. What do you think, Granddad? Can you go to heaven if you're stuffed full of concrete?'

Granddad said, 'I think there's just time to try and launch the rocket before it starts to get dark. Coming?' and got up from the table followed by Jack and Phil.

Grandma said, 'Who's for a cup of tea and a Jaffa Cake?'

and eased herself up from the table by her spindly arms.

Mum and Aunty Vicky said, 'Sit down, Mum, we'll do it,' and went into the kitchen.

Maddy leant over and switched the camera off, shot me a look and we started to clear the table.

And no one mentioned death or cancer again.

Chapter Twenty-one

Phil pulls off the motorway and into a service station.

We're not actually that far from home but he says tiredness can kill and Mum wouldn't be happy if both her children, her niece and her boyfriend ploughed into the back of a container lorry, just because I whinged about Phil wanting to have a shot of caffeine before driving any further. Anyway, I can buy a magazine from the shop and use it to show Maddy how the S-Scale works. Although I've given up with it on a day-to-day basis, I'll be interested to see whether we give similar scores because we're related.

Phil parks the car under a CCTV camera (apparently there are loads of thieving weasels at service stations) and we troop across the dark and almost empty car park, up some steps and through the automatic doors. Maddy seems to think that this badly lit soulless place is a good filming opportunity and starts the camera whirring, panning around the shop entrance, the toilets, even filming the Employee of the Month photo on which some joker has drawn horns and blacked out a tooth. The place looks like something out of a horror film, as if all the customers have been spirited away. There's just us, some tired lorry-driving-looking sorts, and a few pervy men staring at magazines on the top shelf in the shop.

'Phil Harris!'

A porky man in a fluorescent yellow jacket approaches us carrying a cardboard cup. From what he's wearing, he's obviously another AA man.

'Haven't seen you in ages, Pete!' Phil says, shaking the AA man's hand so hard Pete's other arm wobbles and brown liquid slops out of the little slot in the lid. 'Your rota never seems to coincide with mine.'

Pete smiles at Maddy, Jack and me. 'These your kids, Phil? You're lucky. Mine are all still in nappies and squitting for England.'

'They're not—' Phil begins. He sounds a bit lost. 'My girlfriend's . . . um . . .'

Maddy drops her camera. 'I'm his sort of but not quite niece-in-law,' she smiles. 'And these are my cousins. I'm visiting from Manhattan, New York.'

'Oh,' Pete says, still not having the foggiest idea where

we fit into Phil's life. 'Listen mate. You got a few minutes to share a brew with me?'

Phil looks at us and raises his eyebrows.

'Go ahead,' Maddy says as I nod in agreement.

Jack grabs the hem of Phil's jacket in case he gets left with girls whilst the men talk about engines and tyres without him.

'Meet back here by the employee photo at half-seven,' Phil suggests, and we look at our watches. We've got fifteen minutes. 'Don't leave the building. Stay on this side of the road and don't cross the bridge.'

'Er, like we're really going to get into trouble here,' I mutter, shoving Maddy towards the shop.

We're browsing through footie mags, not because I'm the slightest bit interested in football, but because it has more men per page than most mags and therefore is perfect to demonstrate the S-Scale. I'm just explaining that level 3 is a take-it-or-leave-it-could-do-better type of snog, when Maddy nudges me.

'Eyes left,' she whispers. 'There's a guy staring at you.'

'Me? Yeah, right,' I giggle. I'm standing next to a Teen Beauty Queen so any lad looking in my direction is clearly *not* looking at me, not unless he's employing the Befriend The Ugly Friend technique and is using me as a human shield whilst he ogles The Goddess.

'No, honest, he is,' Maddy urges.

I give her an *As if!* eye-roll. Making out someone would prefer me over her is stretching the Caring Cousin act a bit too far. Still, I can't help having a sneaky sideways glance at who's flexing his eyeballs in our direction.

Oh. My. God.

It *is* me he's staring at!

Of all the service stations in all the towns he has to walk into mine!

It's Freak Boy hovering by the computer magazines, which are dangerously close to the footie section.

I'm going to just ignore him and study David Beckham's tattoos in great detail.

'Don't look now!' Maddy squeaks. 'He's coming over!'

'Hi!' Maddy says to the hovering Freak. 'I'm Maddy from Manhattan and this is my cousin Electra.'

'*Buenas tardes.*'

Why on earth is FB speaking like an alien? Is it Klingon or Freakon or . . .

Oh. My. God. It's Spanish! Freak Boy obviously took the whole pretending-to-be-my-Spanish-boyfriend thing seriously. He's been learning the language for just this moment! Never in a million years did I really think he

191

thought I meant he could pretend to be my pretend boyfriend.

I stand behind Maddy and impersonate a red-cape-wielding matador, and even, in desperation, a ground-pawing bull, shaking my head and making wild arm-crossing movements . . .

'*Bienvenido a Inglaterra. Me llamo Jags.*'

. . . which clearly hasn't worked.

I want to die, right here, right now, in a scummy motorway service station. Perhaps fate will be kind and I will spontaneously combust, a meteor will crash through the roof and instantly kill me, or all that fiddling with a chicken's arse has given me bird flu and I'll just expire, crashing to the ground still clutching David Beckham. I wish Phil hadn't stopped for a coffee so that we *had* ploughed into the back of a container lorry. I know that sacrificing other lives just to get out of this mess is totally selfish, and I know it would leave Mum alone and heartbroken, but it just shows how *terrible* I feel. I should never have lied in the first place, but as I did, I should have fessed up to Maddy the *moment* she hit English soil.

'Jags?' Maddy says. 'Jags as in Electra's Spanish boyfriend Jags?'

'*Si!*' Freak Boy beams. '*Me llamo Jags.*'

As I'm clearly not going to spontaneously combust, be

targeted by space debris or killed by instant bird flu, desperate diversionary measures are called for.

'I'm ill,' I gasp, throwing down Becks and clutching my gut. 'Must be the raw poultry. Got to get to a loo. Quick.'

I dart out of the shop hoping that A: Maddy has followed me and B: She hasn't filmed my pretending to have the sudden trots when . . .

'Electra. Are you OK?'

Dunc The Hot Dad Hunk and Glam Doc are standing in front of me looking concerned. I've practically knocked them over in my rush to get away from their freaky son.

Just seeing Hot Dad makes me feel better, not that I was ill anyway.

'Oh, I'm fine,' I smile as Maddy turns up looking worried.

'She's not fine, she's got diarrhoea.' She puts an arm around me and I take back my opinion that Maddy always says the right thing at the right time. 'We had an incident with an uncooked chicken earlier. It could be salmonella.'

Glam Doc puts her hand on my forehead and swings into major medical mode whilst Maddy whips her camera out and films the impromptu examination. 'Have you vomited? Would you say the diarrhoea is watery or with mucus in it?'

'Put the camera down!' I hiss at Maddy, drawing the line at my intimate bowel habits being discussed and captured on film. I smile weakly at FB's parents. 'I'm fine, thank you. It was just a bout of trapped wind and I panicked.'

'Well, if you're sure you're OK . . .' As I haven't got a hot head or the raging trots, Glam Doc seems to be convinced by my wind excuse and as she and Hot Dad wander off towards the car I pretend to Maddy that they're old friends of my dad's and that *yes*, I'm fine because I managed to silently but violently expel the trapped fart without anyone knowing.

We hang around waiting for Phil and Jack. I've been continuously scanning the area for any signs of FB activity so I'm freaked when he appears from nowhere. He's obviously been silently lurking. Before he can say anything, Maddy sees him and steps forward to stand in front of him, cute button nose to big glowing beak.

'Listen, numbnuts!' she growls. 'Translate *this* into Spanish, you jello-spined jerk! My cousin can do *way* better than a loser like you'

Freak Boy looks shocked and scuttles off, and I have an overwhelming desire to run after him and tell him there's been a mistake and that he doesn't deserve to be called numbnuts, but I don't.

'What a louse,' Maddy says as we see FB practically throwing himself through the glass door to get away from us and out into the car park. 'I can see why you were upset though. He's totally cute.'

Chapter Twenty-two

'Hey, Missy B, what's the plan?'

I open one eye to see Maddy leaning over me, filming. When we got home last night we decided it would be more fun to share a room all week, so I'm still on the farting airbed, even though she offered to take her chance with the marauding arachnids.

'Mads, don't!' I pull up the sleeping bag. 'That's gross. What if I was dribbling or snoring or something?' I peer over the top to make sure the camera is out of nostril-filming reach.

'Then I'd do a close-up,' Maddy laughs and leans even closer.

I fling my pillow up at her and she flings it back at me and we collapse in fits of giggles.

'So, what's the plan?' she says again, dangling her crimson-painted toes over my face. 'I need to film something other than you lying in bed!'

I push away her toes and sit up. 'There is no plan,' I say. 'I thought the idea was just to do what I do on a normal half-term.'

'Which is?'

'Not much. Sleep in. Get dressed. Text the girls. Talk on MSN. Mooch about . . .'

'Well, we can cross sleeping in off the list!' Maddy giggles, nodding towards my alarm clock. It's almost noon. 'My excuse is jet lag, what's yours?'

'I couldn't get to sleep,' I say as Maddy gets up. 'Look, there's something I need to tell you.'

'I'm bursting for a pee!' she says, heading out of the door. 'Tell me later!'

I stick my head under the sleeping bag but quickly come up for air as it smells a bit rank down there. It had taken me ages to fall asleep as I'd been thinking about how I was going to fess up to Maddy that I'd lied about having a boyfriend. I was just at the point of switching on the light and getting it off my uneven chest when she started snoring, and it didn't seem right to wake her up just to tell her I'm the female equivalent of a numbnut. When I finally fell asleep I had terrible dreams about getting my hand stuck up a chicken's backside even though it was still alive and trying to peck me to death.

I decide to get dressed and *then* get washed, so I reach under my bed, drag out the nearest pair of jeans and a black sweater, brush the dust off, haul myself to my feet, prop the airbed against the wall as otherwise there's practically no room to walk, sniff a bra which is hanging over the back of a chair and fish out a pair of clean knickers from the drawer. I put it all on and then see Maddy's bra on top of her suitcase. I prod it and poke it and generally have a good feel. She's not naturally pneumatic! The bra is padded, filled with what feels like air.

I loop it over my arms and stare at myself in the mirror inside the wardrobe door. I very rarely look at myself full-length and now I remember why, although to be fair, I can't imagine anyone looking good with a bright-pink satin bra worn on the outside of a black polo-neck.

'Is that the style of a typical Brit teen as if so, I've *so* got to capture it on camera!' Maddy teases. I was so busy looking horrified at myself, I hadn't heard her come back in. 'Victoria's Secret. It's like strapping a couple of air bags across your front. I'm practically flat without it!' She pulls her tartan pyjamas tight over her chest, and although I would hardly say she's sporting a couple of fried eggs, possibly bread rolls, the Stafford Mighty Mammary Gene has clearly not sprung into life.

'I've brought some photos with me, if you're

interested,' she says, pulling her jeans on as I take her bra off. 'Just pics of Max and my friends. They're on a disc.'

This is the first time she's mentioned the Abercrombie & Fitch model.

'Are you missing Max?' I ask, clearing a pile of mags from the Thigh Crusher and switching it on whilst she finishes getting dressed.

'Well, to be honest, I'm missing Rufus more.' She hands me the disc to load. 'Max knows I'm coming home but a dog doesn't. He's probably wondering where I've gone and Dad's not a dog cuddler.'

I click open the first image. It's a group of girls standing outside a wooden door, framed by a sweeping grey stone arch over which the American flag is fluttering. There are green plants in grey stone troughs, no graffiti and it looks mega posh.

'That's us outside school, but you can't really see much,' Maddy says, looking over my shoulder. 'Go on to the next one.

'This is when we were at camp last summer,' she says as I look at a picture of girls with long brown legs poking from the bottom of short shorts. 'Max couldn't go.'

As Mads gives a running commentary, I flick through shot after shot of gorgeous girls at parties, crammed on a sofa, in a bedroom, at a softball game, in the park. All of her friends have names like Brianna and Savannah and look so groomed and gorge I'm beginning to wonder if the first thing that happens when they go to school isn't registration but a professional blow-dry.

There are shots of Uncle Hamp looking smooth and smarmy in his golf clothes with his coppery-coloured hair slicked back, a few of Aunty Vicky and Uncle Hamp in restaurants, some of their enormous apartment on the Upper East Side of New York and masses and masses of a tiny red sausage dog doing things with a ball in a park.

'Oh and there's one of Max and me in bed when we went on vacation to Bermuda last June, just before I went to camp. Dad took it so it's a bit fuzzy.'

Maddy turned fourteen the previous April. No *way* would Mum and Dad let me share a room with my boyfriend when I was barely fourteen, or even eighteen come to that. I'm shocked that Aunty Vicky allowed it and that Uncle Hamp photographed it.

I look at the photo.

Maddy is on the bed in a hotel room in her nightie, her arms wrapped around . . .

'Max is a *girl*?'

I stare at the photo of the pretty oriental girl hugging my cousin.

'You thought she was a boy?' Maddy shrieks with

laughter. 'She is *so* going to think that's hysterical when I tell her.'

She can't stop laughing. Tears are pouring down her cheeks. I don't find it funny. The Jags lie I made up was, in part, because I thought Maddy had a boyfriend, and all the time Max was a girl.

'Well, she shouldn't have a boy's name then,' I say sourly.

'She's really called Maxianne. Maxianne Setsuki. Fifty per cent Japanese, fifty per cent Canadian and, according to you, one hundred per cent male!' Maddy shrieks again. 'What time is it? I must get my cell and text her immediately!'

'I thought Max was your boyfriend,' I say, wanting to laugh, but freaked at the trouble I'm in. 'Mum did too.'

Maddy shakes her head as she taps out her message. 'That area of my life is a total disaster! I'm fourteen and I've been on like, three dates with two boys in my entire life and both of them have had such bad breath I couldn't bear to kiss them!' She nudges me in the ribs. 'I'm barely at first base whereas it sounds as if you have had a home run!'

I'm going to tell her about Jags and Freak Boy. I can't lie to her any longer. When Maddy arrived she was just my stuck-up cousin I had to put up with for a week. Now she feels like a friend, the sort of friend who could become a best friend. And I can't lie to a best friend.

'About Jags,' I say.

'Numbnuts,' Maddy corrects me, snapping shut her phone.

'Whatever. The thing is—'

'Girls, can I come in?' Phil puts his head around the half-open door. 'I need to go to the supermarket. Fancy helping me? I'm going now.'

I'm sure that when Maddy said she was happy to go along with whatever I would normally do in the hols she thought I was the sort of girl who you see on the TV or read about in the papers. The sort that spends their holidays producing a full-length musical, or plays in an international badminton tournament or does something useful for humanity whilst also completing fabulous homework. She didn't expect to come three thousand miles to be pushing a trolley around Tesco with me, Phil, Jack and Sorrel, who we've picked up on the way, not because she wanted to go shopping, but because she had a message from her mum to give to Phil about him inspecting the car she wants to buy. If he looks at it and says it's OK, Yolanda's going to take everyone to London on Friday.

I'd warned Maddy that Sorrel takes a while to warm to new people so not to worry if she either stared at her or ignored her, but so far they seem to be getting on well, probably because the first thing Maddy said when Sorrel squeezed next to us in the back of the car was, 'Fantastic nails,' and it's a bit hard to be a stroppy cow to someone who's just admired your manicure.

Actually, it's not so bad shopping with Phil because he clearly has no idea what we usually buy, so we're filling the trolley with the sorts of things Mum never lets us eat regularly. Turkey Twizzlers, jam doughnuts, huge bags of Cheesy Wotsits and multi-packs of Pot Noodles for Jack, who's running up and down the aisles grabbing food filled with sugar and saturated fat and preservatives as if all his Christmases have come at once.

'What do you fancy eating tonight?' Phil asks, staring at row upon row of pinky meat worms. 'I could get some mince for spag bol.'

I get the impression Phil can only cook with mince.

'I need the loo,' Jack says in an urgent voice.

'Didn't you go before you left?' Phil sighs, and The Little Runt shakes his head and makes a butt-clenching face.

'Come on then. Let's see if we can find somewhere.' He looks at us. 'Just keep going round and we'll catch up with you.'

It's only Monday and already Phil looks tired. I feel a bit sorry for him actually. He'd booked this week off to fly to Miami and have fun. Instead, he's been landed with a whole load of kids he's not related to, one of whom still hasn't got the hang of toilet-training.

I give the trolley a really big push and stand on the back, whilst Maddy films me and Sorrel mutters on about possible reasons for the lack of recent Warren-sightings, despite spending all her time hanging around Macky D's and The Oaks. She's thinking along the lines of him having stacks of coursework now he's at tech and being too busy to work, but I've got other ideas.

'Perhaps he's seriously ill in a coma,' I say as we turn into another aisle. 'Or maybe he's lost his memory and no one knows who he is. He could be wandering the streets crying, '*Sorrel! Sorrel!*' and people keep offering him bunches of the herb.'

'Why don't you ask one of his friends where he is?' Maddy volunteers from behind the camera. 'They might know.'

'I've never met any of his friends,' Sorrel says gloomily.

I grab a bag of muesli and hold it up to the camera.

'Fill your gut and then your butt with our fibre-packed rabbit food for humans!'

Maddy giggles and even Sorrel cracks a smile.

'Mads, let me film you!' I say, sticking my hand out. 'You pretend you're in a commercial.'

She hands me the camera, I raise it and she points at a row of Pop-Tarts.

'British tarts are *so* much tastier!' she says, flashing a cheesy grin towards the lens. She's talking away but I've stopped listening. I'm not even watching what she's doing. I'm staring in horror at the image in the viewfinder. Behind Mads a short dark-haired woman in a red coat is scanning the breakfast cereals. She takes a box down, looks at it, and throws it in the trolley next to her. The trolley that is being wheeled towards me by Jags. Not the pretend Freak Boy Jags, but the proper Slough via Spain Jags. The Spanish Lurve God. My virtual boyfriend.

My first thought is, *I have to hide*. I have to turn this trolley round and get out of here before the Spanish Armada get level with the Pop-Tarts. But then I think, *So what?* On past performance I could be rolling naked in a pile of Rice Krispies and however much snap, crackle and popping was going on, Jags *still* wouldn't notice me. He's hardly likely to come bounding up and say, 'Hi, I'm Jags,' is he? Sorrel won't speak to him and, as things stand, Maddy thinks Freak Boy is Jags. I'll just slowly hide the camera in my bag, take a great interest in the list of ingredients on a random box of cornflakes until the danger has passed, and then the moment I get home, I'll tell Mads *everything*.

'Electra!' Sorrel hisses beside me.

She's obviously spotted Jags.

'I know,' I hiss back. 'Just ignore him.'

'Electra!'

'What are you doing?'

I swing round to see a security guard and a man in a shiny grey suit standing behind me.

'I think she's filming undercover for a TV documentary,' says the security guard. He points to my bag. 'I know you have a camera in there. Hand it over.'

I pull the camera out.

Sorrel glares at the men.

Maddy gives them her best toothpaste-white smile. 'It's my camera,' she says. 'That's my cousin and I'm visiting from New York. I'm making a video diary of everything she does. It's for a school project.'

'Well . . .' begins Shiny Suit, his face softening.

'Yeah, right,' I butt in. 'Like three fourteen-year-olds are really filming a box of your crappy cornflakes for a TV company.' I give a sarcastic laugh, but then rapidly regret it as I get the impression that if I'd kept my mouth shut we might have been let off.

'Let's take you to the office and have a look at what

you've filmed,' Shiny Suit says briskly.

'This is ridiculous!' I say, not moving. 'We're schoolgirls not a film crew!'

'I'll run the film back and show you,' Maddy volunteers, fiddling with her camera.

'What's up?' Jags is standing next to me clutching a packet of Cheerios.

I haven't the foggiest who this question is directed at. Jags has never really talked to me apart from the one-and-only-and-never-again time I was so drunk I could barely remember the conversation, though I can still remember sliding down his body and pulling his jeans down as I collapsed on the floor at his feet. My face begins to burn with humiliation at the memory and I stare at the ground.

'Who are you?' one of the men asks. 'Do you know these girls?'

'Jags. I sorta know them. Well, I've seen a couple of them before.'

'Jags?' It's Maddy's voice.

I want to bolt for the exit. I *need* to bolt for the exit as my bowels have sprung into life. I *would* bolt for the exit if my legs hadn't gone to jelly.

'Yeah. Electra's ex-boyfriend.'

That's it! I'm dead!

Sorrel has suddenly remembered all those

207

conversations I'd had with her and Luce reminding them to pretend Jags was my boyfriend. I hadn't meant her to lie for me in front of my pretend boyfriend, only in front of my real cousin!

'I've never been out with her,' Jags says in a tone of voice which makes it sound as if he'd rather eat a pile of festering beetle dung than go on a date with me. 'She's just a friend of my mate's kid sister.'

'Oh, just brush away the last seven months,' Sorrel snarls, clearly thinking she's helping when really she's making things a million times worse.

I'm wondering if my heart beats any faster whether it will just give up or explode through my chest and splatter everyone with blood and heart-gore. It's an extreme way to die, but at this moment it's better than the slow lingering painful public death I'm experiencing.

'I think we should go to the office.' It's either Thin Face or Security Guard but I'm too panicked to work out which is which. 'We're getting nowhere out here.'

'Javier, 'ave you been dating zis girl?' A woman with a heavy Spanish accent is calling above the noise of an announcement that there's a special offer on Sour Cream and Chive Pringles in aisle eight. 'What ees going on?'

'That's what I'd like to know,' says a voice which is unmistakably Phil's.

Chapter Twenty-three

'Five minutes. I was away for five minutes, and I come back to that!' Phil crashes through the gears on his car after we've dropped Sorrel off for more Warren-stalking. 'Five minutes and there are people shouting at each other and security guards and—'

'It was totally my fault, Phil,' Maddy says from the back of the car. 'I started the filming.'

'I was involved too,' I mutter, slumping further down into my seat. 'Sorry.'

Jack is in the front. He keeps turning round and making smug faces, delighted that I'm in trouble. I'd really like to kick the back of his seat, but I don't dare. I'll kick him later though.

It hadn't helped that, when Phil returned, Thin Face turned out to be a store manager called Mr Potter who recognized Jack as being the kid who'd stolen a box of forty Super Plus Tampax months ago, and when Phil introduced himself as 'Jack's mother's boyfriend' there was muttering between Thin Face and Security Guard about *problem families* and we were let go.

'Do you *always* cause trouble when your mum's away?' Phil says, glaring at me through the rear-view mirror. 'As if there's not enough going on at the moment!'

I do feel bad for Phil, but I'm also worried about what we're going to eat for the rest of the week, as after we left the store manager's office Phil marched out, leaving the junk-food laden trolley abandoned in the breakfast cereal aisle, and there's not much in the freezer. But most of all I'm freaked about what I'm going to tell Maddy.

I give her a sidelong glance. She's fiddling with her phone, no doubt texting Max to say she's staying with a lying cheating minger of a cuz and can't wait to come home.

I've ruined *everything*.

I've got Maddy into trouble. I've caused rows. I've not taken her anywhere exciting. She caught me wearing her bra. But worst of all, I've lied.

I'll always be her cousin, but now I can never really be her friend.

* * *

'So let's get this right,' Maddy says after I tried to explain the difference between Freak Boy Jags and Lurve God Jags and the fact that neither of them were or had ever been my boyfriend, and the reality was that other than the spitting-Frog I've got zero boy experience. 'Before I came here *you* thought I was a stuck-up-my-own-butt Teen Queen dating an Abercrombie & Fitch model called Max?'

I nod. 'But you're not! I realized I was wrong about so many things after the first day!'

'And before *I* met you I thought you were some slutty Brit girl who was probably having underage sex with a Spaniard.'

Put like that it sounds so sleazy. It hadn't been sleazy in my head. 'But I'm not,' I say. 'I'm not slutty and there's no sex!'

We're up in my room, sitting on the bed, door closed, trying to block out the tense atmosphere seeping up the stairs from the kitchen where Phil's trying to be creative with what's left in the freezer. I don't know how he's going to make tea for four from a few frozen pitta breads, some ice cubes and an out-of-date moussaka which Mum bought forgetting it was packed with food-of-the-devil aubergines.

'I guess we both got each other wrong,' Maddy smiles.

'But what was with the dot dot dots and why did it matter so much that I might be dating when you're not?'

'It just did,' I say, biting my lip to stop myself crying. '*Everyone* seemed to be close to dot dot dotting except me. I thought you were dating, Lucy had this summer snog with Pascal the Frog and then there's this whole Warren and Sorrel thing . . .'

'The Sorrel–Warren thing sounds as if it's going nowhere and this Pascal guy lives in France.'

'But they *could* be going out with someone if they wanted to!' I say. '*I* don't even get the chance to turn someone down. I'm never asked out in the first place.'

'Jags One fancies you,' Maddy says hugging her knees. 'I promise you I could see lust in his eyes.'

'Freak Boy?'

'Freak Boy?' Maddy sounds genuinely surprised. 'What's freaky about him? If he smiled and stood up straight he'd more Fit Boy than Freak Boy and much cuter than that greasy little munchkin we met in the grocery store.'

'You're winding me up!' I giggle.

Maddy shakes her head. 'For me, Jags One would be near the top of your Snogability Scale whereas I'd only snog Jags Two if my life depended on it.'

'FB has got nice green eyes,' I say, strangely finding that

I'm not offended by my virtual boyfriend being referred to as a greasy munchkin and getting a minging S score. 'And when he smiles, he's not so freaky.'

'So, go out with him!' Maddy laughs. 'You know you want to!'

'I do not!' I say, which is absolutely true. Even if by some faint stretch of my overactive imagination I did go out with FB, I couldn't cope with all the teasing at school, plus no one decent would ever ask me out because they'd think a freak was all I could get, and all the zitty-bum-fluff saddos would pester me because they'd think I was so desperate they'd be in with a chance. '*Everyone* thinks he's freaky,' I say. 'If I went out with him, everyone would think *I'd* freaked.'

Maddy shakes her head. 'So, ignore *everyone*! Swim against the tide!'

I'm about to point out that going out with FB wouldn't be so much swimming against the tide as drowning in a tidal wave of school disgust, when my moby goes.

It's Dad.

'What are you up to?' he asks.

'Just gabbing with Maddy,' I say, mouthing *Dad* to her.

'About Madison,' Dad says. 'Caroline has suggested you and she might like to join us for a Chinese on Wednesday evening. We thought the Golden Chopsticks just near the flat? Pick you up from the house about seven?'

And then he rings off. No mention of how Grandma is or whether Wednesday is OK for us.

'Mads, you're going to meet The Evil Kipper on Wednesday night,' I say. 'She's probably going to poke me in the eye with a pair of chopsticks.'

As I say it I wonder why I'm bothering. Dad doesn't believe The Kipper is a bitch to me. My best friends think I'm the one with the Kipper problem. Even The Little Runt likes her. I thought at least Maddy would understand, but now, after lying to her about Jags, how can I expect her to believe me?

Chapter Twenty-four

Tuesday. The day of Grandma's butt op. Mum rang last night and said Grandma was settled in hospital, she was first on the operating list this morning, Granddad was fine but obviously worried as he kept popping out to his shed and coming back with damp red eyes and she'd ring as soon as they had any news.

Mads and I slept in until ten, I texted Luce and Sorrel to tell them Maddy knew everything, Luce texted back to say Ireland was wet and she couldn't wait to see me on Thursday, Sorrel texted to say she was being forced to work at the café, Maddy texted Max to tell her I wasn't a teen slut after all, we got dressed in each other's clothes (all except bottoms as Mads is much more twiggy than me and I couldn't face the thought of busting her jean seams), spent some time filming each other measuring our tongues next to a pink ruler for no other reason than it seemed a fun thing to do, and then we wandered downstairs where Jack was sitting at the kitchen table surrounded by paper and crayons and bits of stuff.

'What's up, Jack?' Maddy asks. I've told her he responds better to terms such as Runt Features or Scroat Face but she doesn't listen.

'I'm making Grandma a get-well card,' he says, pointing at the table. He's cut a picture of David Beckham out of one of his footie mags, stuck it on a piece of card and drawn a speech bubble next to it so that Becks is saying, *Get Wel Soon Grandama*. Actually, I think he must have drawn the bubble *before* he wrote the words, as *ama* is outside the balloon. Still, it's the thought that counts, not the design or the spelling, which is just as well.

'Are you girls coming with me to look at Yolanda Callender's new car this afternoon?' Phil asks. He's at the kitchen sink up to his elbows in soap bubbles. 'I'm meeting her at her café at three.'

'I don't think sniffing round some old motor is going to be very exciting, Mads,' I say. 'But we should probably go and rescue Sorrel from lentil duty.'

'It's fine by me, Missy B,' she says, pouring Shreddies into a bowl. 'It all goes in the viddy diary.'

The house phone rings and we all jump. It's the call we've been waiting for. The call about Grandma.

Phil goes over to the dresser and picks it up.

'Ellie?'

I'm holding my breath, looking at Maddy, who isn't even blinking but is poised in mid-Shreddie crunch-down.

'Yes, she's here. Hang on a moment.'

'It's your dad,' Phil says, handing me the phone as everyone sighs.

'Is that the grease monkey?' Dad barks. 'What's *he* doing there?'

I don't want to get into all this in a kitchen full of people ear-wigging so I just say, 'Why didn't you try my moby?'

'I did,' Dad replies. 'It just went on to the answerphone.'

I must have left it upstairs.

'Well, can you be quick as we're waiting to hear how Grandma's operation has gone,' I say. 'We need to keep the line clear.'

'Oh, well, about tomorrow. You know we were going out?' For one glorious moment I think that perhaps he and The Kipper have the lurgy and the meal is cancelled. 'Rather than go out, Caroline's suggested she cooks. See you at seven as planned.'

And then he rings off, which is I suppose what I asked him to do.

'We're not having a Chinese meal in a restaurant,' I say, slamming the phone down. 'Dad's girlfriend's cooking.'

'It's nice of her to make an effort,' Phil says back at the sink.

'It's not nice!' I snap. 'It's horrid. She's probably only doing it to kill me. You wait, she'll make sure she serves me first because my bit will be laced with poison! I am not going to eat *anything* that chain-smoking cow has touched.'

Everyone stares at me as if I'm nuts.

'Don't look at me like that!' I squeal. 'She's only cooking to make Dad think she's Mary Poppins when really she's an evil kipper!'

'What's a kipper?' Jack asks as the phone rings again.

'A smoked orange fish with lots of bones,' Maddy explains.

'She's a psycho,' I hiss, picking up the phone as I'm still next to it. 'She'll probably use arsenic to kill me.'

Now it's Mum. She says Grandma's sleepy and hasn't said anything other than make the odd grunt but she's through the operation and everything went well.

'How's everything there?' Mum asks. 'Anything to report?'

'Everything's fine,' I say. 'Do you want a word with Phil?'

'Just a quick one,' Mum says. 'If he's around.'

'Phil!' I say. 'Mum wants a quick word.'

I look back at the table where Phil is bending over a sobbing Jack who's leaning back across his chair, a glue stick stuck up his left nostril.

'Can he phone you back?' I say. 'He's just up to something.'

'Sorry we're late,' Phil says as we troop through the bright-yellow door of the Bay Tree Café. 'We had a bit of a detour.'

'Phil!' Yolanda rushes from behind the counter and hugs him, even though they've never met before, not unless you count the time he ran a voddy-soaked Sorrel home from Mortimer Road in the early hours of the morning and carried her practically unconscious to the front door. 'Sorrel got the text and told me.' She lets go of Phil, which is just as well as he was in danger of turning blue from lack of air. She pushes her brightly coloured scarf back from her forehead and bends down towards Jack. 'How are you, lamb?'

The Little Runt ducks before Yolanda can press his head into her tummy.

Our 'bit of a detour' was taking Jack to hospital. Phil pulled the glue stick out of Jack's nose but The Little Runt had wound the stick right up before he rammed it in, so

219

that as it came out, some of it broke off and stayed stuck. I pointed out that Jack had another nostril to breathe through so it wasn't exactly life or death, but I guess Phil was worried that Jack might somehow be permanently injured by a combination of glue and snot in his airways, so we headed off to the local A&E. Jack and Phil were taken to a cubicle whilst Maddy and I sat in reception surrounded by people looking sorry for themselves. It was a bit boring as it took ages for them to treat Jack, there weren't any limbs falling off, there was no sign of Glam Doc who works in A&E and a stern-looking nurse told Maddy off for filming a man doing wheelies in his wheelchair in the corridor.

'He's fine now,' Phil smiles. 'He's learnt his lesson.'

'And you have to be cousins!' Yolanda shrieks at me and Maddy. She goes to hug us both at the same time and manages to bang our heads together. 'Peas from a pod! An organic, ethically farmed one hopefully!'

As Maddy and I rub our foreheads, Sorrel stands glowering. Her mother is forcing her to help out in the café today and tomorrow, saying she wouldn't pay her moby bill unless she did, so she's probably spent the morning up to her elbows in lentils and wheat-grass sludge.

'Are all the herbs coming?' Yolanda asks an assortment of children on a nearby table.

Sorrel's younger sister Sulky Senna shakes her head, stays put and glowers through her thick glasses, but the twins, Orris and Basil, shriek, 'Yeah!' and rush for the door.

'Celeste, hold the fort for half an hour, can you?' Yolanda throws her apron towards a grungy-looking girl with a gold star painted on her forehead. 'We won't be long.'

'It's just round the corner,' Yolanda says as we follow her out of the café and along the road. 'I'm pretty sure it's fine, Phil, but I'd find it a comfort to have a real professional give it a once-over.'

She turns into an alley where she stops outside a large green garage door with peeling paint, and rings the bell. A small hatch cut into the garage door opens and a man with a shrunken face and a few strands of grey hair combed over his bald head looks out.

'Ah, Mrs Callender, come in,' Comb Over says. 'She's through here. Follow me.'

He opens the garage door a fraction and we walk into a courtyard where the car is parked, its black paintwork glinting in the early autumn sunshine.

'Cool!' Jack shrieks.

'Oh my God!' I gasp under my breath.

The twins burst into tears and hide under Yolanda's skirt.

Maddy lifts up her camera and starts to film.

'It will have been meticulously maintained,' Phil says, clearly gobsmacked.

'Naturally,' says Comb Over. 'We can't risk breakdowns.'

'So, what do you think?' Yolanda asks, beaming. 'Isn't she a beauty?'

'Mum, how could you do this to us?' Sorrel cries. 'I can't believe it!'

Yolanda gives Comb Over a look that seems to imply *Teenagers! They're never happy*, and says, 'It's second-hand, in beautiful condition, carries eight people, will run for years and is cheap. That's more than you can say for beast cars and buses.'

'IT'S A FREAKIN' HEARSE!' Sorrel screams so loudly, she could wake the dead. 'YOU'RE BUYING A FREAKIN' COFFIN CARRIER!'

'No, no!' Comb Over corrects. 'It's a funereal stretch limo. It's never carried a coffin. Only mourners *behind* the hearse.'

'It's a Goth stretch limo,' Sorrel snarls. 'No wonder it's cheap! Who other than us and gravediggers would buy one?'

I'm standing close to Comb Over and hear him mutter,

'Funeral directors, not gravediggers, if you please,' under his breath.

'And with the money I've saved I'm going to convert the engine to run on vegetable oil!' Yolanda beams. 'What do you think, Phil?'

Phil has had his head under the Goth limo's bonnet and is now lying on the ground shining a torch underneath. He's got to at least *pretend* that something's wrong with the car. He *can't* let Yolanda buy it. Sorrel will be totally humiliated. Phil will have to lie and say that years of mourners wailing in the back has bent its suspension or something.

'Well, if you want an eight-seater saloon with a full service history, I'd say you couldn't do better.'

Sorrel kicks one of the tyres and shoots Phil a *Drop dead* look.

'It's got leather seats, Yolanda,' I say as a last desperate attempt on Sorrel's behalf to put her mother off. 'Animals have been slaughtered for this car.'

Knowing how anti-meat Yolanda is I can't imagine that she's happy to park her butt on dead animal skin.

'I have wrestled with my conscience on that subject, Electra, but as I see it, the innocent beast has already been killed and skinned, but continues to serve in death as it did in life.'

From Sorrel's face I can tell she's storing that one up for the next time she asks for a pair of leather boots and her mum says no.

Yolanda and Comb Over start exchanging paperwork and Yolanda hands over a banker's draft, which means she can drive the car away immediately. She jangles the keys in the air.

'So, are we still on for our London trip on Friday?' Yolanda asks. 'Just my way of saying thank you to Phil.'

'Yes, please!' Maddy nods enthusiastically. 'I'd love to see Big Ben.'

It's OK for her. Riding around in a Goth limo is fun on holiday. You can do it if you're a tourist and no one knows you. It would be just about OK for me, as I can say I'm friends with the girl with the eccentric mother who drives a saloon of sorrow knowing that mine runs around in a bog-standard silver Ford Focus. But for Sorrel?

'As if!' Sorrel snaps. 'I'm never setting foot in that coffin-chasing Gothmobile *ever*!'

Chapter Twenty-five

We just larked around today.

First, Maddy made me put my school uniform on so that she could film me in it. I did point out that her project is supposed to be about what a typical British teen does in the holidays and that I was creating entirely the wrong impression by suggesting it's perfectly normal to dress up in school uniform when you don't have to. She said she wanted to use the footage as a retrospective, as if the film started from the Friday before she arrived, even though that's nuts because she wasn't there to film me coming home, and since when did I race up to my bedroom, throw my uniform off from behind the wardrobe door, stick out a naked leg, and then appear fully clothed in party stuff, which is what she got me to do. I'm still painfully aware that The Glam Plan has been a disaster so I blow-dried my hair and did my make-up and nails *before* she filmed me, so now her friends will think I go to school with a face full of slap and enormous earrings, which, thinking about it, isn't that far from the truth.

I put my foot down at wearing my school uniform outside in the holidays, and we went on the bus to Burke's where Maddy was disappointed to see there wasn't a Union Jack flying above the entrance, surprised that instead of plants in posh pots outside we had a Gum 'N Butt Bin, and amazed that rather than a stone arch framing our entrance, there were metal gates with spikes on top. It didn't help the overall impression that someone had written *Tosser* next to Mr Thomson's name on the sign outside.

We walked around the side and saw Pinhead, Gibbo and Spud on the playing field, larking around with spray cans. They must have climbed over the railings to get *in*, which is well odd, as during term time they're always climbing over the railings to get *out*. We then wandered around the streets gossiping as Maddy filmed random dogs and buildings and then went home and spent the afternoon playing bowling on Jack's birthday Wii whilst stuffing ourselves with Pringles. We had fun, but all the time I was dreading seeing The Kipper this evening and now Maddy and I are in the front room waiting for Dad's bling car to pull up. I'm peering behind the curtains, keeping guard so there's no need for him to come to the door, and I've given Phil strict instructions not to come out as I can't face a confrontation between him and Dad, although it might make good film material for Maddy if they started pushing and shoving each other on the street.

'Why are you hiding?' Jack kicks my backside through the curtains. I spin round to try and hit him, and whilst I'm still trying to kick him in his soft bits and he's trying to butt kick me, the bell goes.

I dash to the front door followed by The Little Runt.

'Hi, Dad! We're ready.' I do a fantastic backwards kick which gets Jack right where I hoped it would.

'I'm stabbed!' he howls, jumping around, clutching his bits. 'Poo Head's stabbed me!'

'I didn't stab him, I just kicked him,' I explain to Phil, who's bounded up from the kitchen wearing the pink flowery apron and carrying a wooden spoon.

'Hello,' he says to Dad.

'What's he still doing here?' Dad says sourly, ignoring Jack who's still behaving like a snivelling grub. 'Where's your mother?'

'I *told* you Grandma was ill. That's why Aunty Vicky and Maddy are over.' I glare at Dad, willing him not to cause any aggro. 'Grandma's operation was yesterday.'

'Mum's away for a week!' Jack says, which is *so* not helpful and deserves another kick in his privates.

'I didn't realize *he* was staying,' Dad says. He sneers at Phil. 'So *you're* looking after *my* kids?'

'That's right,' Phil replies, and I notice he's holding the wooden spoon in a defensive manner, dropping bits of mince on the green Axminster.

'Come on, let's go!' I say, sounding falsely cheery at the prospect of The Kipper's cooking, but trying to get out before there's a tussle over ownership of cooking utensils.

'I'm coming too!' Jack says. 'I'll get my DS!'

'Weedy kids can't come,' I snap.

'Of course he can,' Dad replies. 'My son would be much better off spending the evening with his family than with some bloke in a girly pinny.'

Dad pulls up outside the flat in Aldbourne Road.

Maddy wanted to film, even though it's dark, so she's been in the front seat whilst Jack and I have been squashed in the back, pinching each other's thighs all the way, my knees practically round my ears there's so little room. Dad helps Jack out and holds out a hand to me, but I wave it away and snap, 'I can manage!' though, in truth, trying to get out of a tiny seat in the back of a low-slung sports car whilst wearing high heels and tight jeans is not easy. Your centre of gravity is based around your butt and mine seems stuck to the seat, but I'm furious with Dad for inviting The Little Runt and mega furious he tried to humiliate Phil over the apron.

'What are you doing out here in the cold?' Dad says as The Kipper appears from the darkness whilst I'm still trying to wriggle free from the Porsche.

'Just putting some rubbish out,' she says brightly. 'Hi, Jack! I didn't know you were coming. This *is* a nice surprise. And you must be Madison. I'm Caroline.'

I finally stagger free of The Black Bullet, thankful that I'm not wearing a skirt as otherwise in getting out I'd have shown my lady-bits to everyone. I slam the car door behind me for which Dad tells me off, he bleep-locks the car and I troop up the stairs after them.

'Come in and make yourself comfortable,' The Kipper says. 'I've just got a few things to do before we eat, but do ask if you need a drink or anything.'

To avoid The Kipper I haven't been in Dad's flat since the early summer, and if I'd been parachuted in through the window I wouldn't have known where I was. There's no sign of the red velvet sofa piled high with tassel-trimmed cushions. Instead, a couple of boxy brown leather sofas dotted with turquoise silk cushions sit at right angles to each other. The heavy cream curtains are now slim wooden blinds, and the cream-and-gold-flocked wallpaper has been stripped and the walls painted white. There's a long brown-wood table set for four with white china and sparkling cutlery instead of the old glass dining table with its bowl of plastic fruit and crystal candlesticks.

Any trace of Candy Baxter and her dodgy decorating has been completely erased.

'What a beautiful apartment,' Maddy says to Dad as they sit on the sofas.

'What's happened to Candy's stuff?' I ask. 'All the tassels and fringing?'

Dad looks uncomfortable and glances over his shoulder to the kitchen where The Kipper is preparing to poison me. 'Candy wanted some of her things back, so Caroline decided it was an ideal time to make a fresh start and completely redecorate,' he whispers. 'She got an interior decorator in.'

I get the impression that The Kipper doesn't like Candy's name being mentioned. I'll make sure I bring it up as often as possible.

Whilst Maddy and Dad are talking about her trip and Jack is sitting on the floor (now stripped wood rather than cream shagpile) playing on his Nintendo, I wander through to the kitchen. The units are the same but the stencilled grapes have gone and everything has been repainted a sort of muddy cream colour.

'You got rid of Candy's frog magnets,' I say, looking at the blank white fridge. 'And Candy's grapes. Oh and Candy's—'

'Set an extra place.' The Kipper shoves a knife and fork at me, blade and prong forwards. Perhaps she's going to start by stabbing me and if that doesn't work, she'll move on to the poisoned grub.

'Candy bought these,' I say, waving the cutlery in her face before taking them in to the living room.

'We'll eat in about five minutes.' The Kipper's followed me in carrying a large glass of white wine. She's all sweetness and light and false smiles. She dips her hands into a bowl of peanuts. 'So, Madison, what have you done so far? Been up to London? Seen the sights of our capital city?'

'No, but I've had a great time.' Maddy smiles. 'We've been to Gram-ma's, a grocery store, the neighbourhood hospital, bought a funereal car, been to Electra's high school on the bus . . .' Maddy counts these thrilling events off on her fingers. Even I can see that put like that, it sounds a grim trip.

'We *were* going up to London on Friday with Sorrel's mum but that's been cancelled,' I say. 'Phil might take us instead.'

As Sorrel is boycotting the Gothmobile and says we have to too, Phil said he would take us to London, but the downside of this is that The Snivelling Grub would have to come.

Dad's eyes narrow.

'Well, *we* should do something,' he says, obviously desperate to get one over on Phil. 'Caroline and I could take you and Electra up there on Saturday.'

'Oh, that's so sweet, Uncle Rob, but I leave at noon on Saturday,' Maddy says. 'The flights home on Sunday were full by the time we booked.'

What a relief! The thought of having an entire Kipper-filled day is enough to make me want to poison myself.

'Well, how about I take the girls up there?' The Kipper trills. 'I could take Friday off, combine it with a trip to see my old friend from university, Fiona Sheldon. We could go on the train, have a meal in Chinatown—'

'Well, if you're sure,' Maddy butts in, sounding excited. So much for her saying she just wanted to do ordinary things.

Dad goes in for the hard sell. 'You could see the dinosaurs at the Natural History Museum, go to the V&A, see Downing Street . . .'

'I expect the girls would rather go shopping,' The Kipper laughs, and for once, she's right.

'Isn't she wonderful?' Dad says, beaming at her. 'What would I do without you?'

Probably find some other cold fish to sit in your Porsche, I think.

Whilst The Kipper and Dad make a disgusting public display of affection by cooing and nuzzling each other, I make my excuses and go to the loo. It's no surprise that the pink shaggy loo-seat cover has gone, but it's deeply depressing to look in the bathroom cabinet and see that it's now full of Tampax and deodorant and posh perfume that definitely won't smell like donkey pee, all signs that Caroline Cole has more or less moved in with Dad.

When I come out, everyone is already sitting around the table.

'This looks interesting, Caroline,' Maddy says as I sit down. The four of them are sitting opposite each other so I'm perched at the far end like a spare part.

'What is it?' I ask.

'Aubergine stuffed with mince and topped with cheese,' The Kipper replies as Dad hands me a plate. 'And salad.'

I look in front of me. It's as if someone has eaten masses of aubergine and mince and then vomited it on to my plate from a great height.

I hate aubergines. No matter how much mince or

cheese you put on them they are still evil puke-inducing purple blobs. And The Kipper knows this. Or was it Candy who knew it? I bet The Kipper knows it, which is why she volunteered to cook and terrorize me with these Vegetables of the Devil.

'What's wrong?' asks Dad. 'Why aren't you eating?'

'I don't like aubergines,' I say through gritted teeth. 'You know that.'

'In the US we call them eggplant,' Maddy adds, as if this makes them look or taste better.

'Oh, I'm sorry, I had no idea,' The Kipper says. 'Leave the bits you don't like.'

'She's going to leave all of it because she thinks it's poisoned,' Jack pipes up.

'Jack!' I try to kick him in the shins but just manage to hit the table leg so hard, the table vibrates and the pudding spoons rattle.

'You said that she was a smoking kipper who was going to poison you,' The Little Runt continues, relishing being the centre of attention. 'And you called her a psychic.'

'I did not!' I shriek, looking around the table. 'Honestly, I *never* said that.'

Jack sticks a finger up his nose and thinks for a moment. 'Oh, no you didn't,' he remembers. 'You said she was a psycho who was going to use Arsenal to poison you.' He looks confused. 'I meant arsenic.' He'll be looking confused by the time I've beaten the hell out of him later.

'Electra?' Dad sounds furious. 'Did you say those things?'

I have two choices. I can either fess up to the fact that I did and cause an almighty row, or I can lie my way out of it.

I look at Maddy who's shooting me *Keep calm* looks.

'I just said . . .' I begin. 'I just said . . . that I wouldn't like it if Caroline smoked in the flat because smoke is poisonous, which is why none of the Arsenal team smoke. Jack got the wrong idea.' I glare at The Little Runt. He's got aubergine running down the side of his mouth, which makes me feel so sick I can't think of a reasonable explanation as to why I might have called Dad's girlfriend a psycho.

'Right. Well then.' Dad's obviously not convinced but even he doesn't want a scene in front of Maddy. 'Anyway, there was no need to worry. Caroline gave up the evil weed before the summer, didn't you?'

'Rob hated me smoking,' The Kipper purrs, patting Dad's hand. 'So I stopped, just like that. I didn't need willpower, only love.'

She and Dad give each other lovey-dovey glances over

their plates of aubergine vomit.

'You were smoking on the 1st of September,' I say. 'You were smoking at Jack's birthday party.'

'I don't think so,' The Kipper laughs. 'Not me.'

'You were smoking outside Aqua Splash. I saw you. You blew a smoke ring at me!'

The Kipper looks at Dad, sighs, and rolls her eyes. 'I'm sorry, Rob. This is what I've been telling you. I do my best but . . .' She turns to me. 'Why do you always try and make trouble where it doesn't exist? Anyone would think you had it in for me.'

I'm still on the airbed. Although we said we'd take it in turns I can't have Maddy on the floor when she's a guest. She's sitting on my bed in her pyjamas, running back today's footage.

'I suppose you think I'm lying about The Kipper,' I say, staring up at the ceiling cobwebs and wondering if I'm more at risk from a spider falling into my mouth than crawling into it.

'She's very convincing,' Maddy agrees.

'She really is a liar,' I sigh. 'I know you won't believe me after I lied about Jags, but it's true, it really is.'

'I know.'

'Dad doesn't believe me and nor does Sorrel or Luce

and I really thought you might, but how can you after I fed you all that Jags crap?'

'I do.'

'Now no one will *ever* believe me and The Kipper will be free to persecute me and make my life a misery.'

'Missy B, I love you but just shut up for a moment!' Maddy laughs. 'Here, look at this.'

I get out of the airbed and sit next to her. She presses a button and hands me the camera. 'I took it on the way to Uncle Rob's apartment tonight.'

There's just streaming red tail lights, oncoming white headlights, gloomy street lights, a row of dark buildings. Arty but boring.

'I'm starving,' I say, handing back the camera. 'I couldn't eat anything. I'm going downstairs to gorge on Shreddies and sugar.'

'Keep watching,' Maddy urges, pushing the camera back to me.

As we get closer to Dad's flat there's a woman in the street, the light from an open doorway highlighting her scrawny frame. She's clearly taking drags on a cigarette, puffing warm smoke rings out into the cold night air.

'It's The Kipper!' I gasp.

'She wasn't putting the trash out, she was smoking!'

Maddy says triumphantly. 'She lied and that got you into trouble with your dad. And we've gotten it *all* on film.'

At first I was so thrilled about the incriminating evidence I danced around the bedroom and got completely overexcited and started spraying deodorant and perfume in the air shouting, 'Take! That! You! Kipper!' with each alternate spray, just because it seemed a celebratory sort of thing to do, but then Maddy started coughing so I put them down, picked up a hairbrush and pretended to be a reporter. 'We have breaking news from the bedroom where we have received exclusive footage of The Kipper committing a crime . . .' whilst Maddy filmed me. But now, lying on the floor in the dark, I feel a niggling sense of unease, and it isn't just because the airbed has been gradually deflating under the weight of my sturdy bod and is now so thin I can feel a stray flip-flop underneath it.

'Mads, you asleep?' I whisper into the darkness.

'Almost,' she says groggily.

'The Kipper's a lawyer, right? So I've been thinking about whether that bit showing her smoking would stand up in court as evidence.'

I hear Maddy sit up in bed and yawn. 'It's evidence that she smokes when she swore blind she didn't.'

'Exactly. But *not* evidence that she's a bitch to me,' I say.

'I see what you're getting at.' She turns on the bedside light.

I crawl out of the airbed and climb on to the end of the bed.

'If she was in court and had to defend her fag-lie, what would she say?' I ask, sticking my toes under the duvet. 'She'd say, *I put it to the court that I was so ashamed of my bad habit I lied to cover it up.* She's a lawyer! A paid liar! She could convince Dad she lied because she was ashamed of still smoking. Mads, we've got to get more evidence. You've got the camera, we're with her all day on Friday. Let's launch Operation Catch A Kipper.'

Chapter Twenty-six

I think that if your Dad lies about the date of his wedding or where you were conceived and then leads a double life before leaving his wife and kids to live with his dental hygienist who then is replaced by his divorce lawyer, it no longer gives him the right to have a go at you for bad behaviour, but it hasn't stopped him from ringing and laying into me about what happened last night. Maddy and me have arranged to meet Sorrel and just-back-from-Ireland Lucy at Macky D's at one, and we bumped into Butterface and Tammy Two-Names at the newsagent's earlier and they're coming too, but not Tits Out who's still visiting her father and stepmonster, so Mads and I have spent the morning, well, what was left of it by the time we got up, wandering around the shops at Eastwood Circle. We were in JD Sports so she could buy Max an England shirt with Beckham 7 on the back when he rang.

'I didn't want to say anything in front of your cousin or Jack, but I'm sick and tired of your behaviour, Electra,' he barks. 'It's really upsetting Caroline.'

'Upsetting her!' I shriek, hanging over a rack of tracksuit bottoms as I watch Maddy trawl the store. 'You're having a laugh, aren't you?'

'She claims you're always trying to stir things up and cause trouble.'

'Me!' I squeak. 'She's the excrement-stirrer!'

'That's enough!' Dad orders. 'Caroline's bent over backwards to be nice to you but the fact of the matter is, you can't bear her just because she's my girlfriend. Well, I've got news for you, young lady. She and I are together and you had better get used to it.'

'You don't know what she's really like!' I whine. 'She's a monster.'

'Can I remind you that you might *want* to be a seven-year-old kid, but you're actually fourteen and it's about time you grew up!' Dad snaps.

'But she hates me, Dad!' I say. '*Really* hates me!'

'Hates you? Hates you?' Dad's voice sounds as if this is the most ridiculous thing he's ever heard. 'She cooked for you, she bought you a present from Spain . . .'

'She cooked me devil food and the perfume was donkey pee!' I yell, and then wish I hadn't as people are

241

starting to stare.

'Then why is she taking a day off to take you and Madison to London tomorrow?' Dad asks. 'Answer me that!'

I can't, and in frustration I elbow a rail of T-shirts next to me. They wobble so alarmingly I'm scared they're going to topple over. I can't be escorted out of yet *another* shop whilst Maddy's here.

'I am not having a row with you whilst I'm at work,' Dad snaps, 'but this Caroline-hating has got to stop. I'll pick you both up at eight sharp tomorrow morning and run you to the station. You're to be on your best behaviour. And if Caroline comes back and I find out you've been rude . . .' The threat of unspeakable parental retribution hangs in the air before I cut the call and throw my moby into the T-shirt rack in frustration.

I don't think me and my friends are giving a good impression of what it's like to be a typical Brit teen. We're not usually gloomy depressives, but today we're all sitting in Macky D's with faces on.

I'm depressed because of the thought of spending tomorrow with The Kipper, the row I've just had with Dad and the fact that half-term will soon be over, Maddy will be going home and I've got days of homework to finish and only hours to do it. I've also cracked the screen of my moby from when I hurled it at the stainless-steel shop fitting.

Tammy Two-Names is down because the dentist said she needed to have her braces put back on so she's back to being a brace-face.

Nat looks as blank and gormy as ever so it's difficult to know whether she's depressed or not, especially as she's started holding her hand over her scarred left cheek. It doesn't look so much as if she's covering her face as propping her head up.

Sorrel's depressed partly about the Goth car because now it's parked in the drive the neighbours have been coming round to ask who's died and whether there's anything they can do, but mainly because Warren's gone into hiding. She hasn't seen him for nearly four weeks, not since the emergency summoning to Starbucks. He's not at Macky D's, hasn't been answering her texts and is never at home when she's hanging around outside. All she can do is spend hours doodling hearts and writing Sorrel & Warren 4 EVA on any available surface, including her arm.

Lucy's back from Ireland where she was miserable because she couldn't email Pascal, it rained all day *every* day, she was cooped up with her Irish rellies, James moaned about missing Fritha, Michael moaned about missing uni and when she got back there was an email from Perfect Pascal to say he didn't think he'd be coming over at Christmas because someone had booked the farmhouse and they had to be there.

'He didn't put a kiss on the end of his email,' she says gloomily as we sit making one box of chicken nuggets stretch between six. 'He usually puts masses of kisses.'

'Maybe hith like, met someone elth,' Tam lisps. She's got to learn to talk again with the new ironmongery. 'A foreign minxth.'

'I'm supposed to be his foreign minx,' Lucy wails.

'You OK, Sorrel?' Maddy asks. 'You still haven't heard from Warren?'

'Like I *so* care,' Sorrel snaps back.

I'm totally miffed she's been so rude to Maddy. 'So if you don't care, why are you always stalking him and why are you such a stress-head?' I say.

She glowers at me. 'If he's blanking me then I wanna know why he's blanking me. That's all.'

'He sometimes works here, right?' Maddy says and we all nod. 'So, ask them where he is.'

A scrawny man whose uniform is at least five sizes too big is pushing a mop half-heartedly around the floor near our table.

'Is there a guy called Warren here?' Maddy asks as he thrusts the mop towards us, sending a stray chip skittering across the floor.

'Lanky, braids, huge diamond earstud,' I add.

Sorrel mouths *Shut up!* to both of us and gives me a *Drop dead* glare.

Mop Man thinks for a moment and then says, 'Left to work in Smith's. Something about a girl.'

When I'm upset and hurt I cry. I do lash out at the odd object. A wall. A chair. The Little Runt. But generally I collapse in a snivelling heap of snot and tears and hope someone notices me. There's no point in having a major tantrum if there's not someone around to witness it and offer sympathy.

When Sorrel is upset and hurt she gets angry. *Nuclear* angry.

'Sorrel, don't!' I yell, as she scrambles out of her seat and rushes for the door.

We all grab our bags and shoot after her as she speeds across the shopping centre like a missile primed and ready to fire, heading straight for her target in WH Smith's.

We follow her through the door as she races up the newspaper and magazine aisle, down the adult book section, back up the children's book aisle and round to the stationery area where Warren is filling up a shelf with pink furry pencil cases.

'Warren?' Sorrel's voice is full of questioning menace.

'Oh hi, babes,' he says, stroking the pink fur. He looks at the six of us. 'Yous lot OK?'

'We're fine,' I say. 'This is my cousin Maddy. She's visiting from New York.'

'Hi!' Maddy says, which is mega annoying as I'd hoped she might talk a bit more to put off the awful moment when Sorrel takes one of the furry pencil cases and stuffs it in Warren's mouth.

'You didn't tell me you'd left Macky D's,' Sorrel says accusingly, hands on hips, chin jutting out.

'Soz, babes,' Warren shrugs. 'Like there, I could slip you the odd burger, but it's all different here.'

He waves a furry rectangle in the air and I hold my breath for the gob-stuffing action.

'Actually I'm like, really pleased to see you, babes,' he says. 'I've been meaning to call you.'

'You have?' Sorrel looks confused. 'What's this about a girl?'

'About that. There's something I want to ask you.' Warren looks a bit embarrassed and sheepish, but perhaps that's because he's finished with the pencil cases

246

and is now stacking pink and silver pencils shaped like fairy wands.

'There is?' Sorrel tosses her braids and gives a coy smile. You'd never guess a moment ago she was murderous.

'Yeah, babes.' Warren gives a nervous laugh and starts fiddling with his fake-diamond earstud. 'I've wanted to ask you for like ages but it's kinda embarrassing.'

Hallelujah! Finally Shelf Stacker is going to ask Sorrel out though I don't know why he had to leave Macky D's to do it.

'Go on.' Sorrel is all flirty and girly.

'Will you put in a good word for me with your sister?'

Oh. My. God. Warren did fancy a Callender girl, just not Sorrel.

'My sister?' Sorrel asks slowly.

Even though he's a louse I want to warn Warren he's about to be smothered by stationery. I want to hiss, *Warren, put down the fairy pencils and walk away very slowly. Backwards.*

'Yeah, Jasmine. She said she wouldn't go out with me 'cause of the whole meat-is-murder vibe, so that's why I got a job here, but she's still blanking me, man!'

'*You* want *me* to tell my sister to go out with *you*?' Sorrel snarls.

'Well, yeah.'

Here we go. Remove the pencils. Hide the rulers. War on Warren is declared.

'YOU FREAKIN' CREEP!' Sorrel shouts, scaring the little kid next to us who's been dithering over whether to choose a pink ring binder or a clear one shot with glitter. 'YOU LOUSY LANKY LOWLIFE CREEP!'

'What's wiv the attitude, babes?' Warren says. 'What have I done?'

'DON'T YOU *DARE* BABES ME!' Sorrel screams. 'I AM *NOT* YOUR BABE!'

Maddy, Luce and I huddle together for safety. Nat and Tam hold their bags in front of them as protection. A concerned mother pulls the ring-binder-choosing kid out of the way. Sorrel's anger is going to orbit out of control any second. I can see her hitting Warren, trashing the shop, ending up with a criminal record, never getting into the police. But then something awful happens. Instead of screaming and shouting and stuffing stationery in every bit of Warren she can reach, Sorrel bursts into tears.

'You led me on, you creep,' she wails, tears streaming down her cheeks. 'You made out it was *me* you fancied!'

Warren holds out his enormous hands. 'We was just mates, babes,' he says lamely. 'I half fancied you, but then when I went to tech I realized you was just a kid, whereas Jas is hot and she's all woman!'

I take back the bit about wanting to warn Warren his life's in danger. He deserves everything that's coming to him. I might even grab a glittery ruler and aim for his nearest orifice.

Sorrel lunges at Warren with her bag but he ducks and she misses, hitting a pile of pencil tins which come crashing to the floor around Warren's gigantic trainer-clad feet.

'Come on,' I say, dragging her away sobbing. 'Let's go.'

I'm on one side and Luce is on the other, practically carrying Sorrel out. Nat and Tam are carrying our bags. Maddy is filming everything. We're just at the door, by one of the tills, when Sorrel breaks free from our grasp. I think she's going to head back for round two with the lanky louse, but instead, she pushes in front of a startled customer about to pay for his copy of *The Times*.

'There's a tall black lad in the stationery section,' she growls at the assistant. 'Watch him. He nicks stuff. He did it at McDonald's too.'

Chapter Twenty-seven

I hate Caroline Cole but I have to admit she knows how to give a girl and her cousin a good time.

Dad picked us up this morning and ran us to the station, and then whilst The Kipper sat on the train and tapped away on her BlackBerry, Maddy filmed me talking in an American accent, and I filmed her trying to talk in a British one and then we gave Snogability Scores to the other passengers (no one over a disappointing 2.3), and generally got so overexcited and giggly that the porky woman opposite us started making tutting noises that sounded like piggy grunts, which made us snigger even more.

When we arrived in London we took the tube to Oxford Circus, arranged to meet The Kipper under the clock at Selfridges in two hours and headed straight for Topshop. We intended to start there and work our way along the street, but ended up spending all our time in

The Temple of Style where Maddy shopped as if New York didn't have any shops. I bought a hat and scarf as close to Maddy's as I could find, and a heart-shaped yellow-diamond belly stud to try and cheer Sorrel up, although I think the only thing that might bring a smile to her face is if she heard that Warren and Jas had been crushed against a wall by the Gothmobile. I felt bad about leaving her today, but Luce is going to hang around to make sure Sorrel doesn't do something stupid, like murder her older sister.

After we met The Kipper we went into Selfridges and she bought a fantastically expensive shiny purple Mulberry handbag, which I noticed she charged to Dad's credit card, had a sandwich and a milkshake in a nearby café, and then The Kipper decided that we really ought to do more than just shop and eat on our day in London so she hailed a taxi and told the driver to take us on an hour's trip of all the sights.

'Having a good day, girls?' The Kipper asks as the taxi swings round the front of Buckingham Palace, up The Mall, through Admiralty Arch and towards the bronze lions of Trafalgar Square.

'Awesome!' Maddy gasps, filming everything. 'This has been so great, Caroline. Thanks!'

It has, but I still haven't managed to catch The Kipper

251

being mean to me on film. She's been such fun, so friendly, I'm beginning to worry that Maddy is going to start thinking I've exaggerated the whole psycho bitch thing, despite the smoking evidence.

The cab pulls up outside Covent Garden tube.

'This do you?' the driver calls out from the front.

Maddy and I stand on the pavement as The Kipper fiddles about in the back of the cab exchanging money.

'We still haven't got her,' I hiss. 'We've got to split up to have a chance of Kipper-catching.'

'OK,' Maddy whispers back. 'Next time I go to the bathroom don't follow me, OK?'

She hands me her camera which I slip into my bag.

The Kipper is beside us looking at her watch.

'We're not meeting Fiona at the restaurant until five-thirty,' she says. 'What do you want to do until then?'

'I'd like a drink,' I say.

'I could use the bathroom,' Maddy adds, catching my eye.

The Kipper points along the road. 'It looks as if there are cafés along there. Let's go and see.'

Whilst The Kipper gives our order to the waitress – two Diet Pepsis and a cappuccino for her – I reach into my bag, which is perched on my lap, make sure that the lens is just poking out and press the *Record* button.

There's no time to waste trying to work up to an argument. If Operation Catch A Kipper is going to work I've got to get straight in and get The Evidence.

'Finding it hard not to slip into Cruella de Vil mode today?' I ask. I'm so nervous my thighs are shaking and I'm just hoping that the film isn't shaky too. 'Because you *are* an evil witch, aren't you? Admit it!'

The Kipper doesn't say anything. She just totally ignores me and stares at the photos of old actors that are hanging on the wall. Even though I hate her I feel ashamed at what I'm doing and how rude I'm being. It makes me feel as if I've stooped to her slug-like level. But it has to be done. Desperate times call for desperate measures and all that.

The waitress arrives with the drinks, but still The Kipper stays silent. Maddy can't stay in the loo much longer or someone will think she's locked herself in.

I try again. 'You hate the fact that I'm a reminder that Mum and Dad were married and you're just Dad's girlfriend, or at least you are until I get him to get rid of you.'

The Kipper stands up. For a moment I think she's going to go for a lunge-and-slap move, but instead of hitting me she grabs my bag off my lap, sticks it on the table, brings out the camcorder and switches it off.

'Nice try, kid,' she says, holding on to it. 'Don't think I didn't realize what you were up to. I'm sure your dad would be interested in this footage.' Suddenly she breaks into a smile. 'This is a sexy little piece of kit. Is it tape or memory card or what?'

'Um . . . er . . . I've been using memory cards,' Maddy says, sitting back down. She can probably tell from the look on my face that Operation Catch A Kipper has been a disaster.

'She saw me,' I hiss as The Kipper goes to the loo. 'She grabbed the camera.'

Maddy pulls a face, presses playback and we huddle over the viewfinder. There's just darkness and my voice going, 'You are an evil witch . . .'

'Guard that camera at all times,' I say. 'If The Kipper gets hold of that film and shows it to Dad, I'm doomed.'

We wander around Covent Garden for a bit, no one mentions the secret filming fiasco and then we weave our way through the streets towards Leicester Square and into Chinatown.

I wonder what Yolanda would make of the rows of dried ducks hanging in restaurant windows, brown and wizened as if they've been sunbathing for too long. I try to take a picture on my moby to send to Sorrel, but it's dark now and the shot doesn't come out. It does give me an idea though. I'd forgotten that I can record about twenty seconds of footage on my moby so perhaps I can put Operation Catch A Kipper into action another day.

'Here we are!' The Kipper leads us up some steps and through a door into a brightly lit area where women in long silk Chinese dresses are scurrying around holding armfuls of menus in burgundy plastic folders. 'And there's Fiona.'

As Fiona is a friend of The Kipper's I thought she might be like her. Perhaps not a kipper but another ugly fish. A slippery eel or ugly old trout. But Fiona Sheldon is nothing like The Kipper. She's small and round and smiley with spiky ginger hair and her face is like a globe dotted with hundreds of tiny freckle islands. It would only take a few more freckles for her face to be completely covered. I can just imagine Mrs Chopley making up a Brain Extender about her. *Fiona's face has 300 freckles that cover 75% of her face. If she gets 10 new freckles a year, how long before her face is one big freckly blob?*

The restaurant is vast, busy and *very* noisy.

There's only a round table for six, not four, and they want us to wait for twenty minutes for a smaller one to come free, but The Kipper assures the waitress that we'll eat quickly and they can have the table back in an hour.

'We've got a long journey home,' she explains to Freckly Fiona as a scary-looking waitress yanks the two extra chairs away from the table and practically throws them at the wall next to us. 'And Maddy has a flight to catch tomorrow.'

The moment I sit down, Scary Waitress drops a menu over my head on to the table in front of me. 'You ready order?' she barks.

I want to say, *Give us a chance!* but I don't dare. She might be wearing a pretty silk dress and flip-flops, but I wouldn't want to cross chopsticks with her on a dark night. Even Maddy puts down her camera when Scary Waitress shoots her evil looks.

'How about we just get them to put something together?' Fiona suggests. 'As we're tight for time?'

As long as there's no sweet and sour aubergine, I'm up for it.

Scary Waitress shuffles off and a young scared-looking waitress dumps a huge basket of prawn crackers on the table and starts rearranging the chopsticks and the plates.

'So, have you enjoyed your day in London?' Fiona asks Maddy. 'Bit different from New York, isn't it?'

Fiona's got a proper smile. The sort of smile where it's

not only your lips that look friendly but your eyes too. She might be close to being a total freckle, but she's lovely.

'Hey! You've been to New York!' Maddy says. 'Vacation or business?'

'Strictly business,' Fiona says, pulling a face that rearranges the freckle map into entirely new continents. 'I was involved in litigation between an architect and a property tycoon. It meant I got to stay in a swanky hotel and eat in five-star restaurants on my law firm's expense account, but never got to see Central Park or the Statue of Liberty. Although,' she leans forward as if she's going to tell us something top secret, 'I did pretend I had another meeting to go to and then sneaked out to Bloomingdales and bought myself a fabulous pair of shoes!'

We all giggle, even The Kipper. I wish Fiona was Dad's girlfriend. He chose the wrong lawyer. Perhaps I could set them up on a blind date? The Kipper deals in divorce. From what Fiona's saying, she does commercial stuff. Maybe I could pretend that someone got their toe stuck in one of the taps Plunge It Plumbing Services supplied and is suing him, and then Fiona The Freckle could represent him. I could launch Operation Freckle Face.

'Was that someone's phone?' The Kipper says, rummaging in her bling bag. 'I'm sure I heard a phone ring above this racket.'

We all look at our mobies.

'It's my cell,' Maddy says, brandishing hers. 'It'll be Mom stressing about tomorrow.'

It's so noisy, Mads decides to take the phone outside and I go with her, not that it's much quieter in the street what with a fire station opposite and crowds of people laughing and shouting all around us.

Maddy assures Aunty Vicky that *yes*, Phil will run her to the airport, *yes*, she will remember her passport and they'll meet by the first American Airline check-in counter, and *no* she won't be left alone in a big foreign scary airport at risk of being abducted into an international prostitution syndicate.

'I'll be fine, Mom,' she says. 'I'll call you if there's a problem. Love you!'

We head back into the restaurant where the table is now groaning with food. I recognize the prawn toasts, rice and spare ribs, but there are all sorts of dishes which for all I know could be nasty bits of animal in a sticky sauce such as sweet and sour bulls' balls or stir-fried chicken beaks. I wouldn't put it past Scary Waitress to order the most disgusting thing on the menu just to spite us for refusing to wait.

'Has anyone seen my camera?' Maddy asks as she sits down. 'I left it here on the table.'

We push the plates and dishes aside but there's no sign of it.

'Are you sure it isn't in your bag?' Fiona asks. 'Have a look.'

Maddy starts unloading the contents of her bag on to the table. Postcards she's written but hasn't sent, make-up, hair bands, gum, her MP3, all sorts of pens, but no camcorder.

'I know it was here.' Her voice sounds panicky as she refills her bag. 'It's got days of stuff on it and all the sightseeing shots. Did you see anyone come past?'

'There's been people coming and going all the time,' Fiona says, getting up and ducking under the white tablecloth before coming back up empty-handed.

Maddy's on her feet, pacing and panicking, repeating, 'Ohmygod. Ohmygod. My project. My project.'

I'm staring at The Kipper, who stares straight back at me. She's not helping to hunt for the camera. She's just sitting there, snapping a prawn cracker between her fishy lips, looking guilty as hell. She's been waiting for a chance to whip the camera, and when Maddy and I left she probably distracted Fiona and then swiped it.

'Why don't you ask *her*!' I say, pointing across the table. 'Ask *her* what she's done with Maddy's camera.'

'What are you talking about?' The Kipper says.

'YOU KNOW EXACTLY WHAT I'M TALKING ABOUT!' I yell above the noise. 'YOU STOLE IT TO GET THE FILM TO SHOW TO DAD! THE BIT WHERE I CALL YOU AN EVIL WITCH!'

People are starting to stare.

'What going on?' A small wrinkled Chinese man in a badly fitting black dinner jacket and bow tie is at our table. 'What problem?'

'My camcorder's gone missing,' Maddy explains, close to tears. 'It's a small silver Sony. It was here, on the table.'

'I'm telling you, she stole it!' I say, glaring at The Kipper. 'Search her bling bag!'

The once noisy restaurant has fallen deathly quiet.

Everyone is looking at us.

By this time the wrinkled man has been joined by Scary Waitress and Scared Waitress. Between them there's lots of high-pitched gabbling and waving of arms. Scary Waitress marches over to one of the spare chairs on the wall behind The Kipper on which someone has dropped a stained tablecloth. She pulls it off with a flourish, and there, underneath, on the chair, is Maddy's camera.

'We say sorry,' says the man, as Scary Waitress swipes Scared Waitress across the face with the grubby linen. 'Mistake. Moved camera for food. Not put back. Sorry. Have prawn crackers. Free. On house.'

260

Chapter Twenty-eight

'Hey, Missy B, we promised each other we weren't going to cry, remember?' Maddy says, hugging me. She's with Aunty Vicky at the airport, standing by the entrance to the security queue. 'If you start to sob it'll set me off and my mascara is packed.'

She pushes me back and holds me by the shoulders. Despite what she's said, her eyes are glistening.

'I'm going to miss you,' I sob. 'Message or mail me, won't you?'

'Try stopping me,' she says, hugging me again. 'And I'll send you an air bra ASAP. Feels like you need it!'

We both giggle through our tears, but it's hard to laugh for long.

Any minute now Maddy and Aunty V will be swallowed by doors which you can only get through if you have a passport and a ticket. I'd give *anything* to have both those things right now and go with them to America. There's nothing here for me now, other than Mum, and the girls and maybe Dad when he's not with The Kipper, oh, and I want to find out what's going to happen next in *Hollyoaks* and I don't know whether they have it in America, but other than that, I might as well leave.

Everything's over.

Half-term.

Maddy's visit.

Operation Catch A Kipper.

My virtual love life.

All I've got to look forward to is a ton of homework, an airbed to deflate and the prospect of Dad going completely ape when he finds out I publicly accused his girlfriend of being a thief.

I don't know why I thought Operation Catch A Kipper would succeed. I've made tons of plans over the years and not one has worked. My plan to get Freak Boy to follow Dad to find out why he'd left home backfired spectacularly, as FB thought he was spending time at the dentist because of dodgy gnashers when really it was because he was sleeping with his dental hygienist. I planned Beat The Impostor to get rid of Phil but he's practically living with us. Operation Bald Eagle was supposed to reunite the parents and they're now divorced. My Non-Party Party Plan ended up with the house being trashed by teenage terrorists and a huge repair bill for me, and as for The Glam Plan – I touch my lumpy chin with manky nails – I'm *never* going to make plans, *ever* again!

'Thanks for looking after Madison,' Aunty Vicky says to Phil, kissing him. 'And thanks for looking after my little sis. You're good for her.'

'You're making me blush!' Phil laughs. 'And don't worry, we'll keep an eye on your mum and dad and let you know what's happening.'

'We should go,' Aunty Vicky says, eyeing the snaking queue. 'Come on.'

Maddy gives me a final hug. 'Remember, despite what anyone says, it's Fit Boy not Freak Boy,' she whispers in my ear.

Chapter Twenty-nine

As if life isn't hard enough missing Maddy, spending Sunday morning in the supermarket, helping Phil clean the house for Mum coming back later and with an afternoon of biology, English and history homework ahead of me, I've just stepped in bunny poo and from the look of it it's squidged under my big toenail.

'Jack!' I yell, just as Theo hops past, depositing soft black currants as he goes. 'Get this rabbit out of here.'

'Jack's in the garden,' Phil says, coming down the stairs with the Hoover. 'He's cleaning out Theo's hutch.'

'Well, tell him his rabbit needs a nappy when it's in the house!' I snap, jumping on the draining board and sticking my foot under the tap. 'It's crapping everywhere.'

I run warm water over the offending toe and then dig out the last remains of bunny excrement with the prong of a fork.

'I'll take Theo out if you can run the Hoover around here,' Phil says, following the rabbit around the kitchen until he finally corners it by the pedal bin and grabs its backside.

I nod, jump off the draining board, dry my foot with a big wodge of paper towels, stick my earplugs into my lugs, turn the vol on my iPod right up and plug the Hoover in. Combining music with housework makes cleaning seem easy. I bop around the kitchen sucking up everything as I go, thinking that maybe we could go to New York for Christmas and then I could see Maddy, and really it's only eight weeks away which gives me plenty of time to start The Glam Plan again, even though I said I was off plans for life, when I realize that the poo isn't being sucked up with the hairs and the stray peas and unidentifiable bits of rubbish, it's just smearing and sticking to the rollers. Time for more kitchen roll.

As I go to the dresser, I notice the answerphone light flashing. I've had the music on so loud I've missed the phone ringing.

I look at my watch. Almost two our time, nine a.m. in New York. It could be Maddy. I turn the Hoover off, rip out my earplugs and press *Play*.

You have two new messages, barks the voice.

Message one *is* from Maddy saying she and Aunty

Vicky arrived back safely in New York yesterday and had a good flight, even though she sat next to a man who smelt as if he'd drenched himself in my donkey pee perfume.

Message Two. 'Ellie, it's Rob. I tried you yesterday but you were out. I don't know when you're back from visiting your mother but can you ring me the moment you are? We need to talk about Electra. *Urgently.*'

He sounds as mad as a box of frogs. The Kipper's obviously told him about Friday. I am in *serious* trouble, and this time, I don't think there's any way out.

Phil comes in from the garden. He sees me standing next to the phone.

'Did someone ring?' he asks.

'Just Maddy to say they're back safely.'

And then I press *Delete*.

'Is this really my house?' Mum says, looking round after she's finished hugging us all. 'I can't believe how clean and tidy it is!'

'Phil said it was a pigsty this morning,' Jack squeals. 'Because Electra's a pig!'

Mum laughs. 'Perfect or pigsty it's good to be home. What's been going on?'

The Little Runt bounces up and down. 'Poo Head got

told off in Tesco's and I had to go to hospital and then we bought a coffin carrier and then Electra said she was poisoned and then—'

'Shut up, scroat features!' I snap.

'Get lost, Poo Head!' he snaps back.

'Some things never change,' Mum smiles. '*Is* there something I should know?'

'Oh nothing,' Phil says. 'Nothing important anyway.'

Mum hands him her car keys. 'I've got some boxes in the car, my old school books and stuff that Mum's been keeping. While I put the kettle on for a cuppa, can you unload them for me?'

'I'll make the tea,' I volunteer as Jack and Phil go upstairs.

'Waitress service! If this is what I come back to each time, I must go away more often,' Mum says as I fill the kettle.

'Please don't,' I say, meaning it.

Mum sits at the kitchen table and starts to flick through the post. 'Why? Has there been a problem? Was Phil keeping something back?'

'No, nothing like that and Phil's been great, it's just I've missed you.' I open a boxed chocolate cake we bought this morning. 'How's Grandma?'

'Surprisingly well,' Mum says. 'She's out of hospital

tomorrow and there are lots of friends and neighbours around to help out. I'll probably nip up next weekend to see how she's doing.'

'So now they've cut the manky bit out, is she cured?' I pour hot water into a teapot as Mum coming home seems like a special occasion. 'Is that it?'

She shrugs. 'We won't know for a while and she has to have another op at some point, but her consultant says it's all looking very positive.'

I pour some tea, slosh in some milk and hand Mum the mug.

'Thanks, love. And did you enjoy having Madison to stay? You seemed to get on well at Mum's.'

'She's the best cousin the world,' I say. 'Not a bit like I imagined.'

'That's everything.' Phil and Jack clatter back downstairs. 'It's all piled up in the front room.'

'Thanks.' Mum opens the last of the post. 'Any phone messages?'

'Just people trying to sell you kitchens, oh, and Electra said Madison rang to say her and Vicky got back safely,' Phil replies.

'I'd better ring Dad to let him know I'm back,' Mum says. 'And then let's settle down and try to get back to a normal quiet life.'

I'm upstairs in my bedroom staring at my history homework, wishing I'd started it a week ago and slightly freaked at the thought of telling Poxy Moxy it's not finished.

From the draught around my ankles, I can tell the front door is open. Mum and Phil are probably having a long lingering goodbye on the doorstep, which will give Mrs Skinner next door something to ogle. Mum suggested he stayed but his holiday is over too and he has to be back on call early tomorrow morning so he's going home. I'm really fond of Phil and he's been good to us this week, but I'm happy he's gone because I don't think I can take any more mince. A Million Meals With Mince seems to be the only cookbook Phil has ever read, and other than the disastrous Chinese and a takeaway pizza the day we abandoned the trolley at the supermarket, I've had mince every day since Mum left. Even the aubergine vomit meal had mince in it. And tonight Phil cooked cottage pie, aka mince under a blanket of lumpy potato.

It's odd that he spends so much time at our house and yet I've never been to his. When I mentioned this to Sorrel she said she'd read about a man who had two lives and two families and kept this going for years without either knowing. He'd tell one lot he was away on business whilst he was with the other one and so on. Perhaps Phil's still married to his ex, Debs. Perhaps he's keeping his house out of bounds so we don't meet his other family who are probably happy he's away as they're fed up of mince too.

I look at my homework. Poxy doesn't allow us to type homework assignments; we have to handwrite them, which is a right pain. I decide it would be better if I wrote in black ink not blue biro. I scribble on a bit of paper in black ink. Yes, black is tons better. I write the title: Germany 1918–1945. I have to cover twenty-seven years of German history in a couple of hours. I underline it. Oh no! I've smudged the line. *That's* why I was writing in blue! I'd forgotten that this black pen doesn't dry quickly and I'm always making black smudges. I'll have to rip out the page and start again. But I still don't want to write in blue. I want to write in black ink that doesn't smudge. And I can't find a pink highlighter, only blue, and blue highlighter looks just so *wrong*.

I'm still stressing over my choice of pen colour when Mum comes in *without* knocking which is a total breach of my personal privacy. I could be doing *anything*.

I'm about to go mental when I see her face. She looks upset. Perhaps the doorstep goodbye with lover boy hasn't gone too well. Perhaps he's confessed that he has to go not because he has an early shift and some mince to cook, but because his wife and kids are expecting him home. Perhaps a week with us has made him realize that he doesn't want to be part of the Brown family and he's dumped her on the doorstep.

'Electra, your father's downstairs, in the hall.'

'Dad?' I gasp. 'Dad's here?'

Mum doesn't say anything but goes downstairs. I'm obviously expected to follow her.

When I get to the hall, there's no sign of Dad. The front door is closed and the front room empty.

We both go downstairs and he's there, in the kitchen, standing by the dresser, his arms folded across his moobs, a face like thunder.

'I asked you to stay upstairs,' Mum says sharply. 'You can't just waltz down here. You no longer own the place.' She turns to me. 'Your father says he left a message for me. Did you pick it up?'

I shrug.

Dad reaches behind him, picks up the phone and starts stabbing the keys.

'My number is the last one to ring here,' he says, listening. 'At 1.55 p.m.'

'That doesn't mean you left a message,' I say lamely. 'It just means you rang.'

271

The parentals might be divorced but they're united in their glaring at me.

'I was going to tell you once we'd had tea and Phil had gone and . . .' I start defiantly but my voice trails off. I know I'm doomed.

'So presumably you haven't told your mother that you publicly accused Caroline of being a thief?'

I just stand there trying to keep my *Am I bovvered?* face as intact as possible which is hard as underneath I'm *mega*-bovvered.

'Look, I don't know what's been going on,' Mum says. 'I've only just got back from Mum and Dad's.'

'I'll tell you what's been going on. Our daughter has been bullying Caroline, making up false accusations about her, being rude to her, generally trying to cause trouble. At our flat this week she claimed Caroline was trying to poison her, and then on Friday, in a packed restaurant, she accused her of stealing her cousin's camcorder.'

'Did you?' Mum asks me.

I nod.

'And had she?'

'No! But she's always mean to me!' I shriek. 'It's me that she bullies! Me that she tries to get into trouble! She's Mary Poppins in front of Dad, and Cruella de Vil behind

272

his back. I'm telling the truth! Honestly!'

'I don't think you know the meaning of the word *honest*, young lady,' Dad snaps. 'It's just one lie after another.'

'Oh, that's great coming from you,' I shout. 'You lied about Candy. You and Mum lied to me about when you were married! What chance did I have? I was born, unwanted, into a web of deceit!'

I'm not entirely sure this outburst helps my case, but as I'm up to my neck in it anyway, it's worth throwing every bit of available ammo into the row.

'Blame your grandmother for that,' Dad snorts. 'That was her daft idea, not mine.'

Mum, who's been looking mad, but has stayed silent, suddenly explodes. 'Don't you *dare* bring my mother into this when she's lying in a hospital bed with a bag instead of a bowel!' she yells. 'Now, I want you out of *my* kitchen and out of *my* house, whilst I have a word with *our* daughter.'

Dad stands his ground for a moment but then stomps upstairs, along the hall and bangs the front door so hard, the glasses on the dresser rattle.

Mum and I are both shaking.

'She's really mean to me, Mum,' I say, starting to cry. 'She hates me. Only Maddy believes me and now she's gone.' I'm sobbing really snotty sobs now.

273

Mum sits down on the sofa and pats the cushion next to her.

'Let's deal with the current problem,' she says as I flop down beside her. 'Did Caroline really try and poison you?'

'She gave me mince and aubergine when she knows I hate it,' I say, gagging at the memory of the dollop of purple and brown vomit.

'And did she have anything to do with Maddy's camera going missing?'

'No, but I was worried she'd get hold of the film, the bit where I called her an evil witch, so that's why I thought she'd taken it!'

I'm painfully aware that I'm digging my own grave with everything I say.

'Listen, love, your dad says Caroline is outside in the car. You're going to have to say sorry. Whatever's gone on before, you can't go around making serious allegations like that.'

'I can't!' I cry. 'I'd rather die.'

Mum sticks her hand down her Mighty Mammaries and pulls out a tissue, which she hands to me. It's warm and slightly damp from cleavage sweat, but when I clamp it to my nose it smells like Mum and is comforting.

'Whether you like her or not, Electra, this time you're in the wrong,' she says. 'You *have* to apologize.'

'There, under the street lamp,' I say, nodding towards The Black Bullet.

Mum and I walk towards the car holding hands. I'm not sure whether the hand-holding is to stop me bolting or to be supportive, but it feels good.

When we get to the car, The Kipper is sitting in the passenger seat, next to the kerb, her face as hard as granite.

Mum knocks on the window and it glides down.

'Electra has something to say, haven't you, Electra?'

She lets go of my hand and gently pushes me towards the car. I bend towards the window and Dad leans over from the driver's side.

'I'm . . . I'm . . .' I can hardly speak. There's a whole pond of frogs in my throat. 'I'm sorry about Friday night. I was wrong.'

Chapter Thirty

On the first day back after half-term I found out what Pinhead, Gibbo and Spud were doing with a spray can of silver paint on the school playing fields last Wednesday. It was so enormous you couldn't help but notice it, especially from our upstairs form room. They sent the caretaker out to mow the field to try and get rid of it, but all it did was to make the outline sharper.

'We *will* find out who sprayed this picture of a male member and its associated organs on the football pitch,' The Teapot barked at an emergency assembly during final break. 'And when we do, they will be severely punished. Graffiti isn't street art, it's vandalism!'

'Don't you think graffiti is just art for the common man, miss?' Pinhead asks as we file into the studio for art & design. 'Especially if it's of a common man's—'

'Everyone get their holiday objects out!' Miss

Ainsworth our art tutor announces, ignoring a sniggering Pinhead. 'Hands up if you've forgotten it.'

Before half-term we were told to bring in something that was connected to what we'd done during the hols so that we could draw it in pencil. I only remembered this on Sunday morning.

Lucy has a piece of wood and some shells she found on a beach in Ireland.

Rather worryingly, Sorrel has brought in a box of pins and a figure looking suspiciously like Warren that she's made out of the twins' modelling clay.

'There's a strange smell around here,' Miss Ainsworth says as she approaches my desk. 'Anyone know what it is?'

'It's fishy and it's coming from Electra Brown,' Pinhead sniggers. 'She's penked all day.'

He'd better watch out or I'll tell The Teapot whose hand was on that spray can button.

'It's my holiday object,' I say, unwrapping it from its carrier bag. A boil-in-the-bag kipper I bought when Phil took us shopping yesterday. I didn't think it would smell in its wrapping, but because the chandelier earrings in my bag somehow pierced the plastic, I was wrong. 'Sorry, miss, it stinks.'

Miss Ainsworth pokes the bony orange fish encased

in its plastic tomb. 'Did you go fishing during half-term?' she asks. 'Is this something you caught and smoked yourself?'

'No, miss, I got it from Tesco, but it reminds me of my Dad's girlfriend. Glassy eyes, same skin colour, smells of smoke. Me and my cousin went to London with her.'

Miss Ainsworth sighs and scuttles off to a bench where Butterface is starting to draw a still life with high-heels-and-mascara combination. 'All I did was go shopping,' I hear her explain.

My kipper picture turned out quite well, although Miss Ainsworth thought that putting a cigarette in its mouth was possibly a bit over the top. 'For this assignment you were supposed to draw what you see,' she'd said, and I had to agree that a kipper from Tesco didn't usually have a Marlboro Light hanging from its pout.

I'm rummaging around in my bag, trying to find a rubber to erase the smoking accessory, when I see my phone flash. I'd put it on silent, but it's Maddy so I *have* to answer it.

I stick my head under the desk and whisper, 'Mads, it's me!'

Above me I can hear Miss Ainsworth calling out, 'Electra, what are you up to?'

Something hits my head and lands next to me. It's my kipper. It stares at me with dead eyes as above me I hear Sorrel say, 'Electra's fish has fallen down, miss. She's just trying to get it.' My hair will penk of smelly scales but I'm grateful for Sorrel's quick thinking.

'I'm just going into class, but I had to call you!' Maddy shrieks. 'Check your emails the *moment* you get home. Operation Catch A Kipper has worked, Missy B! Your dad is so gonna dump that evil fish when he sees what we got!'

We rushed straight out of last reg, kicked and elbowed our way on to the first available bus, ran home and headed straight up to my room to boot up the Thigh Crusher. We haven't even taken our coats off.

'Look!' Lucy cries next to me. 'Receiving mail!'

I stab excitedly at the keys to open the email and then the attached file.

There's a small section where Maddy is filming the restaurant and then obviously turns the camera off. Then the film starts again, presumably as the waitress moves the camera. There's a swish of white, then colour and then fuzzy greyness, as if the laptop screen has gone mental.

'It must be a corrupt file,' Sorrel says. 'You can't see anything.'

'I don't believe it' I cry, bitterly disappointed. 'Just my luck! I'll get Mads to resend it.'

Then, above the noise of clinking glasses, rattling plates and people chatting Fiona says, 'They seem nice girls. Electra's not a bit like you described.'

'You can have her,' The Kipper replies. 'I don't want her. I wish *she* was the one getting on a plane tomorrow but with a one-way ticket.'

'Caroline!' Fiona sounds shocked. 'That's a dreadful thing to say.'

'Well, it's true. I've had to be nice to the snivelling kid all day and the strain of that and not smoking is killing me.'

'Why bother then?'

There's lots of cracking sounds which is probably the munching of prawn crackers. I'm starting to get worried that what Maddy thought of as The Evidence isn't really strong enough for a Kipper conviction.

'I need the money.'

What? Even though there's nothing to see on the screen we all lean towards the Thigh Crusher. I feel excited, sick and furious, all at the same time.

'Listen, Fi, I'm a single solicitor from the suburbs, the wrong side of thirty, strapped for cash with a serious shoe, holiday and handbag habit. Rob isn't loaded but when I was handling the divorce I realized once he's paid off expanding the business he will be, and by then I'll be the next Mrs Brown.' There's more cracker-crunching. 'I might double-barrel it. Mrs Cole-Brown would look good on a platinum credit card, wouldn't it?'

There's a high-pitched cackle and more crunching.

'So you're trying to trap this poor guy into marrying you just for his money?' Fiona says, her voice high above the background noise. 'Even though you despise his daughter?'

'Trap is such a dirty word, Fi,' The Kipper says. 'But if Rob thinks I'd make the perfect stepmother he's more likely to marry me, so that's why I'm nice to the kid when he's around. When he's not I'm the classic wicked stepmother and the best thing is, no one believes the silly kid when she whines about me!'

'What's happened to you, Caroline?' Fiona says. 'You were never like this at law school. When did you become so devious?'

'Sssh!'

I can't tell who says that, but it's obviously because Maddy and I are back, as then you can hear Mads say, 'Has anyone seen my camera?' and the file ends.

'The golddigging witch!' Sorrel shouts, kicking the side of my bed. 'She's not a kipper she's a piranha!'

'I'm so sorry, Electra,' Lucy says hugging me. 'I can't believe that we didn't believe you. You kept telling us she was being horrible to you but I was so busy dreaming of Pascal . . .' She's getting all teary.

'It's OK, Luce,' I say. 'She had everyone fooled, especially Dad.'

'What are you going to do?' she asks me.

'What do you mean, *what's* she going to do?' Sorrel snaps. 'She's going to totally and utterly humiliate that piranha so that she lives a life of constant pain and despair and she'll never ever find another mate ever again and die a sad and lonely death!'

Sorrel is *definitely* projecting all this on to Warren and Jas.

'I need to think,' I say, getting up and marching around my bedroom. The marching doesn't last long as there's not much room what with the clutter and the fact that I *still* haven't deflated the airbed.

'Well?' Lucy asks. 'Any thoughts?'

'I'm going to organize a little film show for Dad and The Kipper!' I say, taking my coat off and dropping it on the bed. My mind is racing even if I'm slowly picking my way between the magazines and dropped knickers. 'I'm going to invite myself round to Dad's flat tomorrow night and take the incriminating evidence with me, as well as a huge bag of popcorn. I'm not sure yet whether it'll be salted or sweet. Then I'll suggest that we watch the DVD I've brought, I'll pretend it's *Harry Potter* or something, and then I'll whack it in, sit back and enjoy listening to The Kipper admitting to her crime.'

'God, I'd love to be a bluebottle on that wall!' Sorrel says.

'With any luck, as well as Dad being horrified, The Kipper will be so shocked she'll inhale a piece of popcorn and choke.'

'Go for sweet,' Sorrel urges. 'It's more likely to stick in her throat.'

'Your dad will be gutted,' Lucy says.

'About her dying?' I say, still savouring the thought of The Kipper lying on her own stripped-wood floor turning blue from inhaled confectionery. 'He'll get over it. I've got to get that file downloaded on to a CD to take round.'

Clearly, blank CDs are not the sort of thing I can find easily in my room, but after much rummaging under the bed, through piles of clothes and under stacks of magazines, I find one that hasn't got much on it.

I press the button on the side of the Thigh Crusher, the drive glides out, I put the disc in, the drive glides back, I press a key and . . . nothing happens, not even a whirring noise.

'The keyboard's stopped working,' I say, banging on random keys without any change to the screen. 'I don't believe it!'

Sorrel leans over and starts whacking the side of the Thigh Crusher, which makes zero difference.

'This is terrible!' 'I moan. 'I wanted to humiliate The Kipper asap!'

'What about the computer downstairs?' Luce suggests. 'You could access your email from there and copy it.'

'It's a dinosaur!' I wail. 'It doesn't write CDs!'

'I've an idea.' Lucy slides open her phone. 'I know a computer whizz-kid who can help.'

Sorrel and I glance at each other.

'Fiona? It's Lucy. Yes, yes, I'm fine. No, no, nothing's wrong. Everything's going really well. It was actually Frazer I was after. Is he around?'

'No!' I hiss at Luce. 'You are *not* getting Freak Boy round here!' I jump up and wave my arms around like a windmill in a gale. 'Cut the call! Cut the call!' I've successfully managed to avoid FB since he did his impression of being a Spanish Freak in the service station and now Luce is inviting him round!

'What's she doing with Freak Boy's number?' Sorrel whispers at me. 'How come she knows his mum?'

I say nothing and just pray FB is out walking the mutt

or is still in the school library reading up about how to make an atomic bomb.

'Hi, Frazer. Electra needs you in her bedroom,' Lucy trills. 'Can you come round?'

In the ten minutes between Lucy putting the phone down and FB standing on my doorstep with a pack of small screwdrivers in his hand, I've shoved every bit of clothing into my wardrobe, thrown all the stuff from the top of my chest of drawers under my duvet, sprayed a stack of Anaïs Anaïs around and generally had a complete fit. It's not that I want to impress Freak Boy, it's just that I don't want him to see one of my thongs hanging over a door knob, or Tampax rolling around in between eyebrow tweezers and several sticks of zit cover-up. I don't want *anyone* who's not a girl to see that stuff.

'It's the keyboard,' I explain, leading FB through the hall. 'It's died and I need to get a file downloaded on to a disc.'

Mum must have heard the doorbell go as I'm halfway up the stairs with FB behind me when she shouts up from the hall, 'Electra, is that a boy you're taking up to your bedroom?'

We both stop on the stairs. I turn to look down at Mum and notice FB's face is so red, his head resembles a humungous throbbing zit.

'The girls are up there,' I say through gritted teeth. 'My laptop's bust.'

'Well, leave the door open,' she smiles, which is obviously something she's read about in a magazine. Three teenage girls and one boy are unlikely to do anything if the door is open. She only needs one *look* at FB to know that *nothing* is *ever* going to happen, whatever Maddy says.

When I get to my room, Sorrel is lying on my duvet reading a mag, and Luce is still fiddling with the computer. Actually she's talking to it, saying, 'Please work, little laptop.'

'Hi, Frazer!' she says when FB scuttles in after me.

Sorrel ignores him.

'I was hoping to get a file transferred on to CD tonight,' I say. 'The one open on the screen. I need it asap.'

FB bends over the laptop and starts prodding and poking and unscrewing bits.

'Well, what's the diagnosis?' I say, desperate to get the beaky alien out of my bedroom, especially as I've spotted a stray Snoopy bra lying under the desk.

'There's a lot of dust and grease and crumbs in there, and several keys are stuck down with nail polish,' FB says gravely. 'White by the looks of it.'

That'll teach me not to do a French manicure resting on the space bar.

'I could take it away and fix it, but it might take a few days, longer if I need to order the part.'

'She needs the file *now*,' Sorrel barks from behind her magazine. 'What are you going to do about that, Mr Computer Whizz?'

I want to tell Sorrel to shut up, stop being so sarky. FB's doing his best to help. She's just lying around criticizing him.

'I'll take it away, attach a remote keyboard to get the file off and then copy it and put a CD through the door later,' he suggests. 'And I'll see if I can repair the laptop, or maybe Dad can.'

'Just do it,' I say. '*Please*.'

And he does.

About half an hour after he leaves, and as the girls are on their way home, there's an envelope on the doormat and in it, a shiny silver disc.

Chapter Thirty-one

Mum sticks her head round my bedroom door.

'It's almost quarter to! What's going on?'

'I can't go to school,' I say feebly, wriggling under the covers. 'I'm ill.'

'What's wrong with you?' she asks, standing over the bed, her Mighty Mammaries pointing down at me like a couple of ripe and ready-to-burst watermelons. 'Have you got a test or something today?'

'No!' I say indignantly. 'I've got period pains. *Really* bad ones.'

'You had period pains only a couple of weeks ago.' She shoots me her best Suspicious Mother look.

'They don't always stick to a timetable,' I say. 'When we had that talk at school the nurse said periods in teenage girls can be all over the place. *And* it's a heavy one.'

Mum's eyes become less suspicious and more motherly. 'Have you taken anything?'

'Yes, but nothing's worked,' I whimper.

'Well, I'll go and get you a hot water bottle. But if you feel better later, you must go in, OK? You don't need to have the whole day off for a few cramps.'

I make moaning noises and slide further down the bed.

Mum comes back with the hottie and goes to pull the duvet aside to put it underneath.

'Mum!' I clutch my fifty-per-cent cotton, fifty-per-cent polyester swirly-patterned pink duvet around me.

'Right, I'm off,' Mum says, bending over to kiss me and practically slapping my face with her boobs. She must get a more supportive bap-pack. 'Remember it's Tuesday, a college day.'

She goes downstairs, I hear her call for Jack in the hall, then the front door slams and the house falls silent. Well, silent other than the traffic noise outside and the central heating banging and the sound of a squirrel tap-dancing in clogs on the roof.

And then I throw back the duvet and get up. I'm already fully dressed in jeans and a jumper. I've even got trainers on.

I slap on some make-up, grab my bag, go via the bathroom where I flush a new Tampax down the loo, leaving the cardboard tube in the water for added period-authenticity, go downstairs, get the telephone directory, find Hammond & Able, rip out the page and then look up minicabs.

'I'd like to book a cab to take me to The Oracle Business Centre,' I say. 'As soon as possible.'

The cab pulls away, leaving me stranded in the car park. It's cost me fifteen quid to get here, and other than a few coins I'm now skint and with no idea how I'm going to get home. It's typical of The Kipper to work somewhere I can't get to by bus.

As I walk towards the scrubby red-brick building I feel sick and wonder if I'm doing the right thing.

After the girls had gone, instead of doing geography homework, I lay on my bed and imagined the delicious scenario of The Kipper and Dad settling down to enjoy a Harry P DVD, but instead of watching life at Hogwarts, they're treated to the sound of The Kipper trashing Dad. But every time I imagined it, I got less and less excited at the thought of The Kipper choking on her popcorn, and more and more worried about Dad's reaction. He likes to think of himself as a successful businessman, the sort of guy who's worked his way up from nothing. He was hurt Mum found a new man so soon after he left. He was upset about Phil beating him at swimming. How will he feel when he discovers the woman he loves only loves his money, and that he was part of her elaborate plan to get a posh credit card and fill her wardrobe with designer stuff? He won't just be hurt, he'll be devastated and even though he's been a crappy dad at times, I can't do it to him. I can't see him humiliated and crumble before my eyes.

'I'm here to see Caroline Cole,' I say to the woman on reception. 'She works for Hammond & Able.'

The woman flicks through a book of signatures in front of her.

'She's not signed in yet,' she smiles. 'Is she expecting you?'

'I thought I'd surprise her,' I say.

She glances up at a digital clock on the wall. 8:44. 'She shouldn't be long. Would you like to wait?'

'Please.' I head towards a black fake-leather sofa that makes a squeaking noise when I sit on it.

The post arrives, people come and go, parcels are delivered, but there's no sign of The Kipper.

I don't know what to do. The magazines are all out of date, there are no plant leaves to count, so I look at the list of companies on the wall and whilst I'm counting them (forty-three), I feel my moby vibrate in my bag;

probably the girls ringing to find out why I'm not at school. I haven't told them what I'm up to. They'd think I was mad. I probably am, but then sometimes you have to do what you feel is right, not just what people expect you to do.

I'm just beginning to wonder whether The Kipper has booked a day off to go shopping or top up her fake tan when, 'There's a young lady to see you.'

I look up to see The Kipper signing in.

The sofa farts as I get up.

'I'm too busy to see a school truant,' she says, barely glancing at me. 'I've got a packed diary.'

'Oh, I think you'll make time for this!' I say, reaching into my bag and pulling out the silver CD with a flourish.

I shove it confidently towards The Kipper, who doesn't take it but stares at it.

'A Justin Timberlake album?' she sneers.

Oh! Oh! I've pulled out the wrong CD. That's been in my bag for weeks. I was supposed to give it back to Luce. I shove it back and pull out the proper one. 'I meant this.'

The Kipper doesn't take the disc, but fixes her glassy eyes on me and picks up her briefcase from the floor.

'Follow me,' she orders, clickity-clacking down the corridor.

And, with a heart beating so fast I think it might explode, I do.

I can't say I've spent much time thinking about the office where The Kipper works, but if I'd had to imagine it, I'd have said it would be a temple of high-powered legal style, all slick steel desks and slim flat screens with the odd perfect white orchid dotted around.

It's not.

It's a mess.

Caroline Cole's office is just a bigger version of our cluttered study at home, with towering piles of paperwork, files stacked floor to ceiling, filthy windows and dirty mugs dotted around.

The Kipper dumps her shiny purple bag on a pile of brown cardboard files, tosses her black briefcase on the floor and sits at her desk.

'OK, hand it over,' she says coolly, sticking a bony orange claw towards me.

'Remember you called me Wasp Girl?' I say, passing her the disc. 'Well, prepare to be stung!'

The Kipper's on one side of the desk and I'm on the other, not sitting, just hovering by a pile of paperwork hoping she can't see my thighs quivering with fear.

Her face remains completely blank as she listens to the

short conversation condemning her to a dating wilderness without Dad and his credit card. Then she presses open the CD drive, grabs the disc, and with a swift movement and a loud crack, snaps it over the edge of the desk and throws the shattered halves towards me.

'That's not the only copy,' I say, shocked. It is actually, but I'm banking on Freak Boy making me another one.

'Didn't think it was,' The Kipper shrugs. 'I just enjoyed doing it.'

There's silence. I stare at The Kipper and The Kipper stares into space. I'm wondering whether she's going to beg my forgiveness by concocting some amazing story such as she's being blackmailed by the Mafia over drugs, and needs Dad's money to pay them off, but instead she just says, 'So, what do you want me to do? Admit everything to your father? Finish with him? What?'

'You just don't care, do you?' I gasp, shocked that she didn't at least *try* to wriggle out of this mess. 'You don't care he'll be devastated. You might love Dad's wallet but I love him!'

The Kipper folds her arms. 'You wouldn't believe me if I said I did, would you? That what started out about money actually turned into something worth more?' My face obviously gives her the answer. 'Didn't think so,' she says staring at her nails. 'Go on then. Go and tell him what an evil witch I am. Isn't Halloween tomorrow anyway?'

'*I'm* not going to tell him about all this,' I say.

The Kipper's bony face jerks up. 'Oh, so you want *me* to dump him?'

'Not that either.'

She looks one confused fish. 'What *do* you want then?'

I lean across the desk towards her. 'Dad will be devastated if he finds out that you've been with him just for his money,' I say. 'And he'll be devastated if you dump him.'

'So what are you saying?' she asks. 'That you'll let all this go?'

'As if!' I snort. I'm enjoying this feeling of power. Sitting behind her scummy desk with a chipped white mug perched on top of a pile of paperwork she looks pathetic. 'No. I want you to stop being so two-faced. I want Dad to see the real you. The real you who's been an absolute bitch to me. The real you who can't stand his kids. The real you who lies and then denies it. Because I reckon that when Dad sees what you're *really* like, *he'll* dump *you*.'

That went well. I'm pleased I sacrificed several hours of sleep to practise my speech. It ended on a good flourish, if I say so myself.

'What if I dump him first?' The Kipper says. 'Then your little plan's backfired.'

Damn! I hadn't thought of that. I need to think fast.

'You won't,' I say. 'You'll hang on in there, giving his credit card a final bashing, getting a few more bling bags and swanky hols before the game is up.'

The Kipper doesn't say anything for a moment but then nods. 'You do realize you've made a pact with the devil, don't you?'

It's my turn to nod. This was the last thing I thought I'd do when Maddy sent me The Evidence, but it's the best way. I can't bear to think of Dad hearing Caroline crowing over how she's been trying to trap him, or sitting in his interior-decorated flat heartbroken because she's walked out. I'd rather Dad was the dumper not the dumpee, even if it takes a bit longer to get rid of her.

'Oh, and one more thing,' I say. 'It cost me twenty quid in a taxi to get here and it'll cost the same back. I'd like forty pounds, please.'

Caroline's mouth opens like a gasping fish but she picks up the purple bag, pulls out her purse and hands me two crisp twenty-pound notes.

'Thanks,' I say, heading towards the door, pleased that I've made a tenner profit so easily and don't have to try and walk home.

'The name Electra suits you. It means the bright one, doesn't it?'

I *knew* it! It's the first time I've heard The Kipper use my proper name. She's going to wriggle out of the deal, give me some sob story, turn on the tears, throw herself at my feet, even offer me her cream Chloé if I keep schtum. The promise of designer leather is going to be hard to turn down.

'So?' I swing round to face her. 'What if it does?'

'So, you'd make a good lawyer.'

'Me?' I'm gobsmacked.

'Yeah you. You're bright, smart, good at negotiating, quick-witted and not above a bit of double-dealing yourself.' I'm shocked to see The Kipper smile. 'You'd make a much better legal eagle than me.' She swings her chair round and stares out of the dirty window. 'The sort of lawyer that could easily afford to buy her own designer handbags and shoes, not rely on some poor man to do it for her.'

She swivels back and gives me a weak, wistful smile.

'*You've* got what it takes, Electra. Remember that the next time you're bored witless counting dead flies during lessons.'

'How do you know about that?' I gasp. 'I've never told you.'

'Your father did. He's always talking about you. He thinks the sun shines out of your . . . well, everywhere. It doesn't matter what you do, or what I pretend you do, he always says the same thing. That you're the best thing that's ever happened to him. You're young, you're bright and Rob loves you. Is it any wonder I'm so jealous of you?'

Chapter Thirty-two

'I *so* need a new thong,' Tits Out says as we stream out of last reg. 'This one's cutting my bits in two!' She reaches behind her, sticks her hand down her waistband and does some elaborate tugging around the butt-crack area. 'I'm off to Eastwood. Anyone coming?'

'God, yeah, Claudia,' Tammy Two-Names pants.

'I need more slap,' Butterface says. 'And some stick-on nails.'

'I've got extra French,' Lucy moans, 'but as I've hardly heard from Pascal I'm thinking of saying *au revoir* to Madame La Poodle.'

'I'll come,' Sorrel says. She's in a good mood as Warren told Jas who told Sorrel that since he'd been let go at Smith's no one would give him a reference to get another job but he didn't know why, and as Jas won't go out with someone who has no money she's blanking Warren, who's pining like a lost puppy.

'See you tomorrow,' I say.

The girls stop in their tracks and stare at me.

'What?' I say. 'What's with the face?'

'You going to the library *again*?' Tits Out asks.

'And your point is?' I reply.

'That's almost every day for more than a week!' Butterface says, sounding shocked but looking blank. 'What's wrong with you?'

'Are you like, into lesbionic librarians?' Tammy asks. 'Is that like, why you've become a geek?'

'Get lost!' I laugh. 'I'm just trying to catch up on all the stuff I've missed.'

'Today the library, tomorrow dorky shoes and sensible hair!' Tits Out teases. 'Don't be such a square-eyed swot. Come and look at thongs!'

The word swot nearly makes me turn my back on the library and head with them to thong-land but I stand firm, even though Tits Out has elbowed me in the ribs.

'No can do, Claudia!' I laugh. 'I'll see you lot tomorrow.'

They head off, thinking I'm nuts and not just about studying rather than shopping. When I told them about making the pact with the devil they thought I should have dropped Caroline right in it, snitched to Dad, humiliated her and had fun doing it. Even Luce thought he had a right to know his girlfriend is a golddigger. I know what she means, but I still think I'm doing the right thing, even if everyone else doesn't. Well, not quite everyone else.

FB's still got the Thigh Crusher so I used the old computer downstairs to email Maddy to tell her what had happened. She replied: *You swam against the tide. I'm so proud of you, Missy B!*, which I printed out and stuck in the front of my planner so that I can look at it when I'm finding things tough.

I go to the library and try to find a book on global warming, not just to impress Buff, but so that I have a hope of knowing a bit about what I'm actually supposed to be studying.

There's no sign of FB. When I came last week I thought he might be here, bent over a table, his beak stuck in a book on how to build a computer from an old tin can and a couple of paper clips. But he wasn't, and I was surprised and deeply freaked by the fact that I felt a stab of disappointment somewhere in the region of where my cleavage should be, if I had boobs big enough to make one.

I take out a book on climate change and also a maths book which has lots of Mrs Chopley Brain Extender-type questions, hang around for a bit enjoying the peace and quiet, work out that it would take ten years and four hundred freckles for Fiona The Freckle's face to become one giant freckle, feel ridiculously pleased with myself and head for home.

'That boy that came round last week called,' Mum says when I get home. 'He's brought your computer back.'

She nods towards the Thigh Crusher on the kitchen table. Mum's sitting next to it surrounded by books, her file open, a pen in her hand. It looks as if she's answering multiple-choice questions. It's odd to see her doing homework even if it's about VAT and employment law rather than depressions and anti-cyclones.

'Frazer Burns?' I ask. 'Was it FB?'

'Mmm,' Mum replies, ticking a box.

'Did he say anything?' I open the fridge and swig from a carton of orange juice. 'Ask if I was in or anything?' I try to say this in a casual way so Mum's antennae don't start waving.

'Nope,' she says, flicking through her textbook.

'Didn't he even say whether he'd fixed it?' I sit down at the table across from her and flip open the lid of the Thigh Crusher.

'Nope.' Mum ticks another answer.

'What? He just handed you the laptop and left?'

'Yep.'

Doesn't Mum realize how irritating it is to just get one-word answers to questions?

With a whirr and a tune the laptop bursts into life and starts booting up, finding the wireless network. FB's obviously got rid of the nail polish, the crumbs and the gross grease as the keyboard is working perfectly.

I click on to my emails. Buried amongst the spammy ones there's one from Maddy with an attachment.

To: SOnotagreekgirl1
From: Madaboutnewyork
Date: 7th November 09.31
Subject: Film Star!

Hi Missy B!

Here's the first draft of The Electra Project. You'll need to decompress the file and open it in a media player, blah de blah de blah, but when you get to see it, I hope you like it. I love it! Let me know what you think and if you want any changes before I present it and post it on YouTube!

Luv you lots,

Maddy xxxx $\times 10^6$

The file opens like a dream and music begins to drift from the computer.

'Electra,' Mum moans. 'Can't you see I'm trying to do my homework? These questions have to be in tomorrow.'

'It's Maddy's film of me,' I say.

Mum gets up and stands behind me as the words *My Perfect Cousin* appear on the screen and then melt away.

As I watch the film I'm almost wetting myself with laughter. Maddy's edited it so that, interspersed with film of the girls, the Goth limo, where we live, my school, Dad and The Kipper, Big Ben, Buckingham Palace, the airport and so on, there's shots of me doing weird things with a weird look on my face:

Scowling at the airport when Maddy arrives.

Lying in my sleeping bag, drooling.

Looking shocked to find a plucked chicken on the end of my arm.

Looking freaked when Glam Doc feels my forehead in a motorway service station.

Standing by a box of muesli in Tesco, pretending to be a rabbit.

Careering up an aisle on the back of a supermarket trolley.

Looking like I might vomit over my plate of aubergines.

Wearing a football shirt and jumping up and down with my back to the camera pointing over my shoulder at the name *Beckham*.

Looking cross-eyed balancing a prawn cracker on the end of my nose then flicking it in the air and eating it.

Sobbing at the airport when Maddy leaves.

There's shots of both of us pretending to have huge boobs by stuffing stacks of knickers in our bras, measuring our tongues and generally acting as if we're completely nuts. There's even a quick shot of Jags holding a box of Cheerios looking very munchkin-like which I'll freeze-frame later.

Watching the film I realize that even though The Glam Plan has failed miserably and I'm not a glossy racehorse like my cousin, we still had fun. Probably more fun than if I'd only seen Maddy for a couple of days in New York, worrying about what people thought of me, trying to keep up the pretence of dating someone who's not interested in me and planning what to tell Tits Out and co. back home.

There's a list of credits, and at the end:

Madison Hampshire would like to thank everyone in the UK for making her trip so fantastic, but especially her fabulous cousin, Electra Brown.
Hasta la vista, Missy B!

'I had no idea you'd done so much,' Mum says. 'What an

amazing film. But what's with the Spanish phrase at the end?'

'Oh, just a private joke,' I giggle as Mum goes back to her homework. 'I'm going to take this to my room and email Maddy to thank her for it.'

'And remember to thank that boy for fixing it, won't you?' Mum says.

I get up leaving the laptop where it is.

'I thought you wanted this thing!' Mum calls out behind me.

'I'm just going out,' I say. 'There's something I've got to do.'

I am totally gobsmacked when FB opens the door.

It's not the fact that he's standing in the hall soaking wet, a black T-shirt clinging to his body.

It's not because he's running his tongue around his mouth to catch the water which is dripping from his fringe down his face.

It's not even the way he's rubbing his wet hands on his jeans-clad thighs to dry them.

It's the fact that despite being drenched to the skin he looks *totally* hot and at least a four on the Snogability Scale.

'You OK?' he asks, and I can feel myself going red,

trying not to look at the outline of his chest under his T-shirt and wishing that I'd bothered to change out of my school uniform, all at the same time.

'Umm . . .' I don't seem to be able to get my brain and my mouth to work together. I'm just standing there, gawping.

'I've just given Archie a bath,' he explains, running a hand through his damp hair, which just makes his score go up to a 4.5 and my legs feel wobbly. 'It's always a fight, but he stank. He's been rolling in fox poo.'

From behind him I can hear the sound of yapping and scrabbling at a door.

I've got to say *something*. I can't just stand here ogling FB whilst his dog tries to escape.

'Would you say fox poo stinks more or less than goose poo, or about the same?'

Oh, someone shoot me! I'm unexpectedly faced with a 4.5 (maybe even higher) on the Snogability Scale and I'm discussing the stinkability of animal excrement with him! That's the sort of stupid thing I'd come out with if Jags was standing in front of me. But this isn't The Spanish Lurve God, it's Freak Boy, although he seems to have turned into Fit Boy just by dunking himself in water.

'Look, do you want to come in?' he asks, as Archie

continues to go mental. 'I could just finish drying the dog and—'

'Nah, you're all right,' I say, pulling myself together by trying to think of Tits Out in her wet T-shirt rather than FB in his, and wondering if every freaky geek should try pouring a bucket of water over their heads to see whether it improves their Snogability score. 'I've got a stack of homework to start and even more to finish. I just wanted to say thanks for fixing my laptop. Do I owe you anything?'

'It needed a new keyboard,' FB says. 'Dad got one from his firm but I fitted it. Sorry it took so long. You don't need to pay.'

'Well, thanks. It meant I could see a film my cousin sent me.'

'The American one?' he asks. 'The one I met?'

'Yeah, Maddy.'

'I don't think she liked me very much,' FB says.

'No, she did,' I say desperately trying to think of Tits Out in her T-shirt, Dad in his Speedos, The Ginger Gnome's bloodshot eye, *anything* to stop the racy thoughts that are starting again.

FB doesn't look convinced. 'She called me a numbnuts,' he says. '*And* a jello-spined jerk.'

'There was just a mix-up,' I say. 'She knew who you

were supposed to be but not who you really were. It was all to do with that whole Spanish-boyfriend-lying thing.'

Suddenly there's a bang and the sound of claws on wood. From the depths of the house Archie comes flying towards us like a mutt possessed. In a blur of wet fur he streaks past FB, practically knocks me over, and races down the gravel drive.

'He always goes mad after a bath,' FB says calmly. 'He can't get through the gate.'

'I'VE LEFT IT OPEN!' I shriek.

In a panic, we hare out of the house, down the drive, through the open gate and along Compton Avenue. Traffic-packed Talbot Road is only moments away. But as we reach the end of the avenue we see Archie standing on the corner, wagging his tail while Pinhead, Gibbo and Spud toss crisps at him. And it's only then, when we're gasping and laughing with relief, that I realize that we're holding hands, and that despite the fact that the Grim Reaper and his gang are staring and jeering, neither of us is going to be the first to let go.

About the Author

Helen Bailey was born and brought up in Ponteland, Newcastle-upon-Tyne. Barely into her teens, Helen invested her pocket money in a copy of *The Writers' and Artists' Yearbook* and spent the next few years sending short stories and poems to anyone she could think of. Much to her surprise, she sometimes found herself in print. After a degree in science, Helen worked in the media and now runs a successful London-based character licensing agency handling internationally renowned properties such as Snoopy, Dirty Dancing, Dilbert and Felicity Wishes. With her husband, John, she divides her time between Highgate, north London and the north-east. She is the author of a number of short stories, young novels and picture books.

www.helenbaileybooks.com

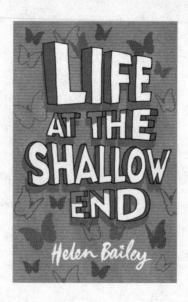

Life as I know it is going pear-shaped.

Dad's having a mid-life crisis.
Mum's given in to her daytime TV addiction.
My little bro (aka The Little Runt) has just been
caught shoplifting. Even the guinea-pig's gone mental.

And all I can think about is whether green eyeliner
complements or clashes with blue eyes.

I can be **very** shallow.

These are the zits-and-all,
no-holds-barred rants of me,
Electra Brown. Welcome to my crazy world.

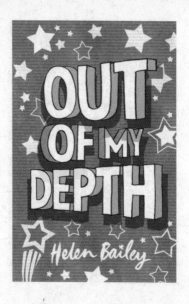

I am *totally*
out of my depth.

Everyone's giving me the third degree!
Freak Boy's dad wants to know whether he's being bullied.
Sorrel's interrogating me about Lucy's stroppy moods.

Even Dad is cross-examining me about Mum's
love-life, over garlic bread and pepperoni pizza.

And all I can think is, *How far can you get a piece
of melted cheese to stretch without it breaking?*

I can be **very** shallow.

These are the real-life,
messed-up rants of me,
Electra Brown. Welcome to my crazy world.

I am finally going to do it.

Lucy's already done it but only in France.
Sorrel thought she'd done it but found out
she hadn't. And Claudia, who's done it
loads of times, has bet me I won't.

I will, though. I'm going to take the plunge
and go out with the first boy who asks me.
But will he be a frog or a prince?

I can be **very** shallow.

These are the weird and
sometimes not-so-wonderful rants of me,
Electra Brown. Welcome to my crazy world.